Praise for *Separ*

"Witty and thought-provoking, *Separ*— — exploration into deciphering personal truths. Karen Brichoux writes with such delightful insight, she reaches past the heart and tugs at your very soul. A highly recommended read!"

—Donna Kauffman, author of *Dear Prince Charming*

"[A] compelling tale of a young woman rearranging her view of the world. Pop this must-read into your beach bag this summer, but don't expect to find breezy fluff between its covers as you while away the hours on the sand." —Curvynovels.com

"Brichoux has managed to break away from the standard 'chick lit' fare to offer literature of more substance [and] innovative ideas. . . . Brichoux deserves kudos for her valiant attempts at reinventing the . . . genre known as 'chick lit.' . . . An author to watch."

—*Lawrence Journal World* (Lawrence, KS)

Coffee & Kung Fu

"*Coffee & Kung Fu* is fresh, lively writing. One of the best parts is its use of metaphor and the elements of folklore gleaned from the Kung Fu universe. After reading Brichoux's debut you might feel, as I do, that you have not given Jackie Chan his due." —*St. Petersburg Times*

"A young woman's guide to life—as seen through classic Jackie Chan films. Newcomer Karen Brichoux scores a coup by venturing into the cliché-strewn, warmed-over waters of Gen-X chick-lit and coming up with a bright, fresh, exciting spin on the genre. . . . Warm, smart and original: a swift Snake in Eagle's Shadow kick to all the Bridget Jones clones." —*Kirkus Reviews*

continued . . .

Other Books by Karen Brichoux

Coffee & Kung Fu

Separation Anxiety

THE GIRL
SHE LEFT
BEHIND

KAREN
BRICHOUX

 NEW AMERICAN LIBRARY

New American Library
Published by New American Library, a division of
Penguin Group (USA) Inc., 375 Hudson Street,
New York, New York 10014, USA
Penguin Group (Canada), 10 Alcorn Avenue, Toronto,
Ontario M4V 3B2, Canada (a division of Pearson Penguin Canada Inc.)
Penguin Books Ltd., 80 Strand, London WC2R 0RL, England
Penguin Ireland, 25 St. Stephen's Green, Dublin 2,
Ireland (a division of Penguin Books Ltd.)
Penguin Group (Australia), 250 Camberwell Road, Camberwell, Victoria 3124,
Australia (a division of Pearson Australia Group Pty. Ltd.)
Penguin Books India Pvt. Ltd., 11 Community Centre, Panchsheel Park,
New Delhi - 110 017, India
Penguin Group (NZ), cnr Airborne and Rosedale Roads, Albany,
Auckland 1310, New Zealand (a division of Pearson New Zealand Ltd.)
Penguin Books (South Africa) (Pty.) Ltd., 24 Sturdee Avenue,
Rosebank, Johannesburg 2196, South Africa

Penguin Books Ltd., Registered Offices: 80 Strand, London WC2R 0RL, England

First published by New American Library, a division of Penguin Group (USA) Inc.

First Printing, July 2005
10 9 8 7 6 5 4 3 2 1

LIBRARY OF CONGRESS CATALOGING-IN-PUBLICATION DATA:
Brichoux, Karen.
  The girl she left behind / by Karen Brichoux.
    p. cm.
  ISBN 0-451-21521-4 (trade pbk.)
  1. Young women—Fiction. 2. Terminally ill—Fiction. 3. Montana—Fiction. 4. Aunts—Fiction.
5. Large type books.   I. Title.
  PS3602.R5G57 2005
  813'.6—dc22   2004027450

Set in Weiss
Designed by Ginger Legato

Printed in the United States of America

For Stripey,
the wild thing who came in from the cold
and made our lives groovy

ACKNOWLEDGMENTS

Writing acknowledgments is a little like accepting an Oscar. Where do you begin and where do you end (and when will you shut up)? So many people take part in the creation of a novel, and someone is bound to be left out. Such is the state of the world, I'm afraid. But, as always, I'd like to thank Ellen Edwards for her kind direction, and Kim Whalen for believing in the book and for her tireless advocacy. I wouldn't make it through alive without the unfailing friendship of fellow authors Jerri Corgiat and Libby Sternberg, or the support of my family, who continues to love me even when I speak in meaningless jargon. A big thank-you to Jan, Lisa, and Beth at Watermark Books for their helpful suggestions for the Readers Guide. And, as always, Dave—the one person who deserves the most thanks and rarely gets it. Never give up.

CHAPTER 1

I know three things about the City of Angels. There are no angels, the beach is too cold for swimming, and despite all the happy pronouncements about clean air, smog exists. Did I say three things? I should have said four. The fourth thing I know about L.A. is that only millionaires can afford to live there in the style presented to the rest of the unsuspecting nation via television programming. I mentioned this to Stephen as he and I loaded the last of our stuff into the overflowing U-Haul trailer. The eviction notice had been taped to the Spanish-style grillwork on our apartment door just the day before.

Stephen shrugged.

And the band around my finger felt tighter than it should have, considering that it fit perfectly when he put it there nine months ago.

In the end, it was the U-Haul business that did us in.

At least, that's how I remember it.

Some Amoco or Conoco or Way-to-go gas station along the 405 freeway. I had the U-Haul trailer attached to my car. I pulled too far past the pump and I had to back up. That sounds easy enough. But try backing a trailer sometime when you just learned this morning that backing a trailer means that everything you know about driving is now backward.

I couldn't do it. Couldn't back it up. So I pulled forward and drove around until I could come at the pump straight on. Stephen, who was standing there holding the pump nozzle, rolled his eyes and muttered something as my window passed by. Maybe I should have cut him some slack. He was driving the old beater. With no air conditioning. In late July.

But Stephen rolled his eyes and I rolled right on by. Just kept going. And I didn't stop until the low-gas warning light came on and I *had* to stop or risk Kitty's and my being stuck on a highway somewhere with psycho serial killers slavering in their black vans as they drive along hunting for unsuspecting girls like Miss Kitty and me. I made sure I stopped by the pump nozzle that time.

Miss Kitty and I have been going ever since.

Like tumbleweeds.

If tumbleweeds could keep going for three years.

Tumbleweeds aren't attached to anything. Most plants in the plant kingdom stay put. Politely burrowing into the ground and propagating themselves by attaching less-polite burrs, pollen, or seeds to fur, bee legs, and the wind. Tumbleweeds refuse to be politely planted. A small family group will scatter in a high wind, rolling haphazardly along until they run up against the fence that borders this highway or the three or four like it that crisscross the Wizard of Oz flats of eastern Montana. The highest point around is the red-tailed hawk on the fencepost. The hawk's head turns as my car rolls on by. There aren't any fences across the two-lane highway for me and Miss K. to run into.

I cross over a bump in the road that passes for a hill and . . . there it is. Silver Creek. Twisting through the grassy mounds and eroded gorges and occasional trees that make up the landscape wrinkles generous people call the beginning of the foothills. Twisting like a silver snake in the mid-afternoon sun.

I used to sit on one of the high points—that bulge of earth with a lone cottonwood just to the right—and watch the creek change color with the sky. I don't know why it's called Silver Creek. As far as I know, no one ever discovered silver in this part of eastern Montana. But maybe the long-dead person who named the creek saw it the very same way I'm seeing it now. After riding or walking long, dry miles, he or she crossed a little bump, and there it was, shining in the sun like a silver snake. And maybe they wanted to name it Silver Snake, but some literalist nearby snorted and said, *"Good Lord, what kind of idiot would name a creek after a serpent?"* Then the literalist shook her head—I'm sure it was a she since the imaginary voice I hear in my head fits so well with the sour-eyed women in the old photos on the wall of Silver Creek's city hall—the literalist shook her head, and the person just like me cringed and fell silent. And the creek became Silver Creek. And the town founded by the sour-eyed women and the mustachioed men became Silver Creek Town. Only no one calls it anything but Silver Creek anymore.

The annoying yellow "you're low on gas" light is on again, so Miss Kitty and I pull into the station near the highway. Silver Creek has been spared the "interstate-ization" of rural America. Because it's not on the interstate. Otherwise it would surely sport the five obligatory fast-food restaurants, competing gas stations, and Best Western—all clustered next to the same-all-across-America four lanes and yellow street lamps—that greet anyone stepping off the interstate looking for food, gas, or lodging. Silver Creek got missed by the railroad in the 1880s and missed by the national interstate system eighty or so years later. Some call it a curse. It might be a blessing.

Miss Kitty and I roll up to one of the two pumps at the Silver Creek Gas and Lube and come to rest.

I turn the engine off.

And spare a memory for that day thirty-eight months, two weeks, and four days ago when I had a trailer hitched to the car and I couldn't back up.

I left the trailer at the first rest area after the Way-to-go gas station. I left a message on Stephen's voice mail telling him where to find the trailer and figured he could hitch it to the beater if he wanted what was in the U-Haul bad enough to hunt it down.

Whack-whack!

I jump.

Miss Kitty yowls and leaps onto the dash.

A gap-toothed teen gives me a little salute.

"Need gas?" he asks.

I roll down the window. "I can get it," I say, hoping to save myself the extra charge of having him do the honors.

He grins. "Sorry. No self-service here."

"Oh. A full . . ." I remember my cash flow problems. "No, better make that ten dollars."

I pop the cover over the gas cap, then slip out because I'm too embarrassed to sit in the car while someone pumps my gas for me. Miss Kitty knows the drill now and stays put on the dash.

Over my head, the station's sign moans and shudders—a sail without a ship, catching the wind but never moving. I lean against the car, wiping the dust from the door with my butt, and look around me. Things seem to spin a little. I've been driving since four this morning after catching a few hours of sleep in my locked car.

A gust of wind rattles the leaves of the cottonwood behind the station.

"Do I know you?" the teen asks as he scrubs the dried bug goo off my windshield. "You look really familiar."

I push my hair out of my eyes, but the wind pulls it back. I look at him.

"I don't think so," I say because I think it's true.

The pump clicks down to ten dollars. I give him eleven and feel like a heel, but he smiles and salutes me again with the bills.

"Take care," he says.

I nod and get back into the car. Wrap my fingers around the steering wheel.

Miss K. blinks at me.

I don't know where to go.

Oh, I know the way, all right. That's not the problem. It's the arriving I'm not sure about. I have a choice. Great-aunt Eva or Uncle Charles. The possibilities for retribution and shame are endless.

Whack-whack!

This time I don't jump before I roll down the window.

"You okay?" the boy asks.

I nod.

"If you need a place to stay," he says, "there's a motel just off the high-way on the other side of town."

Option three occurs to me. I hadn't considered a third option.

"My mom runs it," he continues. "Clean, and you can rent by the week. Assuming you want to stay for a while."

The English language doesn't really allow for three options. On the one hand, you have either. On the other hand, you have or. Neither, nor. If, then. Black, white. Up, down. Yes, no. Maybe it's because humans are bi-lateral creatures. Maybe it's because the humans who spoke the languages that bred and produced the mongrel of the language world—English—led a life so simple they didn't need more than two options.

I need three. But I hadn't even considered the *possibility* of a third op-tion until the gap-toothed, gas-pumping teen brought it up.

Great-aunt Eva, or Uncle Charles, *or* a motel.

A quiet, anonymous motel where Miss Kitty and I can stay—undetected—for about three days. Or three minutes, depending on the speed of the present-day Silver Creek grapevine. I hope I can avoid run-ning into any of the vine's branches. I need a bit of time while I try to figure out what I'm doing here.

If I should be here at all.

I take the back streets to reach the other side of town, even though every block has a stop sign. The houses along the side roads crowd together dustily and reach for the shade of the trees near the edge of the street, but the streets greedily pull back on the shade, keeping it for themselves. As I reach the far side of Silver Creek, the trees and shadows begin to thin until the only thing left between me and the rolling, grassy hills is sunshine and an ancient motel.

The motel keeps up the silver motif by calling itself the Silver Spur. The name sounds shinier than the gray, peeling-paint line of joined rooms that form an L shape around an asphalt parking lot. I park the car so the pine tree by the office shields Miss Kitty from the afternoon sun, then go in to rent us a room.

Cobwebbed spurs jingle as I push open the door.

"Be right with you," says a woman sitting behind the counter. She's watching a game show. "It's Mae West, you idiot," she says as the contestant on the television screen shakes his head in frustration.

I lean on the counter. Under the smudged glass covering the top are postcards from around Montana. *Visit Butte!* one faded red picture orders.

"Just one?" the woman asks, and I look up in time to see her lever her bulk out of the chair.

"One person," I say, unwilling to lie outright, even though Kitty is more human than most humans.

"Twenty dollars."

"I'm staying for a while."

"Do you want a room with a kitchen?"

"How much does it cost?"

She looks me up and down. "Fifteen." She looks me up and down again. "Three days in advance."

I take my money out of the pocket of my jeans and count off two precious twenties and a five.

She purses her lips. "If the money ever gets tight"—I look up from putting the small amount of cash I have left back in my pocket—"not that I think it is or anything, but if you ever happen to be short on change, I could use some help around here."

"What kind of help?"

She steps back, lifts her skirt to just above the knee, and points to her legs. They're swollen so that the knees and ankles are barely visible under the white, blue-veined poufs of flesh. "I don't get around very well," she says, quiet dignity in her voice. "I can take care of the office, but cleaning takes a lot out of me. Dustin helps, but he's got his own work to do."

"Is Dustin the one I met at the Gas and Lube?" I ask.

She smiles and drops the skirt. "You met him?"

I nod.

"He's a good kid."

I nod again.

"It's usually not much," she continues. "Just a few rooms to do up before noon. Some are renters, like yourself. Part of the road crew. Some are just passing through."

"I have a cat," I say. "She's clean."

She bites the inside of her right cheek. "Were you planning on telling me this?"

I open my mouth. Close it. "No," I say after a bit.

"The cat can stay," she says. "I would have appreciated you telling me about her up front, but I've got nothing against cats. Dogs put holes in the sheets." She looks me up and down a third time. "Three-fifty a room. There are usually three or four during the summer. And you do your own room for free. Because of the cat."

"Okay."

She holds out her hand. A silver and turquoise bracelet forms a tourniquet around her wrist.

We shake hands on the deal, I sign the book, and she gives me a key attached to a plastic, spur-shaped key ring. "Number eighteen," she says. "Just across the parking lot. Come in tomorrow morning about nine and I'll tell you what to do."

Kitty and I set up shop with the smooth division of labor of two carnys setting up the Ferris wheel at the county fair. Miss K. tries out the window ledges and the bed springs before sniffing out the dust bunnies. I drag in my duffle bag from the car and set up Miss K.'s litter box next to the porcelain throne. Then we have a rousing game of feather-on-a-string, with Kitty flopping on her side every once in a while to say *"I'm only doing this to make you happy. It really is demeaning"* before she's off after the feather again. We eat a snack of canned peaches and tender liver bits in gravy—respectively, since I don't like liver—then I give Miss K. a scratch behind the ears and go out to look for gainful employment.

I leave my hair down and hunch my shoulders. Silver Creek has a large enough population for a person to remain unnoticed as long as she isn't the youngest surviving member of a family line stretching back to one of the sour-eyed women pictured on the wall of city hall. I avoid Main and continue my hunch-shouldered walk toward the *Creek News* office, where the blue newspaper boxes with the afternoon's paper neatly stacked inside are chained to the exterior of the building. I need a job outside the service sector. No point in advertising my presence by hiring on as a busboy at the all-night restaurant. Dustin's mother—I didn't think to ask her name—said something about some of the motel renters doing highway work.

HELP WANTED.

I subconsciously see the sign and have to walk backward two steps to take a closer look. The sign is taped to the glass-front door of—I look up—THE WATERING HOLE. I haven't been in Silver Creek since I attained the much-heralded legal age for consuming alcoholic beverages. And this particular service-sector job doesn't have a lot of crossover with the local grapevine—the branches of which are all fine upstanding members of the local Society for the Concern of Morals (Other than Gossip) in Our Community.

I pull open the door and step inside. Outside, the late-afternoon sun still has the clarity and heat peculiar to the high plains. Inside, the light comes from a dozen candles, a red-shaded lamp hanging over a threadbare pool table, and some neon beer signs. I feel like the only person in the room, but that's because the two men sitting at the bar are staring at me. I hunch deeper into myself and force my feet to carry me forward. The closer I get to the bar, the brighter it seems. Two more red-shaded ceiling lamps light up the bottles on the wall.

"Nice evening, isn't it?" one of the men asks.

I nod. Then say, "Yeah, it is." I slide onto one of the tall wooden stools and try to figure out the situation. A few years ago, I would have had fifteen minutes' worth of things to say on the weather before asking about the sign taped to the door. But Miss Kitty doesn't do a lot of vocal communication, and she studies things before deciding whether to pounce or go her merry way. Maybe the habit is catching.

The top of the bar is clean. The entire bar is clean. Everything seems to have a place and everything is in its place—

"Do you want something?" the man asks. "Lil's in back, but I know how to pour a beer."

His eyes are dark under the billed cap splashed with the logo of an agricultural implement company that has a dealership on the edge of town, but the lines around his mouth deepen as he smiles.

I smile a little in return. "I'm actually here about a job."

"Thad, give me a hand, will you?" a voice says from the swinging doors behind the bar.

The man speaking to me gets up and walks around to help a woman roll and heave a silver container of draft beer into place. She's hooking the keg up to the tap advertising a premium beer when he leans forward and says, "You've got someone here about the job."

The woman—Lil, I guess—looks up. She has short, curly white-blond or gray hair, and she's wearing a flannel shirt, jeans, and the ubiquitous silver rodeo buckle. Barrel racing, I think, but it's hard to make out the design from here.

She looks me up and down, just like the woman who runs the motel. I try not to hunch my shoulders.

"Have you ever worked in a bar?" she asks.

"No. Ma'am," I add as an afterthought.

"Restaurant?"

"A few times."

"Do you get on well with people?"

I look into her eyes. I'm already hired. I'm close enough to see that. Somehow, she's looked me up and down and made her decision.

"It depends on the people," I say out loud.

She nods. "Thaddeus," she says, "cover Lyle's ears, will you?"

Thad makes a show of covering the other man's ears.

"This is a cash job," Lil says to me. "I pay you in cash. Do you understand?"

I understand. But I haven't had an income-tax kind of job for a while now.

"Fine with me," I say.

"Good. You can let go of Lyle's ears now," she says to Thad. "Lyle's my accountant," she says to me, "and I wouldn't want him to hear anything that might hurt him."

"I heard that," Lyle says.

"Three to two Monday through Thursday. Three to three on week-ends," Lil says to me, ignoring Lyle. "Sundays off and I pay for your supper."

"I have a cat," I say, not sure why I say it. Maybe it's Lil's green eyes.

"Can she keep her tail out of the beer?"

"I don't know."

"She hasn't worked in a bar either?"

Lyle laughs, but it's a nice laugh.

"Bring her on in," Lil says. "Maybe it's time we had a mascot."

"I'm your mascot, Lil," Thad says. Then he starts singing "Rocky Rac-coon." About the point where the songwriter claims everyone knows Magil/Lil as Nancy, Lil throws a damp towel at his head.

"Shut up, sheep lover!"

Thad pulls the towel off his face, but his cap is pushed back and I see gray hair around his temples that says more about his age than his ageless smile.

"You can start tomorrow," Lil says to me.

"Okay." I slide off the stool and walk through the dim coolness to the door.

"Hey!" Lil's voice stops me at the door and I turn around. "What's your name?"

Embarrassment at forgetting a little social nicety crawls into my cheeks. "Katherine," I say. "But call me Kat."

CHAPTER 2

I have an honest face.

That's what Newell said. *"You have an honest face."* He said it 325 miles away from Silver Creek. Stephen sat next to me on the hard bench seat of the van—the seat just behind the driver. And Newell pulled up to the motel, cut the motor, turned around, and said, "Send her in to rent the room." Stephen didn't even protest, just handed me the cash.

"Tell them it's for two people," Newell said to me. "They'll believe you. You have an honest face."

And his upper lip twitched.

For a groupie.

The unspoken words passed between us.

I wasn't a groupie. I was in love.

But Newell was right about one thing. I have an honest face. I was only eighteen, but the desk clerk took my cash. He never asked how old I was. He charged me for two instead of five. I don't think I even signed the register.

My honest face.

I step out of the Silver Spur's scuffed aluminum shower stall and dry off with the hand towel passing itself off as something bigger. Leaning against the sink, I rub the damp terry cloth over the bathroom mirror until the face in question comes into focus.

Things seem to come easy for me. Like this room-cleaning arrange-ment. Like the job at the Watering Hole. It's as if something bigger than me is pushing me along. The wind pushing the tumbleweed until it runs into a fence and can't go any farther. And all along the way, the tumble-weed's honest face keeps it out of trouble and helps pave the road with other people's good intentions. Helps pave the road to . . .

. . . to nowhere.

To Silver Creek.

As good as nowhere.

I was born just outside of Silver Creek's bare-essentials hospital. In the town's lone ambulance. The doctor who ran out to deliver me has told me the story a dozen times. Once for every time I saw him in my first eight-een years of life. *"I got there just when you did. You were a beautiful baby. I told your mama so."*

But my honest face didn't help me two years after I entered the world. Technically, I was Uncle Charles' responsibility. But when he signed the guardianship papers, no one, least of all Uncle Charles, was expecting a flash flood and subsequent orphan status of Will and Meddie's screaming toddler. Great-aunt Eva—last of her generation—offered to step in and take over the parental duties. A grateful Uncle Charles accepted the offer, and I moved in with Eva.

I came in screaming.

I left without a sound.

Sometime in the middle of the night.

With Stephen.

Which is how I came to be 325 miles away from Silver Creek in a van outside a motel. Eighteen years old, on my way to the golden city of Los Angeles, riding in a busted-down van with four guys in leather jackets, and staring at Newell's silent twist of sarcasm.

I rub the damp terry cloth over the mirror again. The movement causes the hemp string around my neck to shift. In the dim light from the bathroom's lone bulb, the gold ring that hangs from the twisted hemp bounces sparkles of light between itself and the mirror.

I left with Stephen in the middle of the night.

Which is how I came to be on a beach a few months later, knee-deep in the ocean and exchanging vows and rings under the dual blessing of a crescent moon and a setting sun. Even the universe ordained that Stephen and I should be together. Until I drove away.

I lean forward and breathe a warm circle of fog on the mirror. The ring swings away from my chest, then bumps cold against the skin between my breasts. I'm twenty-two years old and have an honest face.

The universe doesn't ordain anything.

I pull an old T-shirt over my head and slip into bed. Beside me, Miss Kitty kneads one of the bed pillows into shape while I wad mine up behind my head and reach for a worn spiral notebook.

"Do you ever write your own?" Stephen asks from a memory. We were crunched together on a mattress made for one. On the far side of someone else's no-bedroom apartment. I was carefully copying an Emily Dickinson poem from a library book. Finding peace in knowing that somewhere in time and space, someone knew the feelings swirling in my chest.

The ballpoint pen between my fingers slowed to a halt.

"No," I said to Stephen.

"Why not?"

I shut the notebook. "I'm no good at it."

Lying in the fast-warming sheets of the Silver Spur's double bed, Kitty's purr in my ear, I thumb through the worn notebook. I started keeping it . . . I don't remember when I started copying down poems. Anytime I read or hear a few lines that let me feel the touch of another person, I write the lines in this notebook.

A record of humanity and its soul.

But the poems don't explain the wind blowing me to Silver Creek.

In the middle of the night, I wake up from a dream about drowning to find I've got the ring clutched in my fist.

"If it isn't Little. Miss. Perfect," says a voice.

I'm wiping up smudges left on the bar's polished surface by sweaty beer mugs and dirty forearms. But at the sound of the voice, my hand stops dead.

I look up from the rag and focus on the voice's owner. The strawberry hair is the same, but the four years between now and the last day of high school haven't been kind to Summer Jones. The hard wind that dried out her tanned skin seems to have dried out her eyes, too. She reminds me of a cottonwood leaf nearing the frosty days when it will shrivel and fall off dead. How would Poe have put it?

The leaves they were withering and sere.

"Hi, Summer," I say and push the rag back into action.

She leans her arms on the bar and settles in. I feel her looking at my left hand, but I squash the sensation of wanting to hide my fingers behind my back.

"Looks like he swept you up and threw you out," Summer says, reaching into a glass dish for some complimentary honey-roasted peanuts. She tosses a peanut into the air, catches it in her mouth, and smiles around the crunch.

"Could be," I say.

I'm waiting for the rush of anger or indignation or disgust or embarrassment or . . . *something.* Only nothing rushes.

I wipe the rag in a slow circle before looking into Summer's dried-up eyes.

"Could be," I say again. "Could be not."

My old enemy was waiting for this tango of words. She smiles.

"The valedictorian comes to a bad end," she says. "Everyone else knew he'd dump you eventually. Maybe you just weren't smart enough."

I nod sagely, as if I'm agreeing with her. "It's true. I guess getting voted homecoming queen went to my head."

Summer doesn't move, but I can see she still remembers being runner-up—and that being runner-up still stings.

Crowning a homecoming queen is a publicity stunt these days. Nostalgia guaranteed to bring home a few donations from the alumni who can afford to be immortalized with a plaque over the door to a cafeteria or reading room. Standing next to a smelly jock and waving into the lights didn't do a lot for me. But Summer believed the publicity. She wanted to wear the tiara. Wave into the lights. Smelly jock and all.

"How about a couple of beers?" she asks, grinding her teeth. "Before I die of thirst."

I reach for the mugs, but she stops me. "Not that goat piss this place has got on draft. Two Coronas."

I pop the caps off the Coronas at the opener attached to the edge of the bar and stick a wedge of lime across each bottle mouth, just like Lil told me to do during that slam-bang orientation session this afternoon. Setting the bottles on the bar, I realize the rush I'm finally feeling is pity.

For Summer Jones.

It's unnatural.

Like being here. Like the unnatural wind that tumbled me here.

Summer pays me. As she walks back to her table and the muscled man wearing a wife-beater tank, she throws the lime wedges onto the floor.

"Summer's such a lovely girl," Lil says from beside me.

I rub the rag into the wooden surface of the bar.

"This was a mistake," I say as Summer leans in to kiss the man before tilting her head in my direction.

"You just started," Lil says, surprise in her voice. "You want to quit already?"

I realize I said the words out loud. "Not working here," I tell her. "Being here. In Silver Creek. Being here is a mistake."

"The only mistake you're making is letting Summer chew you up," Lil says. "Don't be such a baby. Worse people come in here on the weekends."

I nod, and Lil walks down to the end of the bar where Thad and Lyle are sitting. Lil's advice is great. Or it would be, if I were new to this town.

Summer glances at me and twitches her hair over her shoulder. And I remember a golden morning four years ago when the sunlight caught the red in Summer's hair as she flipped it over her shoulder. Her standard Rapunzel method of trapping men. That golden morning, Summer had the guitarist drooling under her tower. Her sister was getting married and the guitarist should have been on the stage playing music for the bride and groom, but Summer flipped her siren hair and breathed deeply. Sunshine sparkled off the glitter powder dusted between her breasts. She had about three more deep breaths to go before the maid-of-honor dress popped and freed all that skin. Sipping from the little glass punch cup, I couldn't help smiling at the mental image of the explosion.

I was still smiling when the guitarist turned around. Still smiling when I was caught by Stephen McKittrick's brown eyes.

Rubbing the rag over the bar, I blink at Summer and Mr. Muscles. I don't understand why I'm here. In Silver Creek. But one of the things Miss Kitty has taught me is that you have to trust your instincts.

Instinct tumbled me here. Might as well run with it.

"Hey, Kat, when are you planning on bringing in the new mascot?" Thad asks.

I toss the rag and the memories, and wander down to Thad's and Lyle's end of the bar.

"I thought one newbie a night was about all Lil could handle," I say, leaning my elbows on the bar next to my new boss.

Lyle sips his beer. "Lil's tough."

"Tomorrow, then," I say. "If Miss K. hasn't wrecked the room and gotten us kicked out of the motel. Then we'll have to move into the storeroom."

Lil looks at me out of the sides of her eyes.

"It was a joke," I say. "She doesn't even scratch furniture. She's very well behaved."

"Oops," Summer says, her voice raised to reach us. "I just knocked over my beer." The dribbling bottle rolls off the edge of the table and onto the floor. "Clumsy, clumsy me."

The other customers in the bar turn to look.

"Better behaved than some people," I say.

Lil sighs. "God help us if our future mascot can only claim behavior that's better than some people's."

"She's a cat," I say. "People are good companions, but she wouldn't approve of using bald monkeys as role models for kitty behavior."

Lyle blinks. "This is too weird," he says. "I'm going home."

"See you tomorrow," Lil says. After he leaves, she picks up a roll of paper towels and starts to walk around the edge of the bar, but I stop her.

"I'll do it."

"You sure?" she asks, tilting her head to one side.

I nod.

She tosses me the paper towels.

I walk over to the table where Summer is leaning back in her chair, a smirk she has no intention of hiding all over her face. I pick up the bottle from the floor, set it on the table, and give a little bow.

"Quick Clean at your service, ma'am," I say to Summer. Then I turn to Mr. Muscles and touch the paper towel roll to my temple in an imitation of Dustin's salute. "Hi, Nate."

It took me a while to recognize him—the muscles are a new look—but the guy Summer is with used to live down the block from Great-aunt Eva's. By some freak accident, we ended up in different elementary schools and with different friends, then he dropped out of high school. . . .

Nate smiles. "Hi, Kat."

"Still hardheaded?" I ask.

"You *know* her?" Summer interrupts. Her eyes are dried leaves piled up and set on fire.

"Yeah," Nate says to me.

"Old neighbor," I say to Summer. Then I pull a wad of towels off the roll and wipe the table in the middle of the silence that's pushing down on the three of us. I'm catching the puddle of beer on the floor when Summer puts the toe of her lizard-skin boot on top of the damp paper towels, narrowly missing my fingers.

"You know him?" she asks.

I lean back on my haunches, elbows resting on my knees, and look up at her. "He flipped over the handlebars of his bike and landed on his head when he was six. I think it warped his brain."

I don't mean for it to sound like I think only a man with a warped mind would be caught with Summer Jones, but Summer chooses to take it that way.

And maybe that *is* what I wanted.

"Have a bottle," she says. And she drops the still-half-full bottle onto the floor in front of me. Beer splatters. "Welcome home."

I nod. "Thanks. It's good to be back." Then I right the bottle before it can spill any more beer on the sopping paper towel wad.

Nate chuckles.

Summer snarls something unintelligible and pushes out of her chair. She's nearly out the bar door before Nate realizes they're leaving.

"I guess we're going," he says.

I hand him the leather jacket Summer left behind. "Nice to see you again."

He grins. "You, too. Things were getting boring around here."

"Like I'm going to liven them up."

His grin widens. Just before he reaches the door, he turns. "You never know."

Thad and Lil are watching me as I toss the dripping paper towels away and wheel the mop and bucket out of the storeroom.

"Do you think this is the moment when I should say something cliché about our Kat growing claws?" Lil asks.

"No," I say from where I'm mopping the floor.

"Bravo," Thad says. "Encore." Then he and Lil give me a polite round of applause. Theater critics run amok. A few of the bar's patrons—the ones who noticed what was going on—join in a bit more enthusiastically. I lean on my mop and shake my head. It's harder to ignore the warm feeling in my chest.

CHAPTER 3

"You have a message," Dustin's mother says to me as I step into the motel office to pick up the key to the door grandly labeled HOUSEKEEPING.

"A message?"

"On the telephone."

Do I have memory haze—I *am* trying to get by on five hours of sleep—or isn't there a phone in my room?

She sees my confusion. "People who want to be put through to someone's room should act a little less like God issuing commandments from Mount Sinai," she says.

I bite my lip, then give up and grin at her outrage.

She holds up a finger in warning.

"Sorry," I say, pasting a serious look on my face.

"She said that no relation of hers would stay *here*," Dustin's mother continues, her voice changing drastically, horribly, familiarly on that last word.

No need for paste. I don't know why I thought it would be Lil calling me first thing in the morning.

It wasn't Lil.

Shit.

The grapevine took exactly . . . thirty-six hours to report me.

I lean against the counter and press the heels of my hands into my eyes.

"Be careful how you lean on that glass," Dustin's mother says.

"We've never been introduced," I say from behind my hands, taking care not to lean so heavily on the glass covering the postcards.

"What?"

I drop my hands from my eyes and try to smile. "I'm Kat," I say.

"I know," she says, looking at me as though I might suddenly turn into some kind of horned insurance salesman or representative for one of the myriad local churches. "You signed the register, remember?"

"But I don't know your name," I say.

"Melody."

"Nice to meet you." I hold a hand out over the counter. She looks at it. "The woman who called you was my great-aunt," I say. "If I thought the kinds of things she thinks, I would be staying at the house I grew up in."

Melody reaches out and takes my hand. "You can't choose your blood," she says.

"I've never thought of it like that."

She shrugs.

And it's the shrug—and maybe the memory of Great-aunt Eva's voice called up by Melody's imitation—that tosses me back to being eighteen and the golden sunny day when Summer's sister got married.

"You're following me, aren't you?" I asked the guitarist who had been walking a half block behind me as I picked my way down the cracked sidewalk toward Eva's house.

He stopped a few feet away and shrugged. One shoulder tilting up into the sunshine. One corner of his mouth lifting in a smile. "Yes."

"So if I leave town for four years, I can expect to get lost?" I teased. "And have to find my way by following people around?"

"It depends on where you go."

"Katherine," Great-aunt Eva called from the screen door. "You have a phone call."

"You live here?" he asked.

"You knew that."

"Actually, I didn't."

I smiled. "Now you do."

A drawer slams.

"—if I could remember where I put it," Melody finishes, digging around behind the counter.

"What?" I ask. Automatically. Still lost in the memory.

"Here." Melody hands me a bit of newspaper.

I reach out for it. Look at it.

The past drifts away like the elusive scent of springtime honeysuckle.

It's just a piece of paper. A piece of—I look at the date—today's weather forecast. I lift a hand in a bewildered gesture.

"Wrong side," she says.

I turn it over. "Oh."

"That's you, isn't it?"

I nod.

"I didn't know you were a model."

"I wasn't. I'm not. They offered a few hundred dollars for 'suitable-looking' high school kids." I set the paper with the ad for a local department store on the counter. Carefully. As if the glass might crack under the weight. Those few hundred dollars helped pay for the first-and-last rent on the Spanish-style grillwork apartment. Before two jobs couldn't manage to keep the money flowing in fast enough. "I'd think they would have gotten in some different fashions by now," I say to Melody. "That picture is four years old."

"Yeah, but you can't really see what you're wearing," she says. "It's more of a . . . a thought piece."

I reach for the housekeeping key that hangs on the hook board by the counter. "Sure."

"You'll want this," she says before I can reach the door.

I think she means the ad, but she gives me a pink slip of paper with a telephone number neatly—if darkly—printed on it.

"Thanks," I say. "I know the number."

Bridges. Human beings love bridges. We cross them when we come to them and burn them behind us. We build bridges between us and cross the Rubicon to change history. The town of Silver Creek has one bridge. It spans a narrow bit of the snaking river that runs ragged in spring and runs dry around September. The bridge is old and, just like the town, it manages to be overlooked by the nation, state, and county. Otherwise someone would have conceived the marvelous idea of tearing it down and funding some local bridge replacement firm with tax dollars. But when the only traffic is dusty ranch pickups and the occasional scenic-route tourist who has lost his way, no one feels a burning need to rip out one of the few unique landmarks left to the area.

Walking to the middle of the bridge, I swing one leg over the ornate arched guardrail made of cement. No, I'm not thinking of jumping. That would be ridiculous. I'd end up with nothing worse than a broken leg or ankle. The sun-warmed cement soaks heat through my jeans, and under my dangling feet, the last of the summer water trickles between the rocks. Silver Creek isn't exactly picturesque in late summer. Still water collects in small, greasy pools, and the flow is reduced to a thin ribbon of water in the center of a barren moonscape of tumbled boulders.

I lied this morning.

To Melody.

Not exactly lied, I guess. But I used to think the things my great-aunt thinks.

Shame and sunlight heat my face.

I'm ashamed. Not that I lied. Because while lying is bad, at what point does yesterday's truth become tomorrow's lie?

"Katherine? Is that you?"

I nearly fall off the bridge. Looking over my shoulder, I see a smooth, gleaming Cadillac in the latest model and custom color. No Acuras for this old boy.

Pulling my legs up, I turn around so my back is to the riverbed and the grasslands stretching into the distance, and so I'm facing the open window of the car.

"Uncle Charles."

He turns off the engine. I can see him thinking. His forehead wrinkles and he purses his lips.

"Not 'Chaz'?" he asks.

"If you'd rather."

He smiles. "No. Thanks, anyway. But, no." And opening the door, he unfastens the seat belt and steps out of the car. He's a little wrinkled, and he's coming back into Silver Creek from the ranch land to the north and west.

Been out foreclosing?

A summer morning when I was ten. I'd just lost three teeth on top of growing two inches and could have been empress of the world. The downtown was steamy hot, so I slipped into the credit union building. Blue-marble tile met my stockinged feet as I slid across the lobby floor. Once. Twice. From his office, I could hear Uncle Charles moan and hang up the phone. *"Katherine . . . please. Don't you—"* "Hi, Chaz," I said, reaching up on tiptoe to plant a smacking kiss on his cheek. "Been foreclosing?"

Here on the bridge, I keep my mouth shut. Sweat prickles between my shoulder blades.

Uncle Charles stretches, then digs his hands into the pockets of his slacks and leans back against the side of his car. He looks at me. An expanse of dark asphalt road separates us.

"How did you find out?" he asks.

Heat waves shimmy across the asphalt and over the milk-green metal of the car's hood.

"About what?" I ask.

Silence replaces the heat waves.

"Have you told Aunt Eva you're home?"

"No."

"But she knows you're here?" He knows the Silver Creek grapevine, too.

"She called this morning."

"So you've spoken to her?" He looks relieved.

"Not yet."

He sighs and almost runs a hand through his hair, but he catches himself in time to avoid messing up the deliberately casual look fixed with a combination of gel and hair spray. We share the same thick red-brown hair. Only I've taken to braiding the mess and ignoring it rather than beating it into submission with a bathroom full of products.

"Why are you always so difficult?" he asks. His voice is tired.

I don't have an answer. Oh, I have enough fury and emotions and explanations and accusations to fill the void of the sky from one bit of horizon to the other. But incoherent, frustrated babbling isn't communication. The builders who attempted the tower at Babel could tell you that.

"She's dying," Charles says.

"She's always dying."

This isn't callous. This is the voice of experience. Great-aunt Eva believes death is around every corner. For her, anyway. A simple cold is pneumonia. A headache is a massive brain aneurism. Having her foot fall asleep while watching TV is the beginning of debilitating paralysis.

"This time it's real," he says.

I can feel the hot cement under the palms of my hands. Sweat forms between skin and reflected heat.

"I tried to locate you," he says. "I couldn't."

"No."

He frowns and shakes his head. "No explanations?"

"For what?"

"For where you've been."

"Did the grapevine miss me?" I ask. The question is automatic. I'm thinking about Great-aunt Eva sitting in her yellow velvet "TV chair." *I don't know why everyone assumes a woman should suffer in silence. My ankles are definitely swollen,* she's saying in my memory.

"Of course not," Uncle Charles says. "You left town with a man named Stephen McKittrick. I tracked him down someplace in Seattle, but he didn't know where you were either."

"Seattle," I repeat.

Stephen's band was really Newell's band. Only when Newell found out about the recording contract, he mixed celebrating with motorcycles. The band tried to go on without him, but Newell had been the one who wrote the songs and knew that rhythm didn't have to mean a straight 4/4 beat. The contract fizzled. Los Angeles must have fizzled, too.

Uncle Charles pushes away from the car and wades through the heat waves. He snaps his fingers in front of my face.

"Are you here? On drugs? Drinking? Suicidal?" Each question is punctuated by a snap.

"I'm fine," I say, pushing his hand away from my face.

"God!" The word is a small explosion. Then he lets out a sigh that is half moan. "Why won't you ever grow up? Start thinking about people other than yourself?"

"I'm trying," I say. "But it's difficult when other people forget I'm not canine and snap their fingers at me."

He runs his guilty fingers through his hair, leaving tunnels in the fixative.

"I'm sorry," he says. Up close, the lines around his eyes are deeper and his mouth tilts down at the corners.

"Thank you for trying to find me," I say.

He shakes his head in bewilderment and sits down beside me on the guardrail.

"You're nothing like Will or Meddie. Maybe you were adopted."

"Not with this hair."

He continues to shake his head.

"Here, *Chaz*," I say. And I reach out and fluff his hair back into place.

"Promise me you'll go see Eva," he says.

My hand falls.

"Promise?"

"I promise."

"I have to go back to work. . . ." He trails off. "Do you need money? A place to stay?"

It would be so easy. So easy to—

"No," I say. "I'm fine."

One muddy spring day, I was playing with a hoe in Great-aunt Eva's vegetable garden. The blade sank so beautifully into the soft, wet dirt that I didn't even notice when it sank into my six-year-old toe. Until the stinging started and blood mixed with mud. I showed it to Eva. *"That's going to take a tetanus shot,"* she said.

The only word I heard was "shot."

Sitting on the smooth chairs at the doctor's office, I kept my eyes screwed shut. Pretending that somehow, someway, the *shot* wasn't going to happen. The doctor would have an emergency. The office would close. The rapture would happen and the doctor would be left behind. Or I'd be left behind. I didn't care as long as we weren't going to the same place.

"Bad things don't go away just because you want them to," Great-aunt Eva said. "Besides, it's just a little prick. Would you rather have your jaw freeze shut?"

Having my jaw freeze shut sounded better than letting the antiseptic-smelling man in a lab coat jab me with a twenty-eight-inch cattle prod disguised as a needle.

I got the shot. (It was just as bad as I knew it was going to be.) I got a sucker. And the bad thing didn't go away. I just lived through it.

Despite the learning experience, I didn't learn a damn thing.

I sometimes shut my eyes and pretend the shot isn't going to happen.

Sitting on the bridge, breathing the dust kicked up by Charles' car, I shut my eyes and pretend that no one knows who I am and I don't even *have* a great-aunt, much less an obligation to live up to.

I shut my eyes and pray for the rapture. For deliverance from evil.

Because I don't want to go see Great-aunt Eva.

Deliver me unto procrastination, O Lord.

It's only two hours until I have to be at the Watering Hole. It will be Miss Kitty's first day.

I welcome the excuses with open arms.

Two hours later, I open the cat carrier and let Miss K. out onto the bar.

"I'm sure that isn't legal," Lyle says.

Thad rolls his eyes. "Who are you? The health inspector?"

"No," Lyle says. "I'm the guy who has to figure out how Lil is going to pay all the fines if the health inspector makes a surprise visit."

"Sorry, Lil," I say, picking Kitty up and setting her on the floor.

"Don't look at me," Lil says. "I didn't make a peep." She turns to Lyle and Thad. "Don't you two have anything better to do than sit around my bar at three in the afternoon?"

Lyle mumbles something about ungrateful females and slouches out the door, but Thad just grins. "I'm courting," he says.

"She must be desperate," Lil says. "Or a sheep."

Thad goes down on his knees. "Marry me, Lil."

"And give you half my bar? Get out of here."

He laughs and leaves.

"Idiot," Lil says, affection in her voice.

I watch the sunlight kiss Thad's heels as he shuts the door behind him, then look at Lil's face.

Maybe it's the observation lessons I'm taking from Kitty, but if you were looking, you could have seen a thread of deeper emotion under Thad's grin. If you happened to be looking for something that wasn't on the surface, that is.

"You think he's joking?" I ask Lil.

She shuts her eyes, then shrugs a little. "Of course. There isn't a serious bone in Thaddeus' body."

I nod. I don't believe her, but it isn't my problem.

An avalanche of falling brooms and mops hits the storeroom floor as Miss K. streaks out the door and into the bar. She skids to a stop and begins to wash a paw. *"Amazing,"* she seems to say. *"One moment they were just leaning against the wall and the next I was running for my life."*

"Do mascots always trash things?" Lil asks me.

"Only if the other team wins."

CHAPTER 4

My procrastination lasts two more days. But Sunday comes, I'm not on at the bar, and I can only stretch cleaning motel rooms into so many hours. At one point, it gets a little silly. Me telling myself that the faithful washing machine can only make it through the load of king-sized sheets—the laundry service refuses anything larger than queen—if I stand over it chanting, "You can do it, yes you can. If you can't do it . . ."

Like I said, it got a little silly.

I'm standing on the sidewalk at the end of a familiar street. Silly doesn't have to be humorous, and the fluttering in my stomach feels a lot like nausea. The brick street is one of the few in Silver Creek to escape the easy fix of an asphalt covering. Trees planted by the town fathers and mothers stretch out in front of me in imitation of the principles of perspective and viewpoint the junior high art teacher drilled into our hormone-addled heads. It's hard to imagine the town matriarchs caring about something as earthly as shade. But the trees exist, so someone must have searched out the most promising seedlings from the banks of Silver Creek, dug them up, and brought them back here.

I drag my feet as I walk down the sidewalk. Past the immortal crack that brought my Big Wheel to a dead stop and jarred my baby teeth loose the Saturday afternoon Nate and I played Kentucky Derby. Past the tired, dusty spirea shrubs that struggle to grow in the shade of the cottonwoods and bloom halfheartedly every spring. Drag my feet until I reach one of the smaller two-story houses. The gingerbread trim was removed by Great-aunt Eva's father, who complained that the "damn frills"—as she says he called them—were too hard to paint. The removal actually improves the look of the place and makes it fit the personality of its inhabitant.

Taking a deep breath, I swear I meet the ghost of myself running down the porch steps and catching Stephen's hand before escaping into the midnight darkness. Running like two idiots into the unknown.

I climb the wooden steps. The second one still squeaks. At the door, I hesitate, then open the screen and knock twice. I shut the screen and wait, hands shoved into my pockets.

Inside, Pearl barks. I can hear her nails skid on the hardwood floor, scrabbling to find purchase. Silence. Then a soft thump and renewed barking. That was Pearl hitting the area rug and sliding—rug and all—into the door.

"Pearl! Hush." The door opens, and I'm face-to-face with the woman who raised me.

"Hi, Eva," I say.

Pearl pushes out the screen door and sinks her teeth into my ankle. Only I'm wearing jeans, so she ends up with a mouthful of denim. She hangs on determinedly to a fold of material. A poodle pit bull.

Great-aunt Eva ignores her.

"Did you ever think that I might have appreciated a phone call or a letter or maybe even a card at Christmas?" she asks. She doesn't sound angry, just matter-of-fact.

"Yes," I say.

"But you didn't call or write."

"No."

She nods once. "Come in."

I cross the threshold, dragging Pearl with me. Inside, I automatically bend down to straighten up the area rug. Pearl catches a whiff of my hand, lets go of my jeans, and backs up. She's still barking, still saying all the rude things no one would dare say in the warm, lemon-wood-polish gleam of this house.

"Pearl! For heaven's sake . . ." Eva taps her cane on the floor twice.

Pearl stops barking and slinks to a spot beside the stairs where she can watch me while being out of reach of Great-aunt Eva's wrath.

"Would you like something to drink?" Eva asks me, polite hostess inquiry on her face.

I almost say no, but my throat is so dry it hurts to swallow. "Please."

"Tea, coffee, or lemonade?"

"Tea, please."

"Hot or cold?"

"Whichever is easiest."

She stiffens. "They are both equally easy," she grinds out. As if I've insulted her hospitality.

"I'm sorry," I say on reflex. "Cold, please."

"At least you haven't forgotten *all* your manners," she says, turning and walking into the kitchen. I start to follow her, then hesitate, unsure whether going into the kitchen would be a breach in "manners."

How can a house look so familiar and feel so foreign? On the wall beside the door, a tight-lipped woman glares down at me from a family photo posing as a judgment seat. I'm sure the picture used to be there, but I don't remember it. That's not exactly surprising. I didn't pay much attention to what decorated the walls outside of my bedroom.

I step closer to the picture. The woman has my chin, but did she ever wake up in the middle of the night shaking from fear? Not likely, judging by the firm grip she has on her chair. Do I have anything in common with her beyond a determined chin and—I squint to catch the photo details— that Earle hair?

"That's Wilhelmina," Eva says.

I jump, and Pearl, who's spent the last five minutes making sure I don't attempt to escape with the family silver, growls.

"My grandmother," Eva continues, ignoring Pearl. She hands me a glass of iced tea—weak, with a sprig of mint. Her fingers are twisted and bulging with arthritis. She isn't wearing her mother's wedding ring anymore.

I look away from Eva's fingers and into Wilhelmina's accusing eyes. My great-great-grandmother's accusing eyes.

Eva rests her hands on top of her cane. "Your father was named after her."

I sip my tea.

"You didn't used to be so quiet," she says.

I lower the glass from my lips. "I'm just listening."

"I haven't exactly been chattering nonstop since you knocked."

"No."

"Speech has value, too."

"I know. I just don't know what to say."

She nods. "Come sit down."

The yellow velvet TV chair still has the place of honor. Beside the right arm, the knitting bag holds court. On the left side is a doily-covered lamp table. Under the lamp, the last two copies of *TV Guide* are colorful smears on the ecru lace. Great-aunt Eva eases into the chair, one twisted claw of a hand grasping the arm to steady herself. I feel ashamed of the easy way I sink into the couch. Drops of condensation from the glass of iced tea drip onto my knee.

Once Eva has set her cane aside and settled her elbows into the worn grooves in the yellow upholstery covering the arms of the chair, we sit and look at each other.

I sip more tea to wet my throat.

"You were never a quiet child," she says.

I swallow and make a good-faith effort to continue the conversation from the hallway. "I probably drove you crazy. Talking all the time."

"It was the screaming more than anything," she says, a slight lift to one corner of her mouth.

"I'm not sure that stopped with age," I mutter into my tea.

"No. I'm afraid not. I don't suppose you ever went to college?"

Memories of screaming rage flit through my mind. The discovery that my future was mapped out, that success in school meant I somehow had an obligation to expand my mind by following someone else's proven path . . . I stood on the stairs and screamed at Charles, screamed at Eva, screamed at the universe for not giving me a place to belong.

I shut the memories down in mid-flit.

"No," I say. Quietly. "I didn't."

Eva continues to look at me until I'm doing my best to not shift in my seat. I forgive Pearl for the warm welcome at the front door when she attracts Great-aunt Eva's attention with a commanding bark. Eva gives her a bit of dog treat and she carries it to a corner and buries it under a throw rug.

"I'm dying," Eva says, watching the dog. "I suppose that's why you're back in town."

"I didn't know."

She looks away from Pearl and toward me. "Oh? You don't seem surprised about it, though."

"I saw Uncle Charles on the bridge. He told me."

"Three days ago."

"Yes."

Pearl whines and digs at the rug, trying to uncover the treat she just buried.

"Your room is still here," Eva says. "Why don't you leave that . . . place where you're staying and come back home?"

Life as it could be flashes before my eyes: Long evenings watching re-runs on the television, waiting for death in a routine of enforced break-fasts, fully set tables, cloth napkins, curfews, and . . . questions. Lots and lots of questions. Tricky questions that don't actually come out and ask what Great-aunt Eva wants to know.

But it gets worse. Because Eva isn't asking me to stay here. She's asking me to return to the way things were when I was eighteen.

She's making a play to return the world to the way things were when she wasn't dying.

"I can't," I say. "I have a cat."

Eva raises her eyebrows. "A cat."

"Yes."

"And you have this cat with you at the motel?"

"Yes."

"I suppose you need one, what with the mice."

Familiar ground. Disagree with Aunt Eva's plan for global domination, and politeness is nailed to the cross of sarcasm.

Lovely.

"Since I do the cleaning," I say through a calm smile, "I doubt there's much left for the mice."

"You clean . . . the rooms?" She raises her eyebrows. "The . . ."

"Toilets. Yes, I do. I pick the hair out of the tub drains, too."

"Thank you for the small details."

"You're welcome."

She rests her cheek in her hand—leans on it until her fingers crease the papery skin above her jaw—and looks at me.

Unfamiliar ground. I don't feel angry. Not even a little bit. More like . . . amused. I'm even enjoying the exchange.

Her lips twitch slightly. "I think I like you better this way," she says.

And the pleasure disappears.

"Really?" I ask.

"Bring the cat if you want," she says, brusque and determined. "You'll have to keep it upstairs. I wouldn't want Pearl and it to get into a fight."

"*It* and I prefer to stay at the motel," I say. "Her name is Miss Kitty and she's the mascot at the Watering Hole."

"So let *her* stay *there*. Perhaps she can help them with their cockroach population."

"Oh, I clean down there, too," I say.

"I do believe," she says, all trace of enjoyment gone from her tone, "that if the past were to happen again, you would walk out of my house in broad daylight."

"You're assuming I've developed some backbone," I say. "But just because I clean other people's—" I break off. I was going to say *"clean other people's shit out of the toilet,"* but that is way too crude for this house and its pristine doilies and manicured poodle. "Just because I clean up other people's messes," I amend, "it doesn't mean I have enough backbone to stand up to you."

"Obviously. But you have developed a bit of sass," she says. "Sass" being negative, of course.

This stings. Maybe I wanted her to correct me and say that I *have* grown a backbone. That I really *would* leave in broad daylight.

"Despite what you think of it," Aunt Eva says, "this is your home. And it will stay that way."

"Thank you," I say, still wishing I had a spine, and not much caring what she calls the house.

"So you might as well move in now, as opposed to *later*." She places a curious emphasis on the last word and catches my full attention. "Not that I will stand for any changes." Picking up her cane, she fiddles with the ebony handle.

"Don't worry," I say, "I'm not moving back."

The cane hits the floor once. Twice. Pearl leaps away from the throw rug and scurries under a chair, peering out from between the legs to see whether she is the guilty party.

"You are the most—" Eva begins. Then she cuts herself off. Both hands rest on the cane. "This is your home," she says, looking at her fingers. "It always will be."

She sounds like a judge passing sentence.

After leaving Great-aunt Eva's house in the late-afternoon light, I walk the mile back to the Silver Spur and collapse across the bed. I sleep the sleep of the damned until midnight, when Miss K. finally rouses me long enough to feed her.

CHAPTER 5

The Kat is out of the bag, so to speak. No point anymore in pretending I can skulk around the back streets and keep my presence in town a secret. So after cleaning the three other rented rooms at the motel—it's a rare tourist who spends a Sunday night in Silver Creek—I head downtown to the thrift store to see whether I can find some different clothes. I caught Lil looking at the worn-through edges on the sleeves of my shirt the other day. She opened her mouth—I was sure she would say something awful and embarrassing—then closed it again. Her tact deserves a new shirt or two at least.

I'm thumbing through the rack of mothball-scented shirts, trying to find something I would be caught dead in that doesn't have pearl buttons when a voice says, "Well, look who's slumming!"

Summer is thumbing through the shirts on the opposite side of the rack. But she's not looking for clothes. I take in her nametag with its smiling-face logo and HAPPY SHOPPING! GOD LOVES YOU! heading.

"Well, look who's doing community service instead of jail time!" I say.

Her eyes narrow, but then she smiles. The smile is so odd, I look over my shoulder to see who's standing there.

"Hi, Kat," says the person standing there.

"Well, if you need any more help, just let me know," Summer says in a trilling little shopgirl voice.

I ignore her.

"Hi, Jennifer," I say to the person. But the words sound rough. The last time I saw my best friend, I was lying to her. *"Sure. Tomorrow. I'll meet you there."*

"Back in town?" Jennifer asks.

"Yes. For a while."

"Because of Eva?"

"No. Yes. I didn't know about it . . . about her dying, I mean, but I guess I'll stick around. For a while."

Which makes me sound a proper little shit.

"It's hard to believe you're that insensitive," Jennifer says.

I shrug. "It depends on how you look at dying, I guess."

"Still the smartass."

"I wasn't trying to be a smartass. I really don't . . . I just found out about Aunt Eva," I finish.

"Sure." She's being sarcastic, but it's coming from the ghost of pain in her eyes more than a desire to humiliate me.

"I'm sorry I lied to you," I say. "I didn't—"

"You didn't think I could keep a secret," she says. She rests a hand on one cocked hip and looks at me from her superior height. "You were probably right. I would have done just about anything to keep you in Silver Creek."

The honesty surprises me. But it shouldn't. Before Stephen, Jen and I were always honest with each other. The two "poor little orphan girls." One being raised by family in the veritable lap of respectability, the other shuffling from foster home to foster home in the veritable lap of notoriety. The two "poor little orphan girls" who manipulated high school society until it bowed before them. But we never lied to each other.

Until I decided to leave with Stephen.

I knew Jen would do anything to stop me.

So I lied.

"But knowing you were right about me doesn't mean I have to like being lied to," Jen says.

"I'm sorry," I say again, knowing I would do the same thing all over again. It's sobering to realize that I haven't learned anything from the past.

"How about a shake, or a sundae, or something for old times' sake?" she asks.

I begin making rapid mental calculations. Not about money. About drinking the familiar shake with the vanilla-butter taste my tongue will never forget. About renewing a friendship I'm just learning to live without.

"Wait . . ." Jen says, misinterpreting my hesitation. "You didn't come here to see me, did you?"

I swallow. "No. There's no way I could have known you'd be here."

"I work here," she says. "I manage the place."

"Oh."

"If you're too busy—"

There's the sarcasm again.

"No," I say, interrupting her. "No, I . . . was going to look you up—"

"You're lying again."

I grab on to the rack of shirts and look at her. "Yes. Let's go get some ice cream. If you can get away."

"Okay. Let me tell Summer."

Summer flips her hair and lifts a shoulder in elegant dismissal.

"How is it?" I ask Jen when we step out into the noon heat. "Working with Summer?"

She accepts the change in subject as easily as she did when we were kids. "Annoying. She hasn't changed a bit."

"You look different," I say.

"So do you." She stops me by catching my elbow.

I see her grin before she puts on a serious look. "In fact, I'd say our roles have reversed." She plucks the mended spot on my shirt.

"Hey, patches are in, don't you know?" I say.

"You must have given Eva the fits."

"I wore my Sunday best."

She pounces. "So you *have* seen her?"

I hold up both hands. "I didn't try to deny it."

"I know, but I just . . ." She trails off. "I just didn't think—"

"—that I had the backbone," I finish for her. "A lot of people have the same opinion."

"Including you?"

I scuff at a cigarette butt lying on the sidewalk in front of me. "Maybe."

She pushes my shoulder. "Get over yourself."

Looking up from the butt, I smile at her. "A little role reversal?"

"Well, you didn't used to be the moody one."

"Gotcha."

We continue walking toward the ice cream shop. The shop doesn't have a name. There's a sort of sign, but it's just two dripping ice cream cones crossed under a sundae in a dish. The similarity to a skull and cross-bones is remarkable, but it goes unnoticed as no one has ever died from eating the ice cream. That I know of, anyway.

The sleigh bells attached to a scrap of harness jingle as Jen pushes the door open.

"It's trouble squared!" says the man behind the glass ice cream case. He tips his paper hat in my direction. "Heard you were back."

"You and everyone else."

I try to smile, but I never thought it would be this hard to bump into family friends. Donner—the man with the ridiculous upside-down paper boat on his head—and Uncle Charles are fishing buddies. If I'd stopped to think about it, I might have persuaded Jen to go down to the local Stop & Shop for a pint of Ben & Jerry's.

"So you're still working here?" I ask, only realizing how horrid that sounds when Jen moans a soft "Oh, no."

"Work here?" Donner asks, drawing himself up to his full (and impressive) height. "Work here? I dip it, mix it, create it . . . I *own* this shop now. I slave over my recipes into the wee hours of the morning. I—" He stops because Jen is making choking noises that might be giggles only they're too unrefined.

"Sorry," I say, trying to step on Jen's toe to make her stop.

"Vanilla malt?" Donner asks me, rolling his eyes away from Jen. "That was your usual, right?"

I nod.

He mixes the malt, and I stare out the window at the hot dusty street, avoiding looking at Jen so she won't start that embarrassing giggle sound again.

"There you go," Donner says, setting my malt on the top of the counter.

I'm rummaging for money when he hands Jen a single-scoop cone. She leans over and kisses him.

"I might be home late," she says.

He nods. "Sandie and Nora can handle the shop tonight, so I'll make supper."

"Okay." She smiles at him and reaches out a hand to bump my jaw closed. She tastes her ice cream. "Is this the new strawberry cheesecake?"

"Is it good?" he asks, sounding worried.

"Excellent."

Jen waves as we leave. The sleigh bells on the door are loud enough to drown out my mumbled thanks, but not loud enough to cover Donner's laugh as he serves new customers.

I think he's laughing at me.

"It's not polite to stare, you know," Jen says, catching a drip with her tongue.

The noon sun is blinding. That explains the wetness in my eyes and the heavy, strange feeling in my chest.

"Donner?" I ask. "But he's . . ."

"Fantastic. Plus, he owns an ice cream shop. How can a girl argue with that?"

"But he's . . ."

"You're not going to pull that stupid age thing with me, are you? It's not like Stephen wasn't older than you."

"Four years," I say. "That's a lot different than twenty-five."

"Says who?"

I realize how stupid I'm being. How . . .

But home isn't supposed to change. And when you're six or sixteen, forty seems like light-years away. Donner seems like light-years away. He's a different generation. Like Great-aunt Eva. Not like Jennifer.

It's a mind bender.

"Let's go down to the square," Jen says. "Maybe some shade will restore your equilibrium."

"Thanks."

She bumps me with her elbow, and I pretend to stagger a little. Automatically. Eva called it "clowning around." It's something we never outgrew.

I stagger into Uncle Charles as he steps out of the credit union.

He straightens me up, and the blood runs into my face.

"Hi, Chaz," I say.

I'm lashing out. Trying to hold on to something solid in my past. I'm lashing out. I know it. Even as I say it, I know it. The blood runs out of my face, and I really do need to sit down to restore my equilibrium.

Charles nods at me. "Katherine." Then he turns to Jen, and his face relaxes into a smile. "Hi, Jennifer."

They exchange kisses on the cheek. As if they were members of the upper crust. As if they were adults greeting each other in front of a child.

I guess I asked for it.

"Could you have Donner call me about next weekend?" Uncle Charles asks Jen. "I'm not sure about Eva, and maybe I'd better stick around."

"Will do," Jen says.

The sun presses down on my head with its hot fingers.

I want to scream that Charles is *my* family. Eva is *my* family. So why am I the stranger? Why am I on the outside looking in?

Oh, God.

I close my eyes against the painful sunshine.

"—all right?" I catch the tail end of Jen's question.

I smile before I open my eyes and find Uncle Charles gone. Because I'm not sure if I could smile after seeing the empty space where he was standing.

"I'm fine," I say. "I'm just not used to the sunshine at this altitude."

"Being gone makes a big difference," she says.

It isn't an actual, physical backhand to the face, but the pain is just the same.

We're sitting in the shade of one of the flowering ornamental trees that dot the lawn in front of the county courthouse when Jen brings up the past. I'm draining the last of the malt from the bottom of the plastic glass and thinking about how malts and hot days don't mix well with a stomachful of bad behavior.

"You and Charles still aren't getting along," Jen says, licking a spot of ice cream from her thumb.

I look up at the tired green leaves above our heads and the blue, cloud-spotted sky above the leaves.

"You and Charles are getting along now," I say. Not in a sarcastic kind of way. Just an observational kind of way.

"He and Donner are friends."

"I know."

"I'm married to Donner."

"Uh-huh."

"He's a good man." Meaning Donner, not Charles.

I smile. Grab on to this handle. "How did you meet?"

She frowns. "I always knew him," she says. "He's worked in the ice cream shop for years. You know that."

"I meant, how did you *meet*," I say, adding emphasis.

"Oh." She wipes her spit-cleaned thumb with the paper napkin Donner wrapped around the cone. "At church. At the singles group."

"You go to church?"

"Sundays get pretty dull when you don't have anyone to do things with."

"It's my fault you married Donner?"

"You make it sound like a bad thing."

"No, I don't. You made the singles group sound like a bad thing."

She smiles at me. "It was. It is."

"You still go?" I'm teasing her now. Trying to tease her past the lump in my chest, the lump in my heart, the lump in my throat.

She rolls her eyes and stands up, taking my glass and her napkin and throwing them into a nearby trash container.

"What about you?" she asks, sitting back down on the bench.

"I don't go to church," I say, "so the singles group idea never came up."

"Idiot."

"Well, how was I to know salvation and the meat market went hand in hand?"

"You're awful."

"So I've heard."

"What about—?"

She's asking about Stephen. I knew it before I made the crack about church.

"I'd better go," I interrupt. I make a show of looking at the clock on the courthouse tower. "I have to be at work at three, and, as you so nicely pointed out, I have patches on my clothes."

She sighs and smiles a little. "Do you need a shirt?"

I do, but I don't want to walk back to the thrift store and fend off more questions.

"Not immediately," I say. "And I have to pick up the mascot."

She couldn't possibly understand.

But she doesn't ask what I mean.

I walk back to the motel. Try to keep a spring in my step and my feet from catching in the heat waves on the sidewalk.

"You're my friend, right?" Jen asked me the June morning when we were sitting under the bridge. My last morning in Silver Creek, only Jen didn't know it. Yet.

"Yeah," I said.

"Forever?"

"Yes."

"I'm scared," Jen said. "Of the future."

I took a healthy swallow from the bottle of Jack Daniels I'd stolen from Charles' locked liquor cabinet a month ago. It was a regular rebellion. I'm not sure why Charles didn't notice. Maybe he did. "No kidding," I said.

"Just promise me you'll always be my friend," Jen said.

I took another swallow and thought about Stephen. About sitting on this very bridge in the moonlight and his whispered question. About leaving tonight. About whether or not I should tell Jen.

"I promise," I said out loud.

"We can tell each other anything, right?" Jen asked.

I handed her the bottle. "Sure."

I walk back to the Silver Spur, trying to keep my feet from catching in the heat waves. It's like walking through mud.

I pick up Miss Kitty and drive to the Watering Hole.

I hide in the bar's storeroom because the malt sits heavy on my stomach and I can't breathe around the lump in my chest.

Lil catches me at it. Thanks to Kitty, who was sitting outside the storeroom door and howling her displeasure.

"This is going to take an explanation," Lil says. "Or I'm going to get a complex." She sits down on a beer keg opposite me.

"Thanks," I say to Miss K.

She gives me the feline equivalent of a shrug.

"It's not her fault you chose a public venue," Lil says. "If you don't want people to know you're crying, you should do it in the shower."

I nod. "You're right."

"So are you going to tell me about it?"

"If I can figure it out myself. And blow my nose."

"Here." She hands me a tissue. "Blow away."

I blow, then toss the tissue in the nearest trash can.

"I grew up here," I say.

Lil leans back against the wall. "That would have me crying, too."

"I'm a child here. Everyone wants me to do things . . . like I used to."

She frowns. "You mean they're treating you like a child?"

"No, I'm acting like one."

"Oh."

"Everything is the same and yet it's different," I continue. "My great-aunt is dying. My best friend married my uncle's best friend. Everyone is grown up . . . except me. I'm still a child."

"You left," Lil says. "At least, I'm assuming you left and weren't just dropped into a time warp or abducted or anything?"

I nod. "I left."

"You left, you come back, and . . . what? You didn't think anything would change?"

I stare at her.

She raises one silver-blond eyebrow.

"No," I say. "No, I thought *I* was the one who changed. But I'm still the same. It's everyone else who's different."

She starts to laugh.

"Why is that funny?"

"Because that's life, Katherine Earle," she says. "We don't notice how much the trees have grown if we live in their shade."

"That's very poetic," I say. "But it doesn't explain why I'm acting like a baby—"

"You're in your own shade," she says, still smiling.

"—or why I would still make the same decisions I made at eighteen all over again."

"Maybe they were the right decisions to begin with."

"Maybe you should go coach the football team," I say, with a touch more sarcasm than is polite. "You might fool them into thinking they're winners."

Lil lets the sarcasm sail right on by. I think she might even find it funny that she's annoying me. Miss K. certainly does. If all of that chin rubbing on Lil's knee can be interpreted as approval. Lil scratches Kitty between the ears and a loud rumbling sound fills the room.

Kitty definitely approves.

"We've got a bar to tend," Lil says. "If you're done sulking."

CHAPTER 6

On Great-aunt Eva's street, one house sticks out from its neighbors. It's not the fault of the house, which, despite its peeling paint and dirt lawn, looks like the rest of the houses on the block. It's the chain-link fence. And the small child hanging on the chain-link fence and swinging back and forth while ignoring the host of other small children behind him who are playing on primary-colored plastic toys or digging in the dirt lawn with plastic spoons and shovels.

"Hi," the small, swinging child says as I walk past. From his clothes, I'm guessing his gender is male. All small children look alike to me. Especially when they're smashing a chain-link fence to pieces.

"Hi."

"*I'm* escaping," he says.

The chain-link gaps away from the posts, then crashes against them. Give him . . . five more minutes and the chain-link fence will be down and he'll be down the street.

"Good luck," I tell him. "You'll need it."

"*Thank* you."

I'm on Great-aunt Eva's porch when the sound of metal crushing metal stops. Looking back toward the misfit house, I see heels and elbows flashing as the boy runs toward the corner.

"*John!*" A screech follows him, and two women rush out of the house and through the gate.

"Good luck, Johnny-Boy," I whisper as I knock on Eva's door.

Pearl goes through the bark, slide, thump, and bark routine. Eva opens the door. She looks at me.

"Those are the same clothes you wore on Sunday," she says.

"Good morning," I say.

She looks at the porch floor on either side of me. "Where are your things?"

"At the motel."

"I'll get Charles to pick them up."

"I'm not moving in," I say. "I'm visiting."

"You're moving in." I notice that she's breathing hard as she says it. "Because I won't have a stranger in my house."

"Not moving in means I'm a stranger?"

She thrusts the cordless phone I didn't notice into my hand.

"Hello?" I say into it.

"Katherine?"

"Uncle Charles?"

He sighs. "Good. Tell her she has to either have the nurse or the nursing home."

I blink.

"Wait!" he says. "Not like that. She'll throw you out."

"I'm still out," I say. "I'm on the porch."

With extra vexation, Great-aunt Eva thumps her cane into the hardwood floor. I look down, expecting to see a dent, but I see only the tip of Pearl's tail as she runs for cover.

"I am *here*," Eva says. "Don't talk about me as if I were not *right here*."

And I'm standing in the hot sun in front of the bank and I know exactly how it feels to be on the outside of a conversation looking in.

"He says you need a nurse," I say.

"I know that. He's threatening to put me into a nursing home, isn't he?"

I hesitate.

"*Isn't he?*"

"Yes."

"Move in with me," Eva says.

"I'm not a nurse."

"What's going on?" Uncle Charles asks in my ear. "You're not a nurse. You can't do that."

"Move in with me," Eva says. "Please?"

And the last word tears my heart apart.

"*Why do you wear a wedding ring if you're not married?*" I asked Eva as my six-year-old fingers picked at the diamond ring on the third finger of her left hand.

"Stop that," Eva said. "The setting is old." She shifted her hand away from my reach. "It's my mother's ring."

"Why are you wearing it?"

"Because Mother was . . . sick. She needed someone to take care of her."

I laughed. "You can't marry your mom."

Eva didn't smile.

Standing on Great-aunt Eva's porch, holding a cordless phone in my hand, I look down at her arthritis-swollen fingers that won't allow her to wear her mother's wedding ring any longer.

"Please," Eva says again.

The word tears my heart apart. Great-aunt Eva doesn't plead. "Please" is mere politeness. Something to add on to the end of "Pass the potatoes." I swallow and know I will never be able to refuse the woman who took in a screaming toddler in the middle of a rain-swept night.

"Okay," I say. "But Miss Kitty has the run of the place."

She starts to open her mouth in protest, then nods instead. "Fine."

"You can't do this," Uncle Charles says. "You're not a nurse."

"I'm doing it," I say into the phone. "But if you want round-the-clock surveillance, you'll have to hire someone to stay here while I'm at work." I give him the hours I'm at work, but I don't think he's listening.

He isn't.

"You can't do this," he says again. "You're too unstable to stay put—" He cuts himself off as he realizes what he just said.

I close my eyes and resist the urge to hang up on him. He has every right to think those thoughts.

Great-aunt Eva snatches the phone away from me. "She's fine," she says to Charles. "She's just fine. Now go do a foreclosure or two and you'll feel better." She pushes the button to disconnect with just a bit too much relish, then turns to me, a triumphant smile on her face. "Go get your things. You have enough time to move in before you have to go sweep up cockroaches or whatever it is that you do."

"Thanks," I say, wondering whether that last "please" could have been manipulative.

She closes the door in my face.

Walking toward the stop sign on the corner, I pass John the Escapist again. He's back in the yard and back on the fence.

"I'm escaping," he says.

"Next time," I mutter, "take me with you."

"I'm sorry," I say to Melody when I tell her I'm checking out.

Cleaning rooms isn't hard, but it's more than Melody can do on her own. And I feel guilty about leaving her to take care of things alone.

Guilty.

Me.

The person who's thought about nothing except surviving for three years. The person who's drifted and tumbled. How ironic that I finally come to rest on a fence and start worrying about the well-being of the barbed wire.

Melody shakes her head. "Someone will come along," she says. "Someone always does." And she rolls her eyes toward the ceiling. I look up before I realize she's alluding to heaven's help.

"But—"

"I don't care much for your aunt's way of thinking," Melody says. "But even if you can't choose your blood, it's still blood."

"I guess."

She lays her thick fingers over my hand where it rests on the glass-covered counter. "Doing the thankless thing is part of growing up," she says. "It hurts sometimes, but you have to do it if you're going to live with yourself."

I nod.

"If you need a person to talk to, I'm usually here." And she squeezes my hand.

"Thanks."

But I never get to find out what it would be like to live again under the same roof as Great-aunt Eva.

When Kitty and I pull up to the house, we have to park down by the escapee. Only he's too busy staring at the revolving lights of the ambulance and fire truck to bother with escaping from his chain-link prison.

I step out of the car in time to catch Pearl before she can lose herself under the traffic on Main. In gratitude, she buries her teeth in my wrist. I don't feel it. Still carrying her, I walk up to the porch in time to meet the stretcher with its covered body coming out the front door.

"Give her to me," Uncle Charles says, grabbing Pearl and forcibly pulling her jaws loose from my wrist, "before you can fuck up anything else."

And that's that.

Great-aunt Eva is . . . gone.

As if she were waiting for me to acquiesce one last time to her will.

As if she wanted to have the last word.

I sit down on the porch steps and watch the ambulance drive away. A few of the firemen are standing around talking. One of them waves to John the Escapist, who has been determinedly yelling "Hel-lo, Mr. Fie-yer-man" over and over for the last few minutes.

"You shouldn't have gotten involved," Uncle Charles says from behind and above me. "It wasn't any of your business. You had no right—" He breaks off, as if he just realized that Great-aunt Eva was the only mother figure my childhood had.

"I'm sorry," he says.

I shake my head. "No. You're right. I'm sorry."

But the admission of guilt is just words. I'm not sorry I agreed to move in and save Great-aunt Eva from the nursing home or from having her house permanently invaded by a stranger. I'm just saying whatever it takes to smooth over the shock and Uncle Charles' anger.

The firemen climb into the truck and it drives away. The chain-link begins its metallic rhythm again as the diversion disappears around the corner.

Uncle Charles sits down beside me. Pearl squirms, but he doesn't seem to notice.

"She seemed fine," I say. "Fine."

"You excited her," Charles says. Then, more softly, "We excited her."

"What happened?" I ask.

"Her heart. She had lung cancer"—and I realize I never even thought to ask—"but the doctor gave her a good nine months still. Even though she refused chemo. I don't know. Her heart just . . ."

"Stopped," I finish for him. Aunt Eva never lived by anyone else's schedule. Why would she die on someone else's schedule?

"I guess," he says.

We sit in silence. So silent that a cricket under the porch stairs takes the stillness as a cue to begin his raspy song.

Charles sighs—frightening the cricket back into silence—and finally notices that Pearl is squirming very hard.

"Should I let her go?" he asks me.

"No. She'll commit suicide under the cars on Main. It's what she always does when she gets loose."

"Right."

Pearl glares at me and lifts her lips over her teeth.

"The house is yours," Uncle Charles says.

I'm looking at Pearl's yellow teeth, and panic has its hands around my neck.

"I mean," he continues, "the house is mine on paper, but I don't want it. To live in. I doubt . . ." He trails off, looking at me, looking at the frayed edges of my clothing. "It's your home."

"No," I say. "It isn't."

"You need a place to live."

"Not really. I *had* a place to live. I was only coming here as—"

"Let's not talk about that," he interrupts. "I'm still trying to understand why you felt you had to interfere with what was obviously the best option."

"For you," I say. "Maybe not for her."

The tendons on his hands bulge. Pearl yipes and snaps at his fingers.

"Goddamn dog!" he says, shaking the blood off his hand.

I reach out and take her away from him. She sinks her teeth into my other wrist. This time I feel it.

"I don't care what you do," Charles says, still shaking his hand.

I'm too busy prying Pearl's jaws open to answer.

"Move in here or live under the bridge," he continues. "I'm tired of arguing."

"I'll pay you rent," I say. "I don't need charity."

"Yes, you do," he says. "It's not like you have any capital to speak of. Consider the place yours. Do whatever you want." He stands up. "But you'd better take care of those wrists," he says just before he leaves. "You've got blood all over you."

I look down at my wrists and notice the time. There isn't any. Between now and work, I mean. I stand up and remember Pearl. She lifts her hackles to celebrate the return of my memory.

"You're vicious," I tell her.

But vicious or not, I can't stand the thought of leaving her in the house, where she'll pace the floor and sniff the yellow chair and wonder whether anyone remembers her.

So I take her with me to the Watering Hole.

"What is that?" Lil asks as I walk in.

"It's a dog," I answer, just as Miss Kitty begins to tell Lil all her troubles from the confines of her carrier. Miss K. doesn't appreciate being caged, even if it's protective custody.

"Isn't that Evalene Earle's dog?" Lyle asks.

"A cat is cool," Lil says at the same time. "Dogs"—she peers at Pearl—"especially poodles, are not."

"It's Aunt Eva's dog," I say to Lyle, trying to ignore Lil.

"Well, come here, Pearl," Lyle says. And Pearl goes into an ecstasy of wiggling. I hand her off to Lyle.

"Hi, sweetie," he says to her. "I've never seen you out of Eva's sight . . ." He looks up at me.

I shake my head. "This afternoon."

"She's taken a turn for the worse?" he asks.

I shake my head again. "She . . ." I fumble around in my brain for the words people in Silver Creek use to soften a blow. "She . . . she died this afternoon," I finally say.

And the reality hits.

Lil puts her arm around me.

I smile and squeeze her back before stepping away.

Sympathy feels wrong. Given the last few silent years . . . given the fact that I abandoned Great-aunt Eva without a word . . . sympathy feels wrong. I know Lil is being genuine. I'm the one who doesn't feel genuine. Who doesn't deserve sympathy.

Lyle continues to stroke Pearl's head. "I'm sorry," he says. "I didn't know. I've been doing her taxes since my father passed away, but I didn't know she was sick."

"Lung cancer. But I think she wanted it . . . now. She had the last word."

He nods. "She would have wanted it *that* way."

I remember Miss K. and let her out of the cat carrier. I catch Lil watching me. "The dog is just for one night," I say to her. "I couldn't leave her alone."

Lil nods. "She seems to have hit it off with Lyle." Then she catches my wrist. "What's this?"

I tilt my head toward Pearl.

"There's a first aid kit in back," she says. "Come on."

Kitty follows us.

"Dog bites can be nasty," Lil says, turning on the hot water tap over the storeroom sink. "I had to get seven rabies shots in my stomach once, and that was enough to convince me." She takes hold of my hand, pushes my sleeve up, and puts my wrist under the water.

"Convince you of what?" I ask.

"That dogs really do guard the gate to hell."

The hot water stings the open wound. I flinch and hide my other hand behind my back before she can see it and prescribe similar treatment that involves water and . . . touching.

Human contact stings.

But it's too late.

"Your other hand," she says, gesturing. I give up, grit my teeth, and let her repeat the sleeve and hot water action.

"Now scrub them good with soap," she says as she dries her hands on a towel. "I think I've got some bigger bandages out under the bar."

I scrub after she leaves. The soap is a strong, antibacterial stuff that burns all the way through one side of my wrists and out the other.

As if Pearl's tooth marks were holes left by nails. God knows, I feel like a martyr, so I guess it fits.

CHAPTER 7

At three-fifteen a.m., I park my car in front of Eva's too-dark house. Pearl steps all over Miss K.'s carrier while trying to see out the window. Miss K. hisses displeasure.

Sitting in the car, I automatically glance up at the porch to see whether the outside light has come on.

"Why does the light always come on when we pull up?" Gregg asked once when a group of us hitched a ride in his ancient Buick after the homecoming dance. Gregg was hooked up—loosely—with Jennifer at the time. The car was a definite plus.

I adjusted my slipping tiara and reached for Jennifer's half-empty can of beer. "So I'll burn my fingers," I said after drinking the beer down.

Jennifer snickered.

Gregg and the others looked confused.

"The key to the door is taped beside the lightbulb," I explained. "Eva waits until she sees I'm outside, then she turns on the light. If I stay out here too long, I burn my fingers getting the key."

"Why's she do that?" Gregg asked.

"So I don't sit out here doing this," I said just before leaning over the seat and kissing him full on the mouth. Then I kissed Jennifer for good measure. One of the other guys in the car gave a little cheer.

Hanging on to my tiara, I climbed over legs to get out of the back seat of the car.

"Need a glove?" Gregg asked, but I dug down into my bag for one of the paper-covered complimentary sets of chopsticks Jennifer and I had snitched from Silver Creek's lone Chinese restaurant.

I held up the chopsticks. "The brain is creative in its search for pleasure and the avoidance of pain."

Then I bowed and my tiara fell off, rolling drunkenly into the gutter.

At three-twenty-five a.m., I'm still sitting in my car and ignoring Pearl's whines. I don't have to do this. I can drive down to the Silver Spur and get my room back.

But Melody doesn't like dogs. They put holes in the sheets. And Pearl is a definite hole digger.

And even if I could persuade Melody to let me keep Pearl, I couldn't keep going on five hours of sleep a night. The rooms have to be cleaned before noon. Which means I've been getting up at nine. And I couldn't quit cleaning (even if I could bear to stay in the motel and watch Melody clean the rooms), because the bar money doesn't cover fifteen dollars a day for room without board. I might be able to keep going for a while. I might even learn to take naps. But eventually something would give out. Me or the money.

I don't care to bet which one would go first.

I look up at the house. It looks less dark now that my eyes have adjusted to the dim shadows cast by the streetlight on the corner.

Uncle Charles didn't give me a key this afternoon, but Great-aunt Eva isn't the kind of person to remove a method of punishment. Even when the person being punished is long gone.

Holding a wriggling Pearl under one arm, I fumble with the light fixture and pull out the dusty key and a dead spider.

No surprise, I think, immediately feeling guilty for thinking bad thoughts about a dead person. The door opens, and I slide Pearl on in, then go back to the car for Kitty and my bag.

Kitty howls at me, clearly saying *"This is an outrage. The dog has to go."*

"You ain't seen nothing yet," I say to her. "The dog owns this place."

Miss K. turns her head away in a definite "we'll see about *that"* gesture.

"Try to be nice," I say, slinging my duffle bag over my shoulder and picking up the carrier. "Pearl's having a rough time."

I open the front door, and Pearl sinks her teeth into my ankle. She's smart enough to go under the jeans this time. Not smart enough to figure out I'm wearing boots.

"You were saying?" Miss Kitty asks.

"Never mind."

The funeral takes place on a sunny Monday morning. The late-summer sky doesn't even have the decency to be gray in honor of Evalene Earle's passing. Instead, it's impossibly blue and the white clouds stretch forever . . . flat-bottomed boats on the ocean. A hawk makes lazy circles high above the pine trees that line the cemetery road. Generations sleep under the singing needles and leaning markers.

Inside the funeral home limo taking us to the graveside service, I slip one foot out of my shoe and rub the other foot's ankle. I didn't have much to do with the funeral arrangements. Uncle Charles asked me to pick out a nice dress, underwear, and shoes for the mortuary to dress the body in. And even though Miss K. has explored the upstairs of Great-aunt Eva's house, I snuck into the master bedroom and felt like a thief going through the closets. I took along Eva's mother's wedding ring and a favorite piece of jewelry, but the mortuary attendant gave them back. *"The family keeps those,"* he said. "Why?" I asked. He shrugged. *"That's just how it's done."*

I feel someone watching me and look up in time to catch Uncle Charles pretending to not be annoyed by the sound of nylon rubbing against nylon. I stop scratching my ankle and slip my foot back into the shoe.

"It's a beautiful morning," the chubby pastor says. He's nervous. Silver Creek has a church for every denomination, but there aren't enough people to fill up the pews. Pastors paid via the Sunday offering are either fresh out of seminary and willing to work for a dime, or retired and willing to still do their duty. This pastor is Methodist. And willing to work for a dime.

Uncle Charles stares at him in a dismal kind of way.

The pastor clears his throat. "I mean—"

"It's a gorgeous day," I say, looking at Uncle Charles and hating him. "Especially when you look at the sky through the pines."

"Y-yes," the pastor says. He clears his throat and tries again. "Did Evalene like the outdoors?"

"No," Uncle Charles says.

"Yes," I say at the same time.

"Oh," the pastor says, realizing that his innocuous question has gone dangerous.

"She loved gardening," I say. "And flowers."

"She did not," Uncle Charles says. "She only did it for appearances."

"She knew all the flowers' names!"

How did I get in this position? I'm defending Great-aunt Eva from an attack by . . . Charles?

"So?" Charles asks. "Knowing something about horticulture doesn't mean you have to like plants."

"We're here," the pastor gasps. He escapes through the limo door without waiting for the driver to open it.

I stay put and look across the space where loved ones' shoes have scraped the limo carpet bare. Look across at Uncle Charles.

"What's going on?" I ask.

"You get the house," he says.

"That's what you said the other day. That I can live—"

He laughs. "You *get* the house. And everything in it. And everything else, too. She changed her will. She left you everything. Even her savings. You're rich." Hunched over, he starts to climb out of the limo. Then he turns and looks at the black dress I bought at the thrift store and spent all night refitting to a twenty-two-year-old body. "Comparatively speaking, that is. Until you manage to waste it all. Congratulations." Then he's gone.

I stare at the opposite seat.

"Miss?" the driver asks, leaning in to look at me.

"Sorry." I climb out and trip over something. The driver catches my arm and saves me from skinning my knees, ruining my hose, looking like a fool.

"Thank you," I say to him.

He pats my arm, and the touch drives a spike into my chest.

Just a pat.

One human to another.

Signifying nothing. Impersonal.

I shudder and walk over to the green tent where the various scions of the sour-mouthed and mustachioed founders have set Eva's coffin and are taking their places in the fold-out chairs. But I see Jennifer standing next to Donner at the back of the lines of chairs, so I change course and stop beside her.

"Hi," I say.

She reaches out and squeezes my hand. She doesn't let go, even when I relax my fingers so she can. I recatch her hand in a hard grip and keep holding on even when the chubby pastor clears his throat and begins, "'I am the resurrection and the life . . .'"

Uncle Charles' neck is stiff as he sits in the front row by the coffin. From here, I can see the gray on his temples. It's new. To me.

I used to sit on Eva's porch and wait for Charles and Cynthia to arrive. *"Set the table, please,"* Great-aunt Eva would say. And I knew that Charles would pull up in front of our sidewalk in a few minutes. Excitement and impatience warred with fear as I handled the Sunday-best china and crystal. Once, Aunt Eva had complimented me on how careful I was. How I'd never broken a glass or plate. At five or six years old, I had an irrational fear—fostered by some TV movie or childish horror story—that Eva would send me away if I ever broke a dish. But once the table was set, I went out to sit on the porch and wait.

"Uncle Charles!"

And Charles would swing me up. I loved the feeling of leaving the ground while still being safe. Then I would inspect his hair and say, "It's still not falling out." Because Cynthia had told me it would.

Cynthia, Charles' perfect wife who was his perfect fiancée when Will and Meddie met their fate in the flash flood. While I still had baby fat on my arms, I adored Cynthia. Her cool skin, the lipstick in her purse she let me try, the way she smelled. After she left Charles—and my baby fat disappeared— I picked up enough clues to figure out that Great-aunt Eva had taken in a toddler because Cynthia had given Charles an ultimatum. The cool skin came with a price. Actually, it came with a subtraction. One less toddler.

After Cynthia left, Charles had a few discreet relationships, but nothing took. I think he actually loved her.

Charles stopped swinging me up. And I stopped inspecting his hair. Still, I think I would have noticed the gray. On the bridge last week, when I fluffed the tunnels out of the hair so like my own. Or maybe the difference isn't the gray in Charles' hair. Maybe the difference is that I no longer believe in my own immortality.

Charles' neck is stiff and straight, but I know he's aware of me, standing back here with Jen. He and I are . . . it. The last two Earles alive. Only for some reason, Great-aunt Eva decided to throw a final barrier between us. Maybe she didn't mean to. Maybe she was thinking that Charles had money while I probably didn't. That she could offer me one last gift of comfort and security. Fat chance. This "gift" has all the characteristic joy of manipulation from beyond the grave. I just haven't figured out the motivation behind Eva's last wishes.

Yet.

The pastor closes his Bible and the sound of the final prayer reaches me through the cawing of the crow sitting at the top of the nearest pine tree.

Jen gives my hand an extra squeeze, and I release her.

End the first human contact since Eva's death that I could bear.

People are shaking Charles' hand, touching his shoulder, or kissing him on the cheek. A few look up at me, but then they look away.

"Can you give me a ride back to Aunt Eva's place?" I ask Jen.

She opens her mouth, but stops. I follow her line of sight and end up with Donner. He's got one hand on Charles' shoulder, but he's looking at Jen. Silent communication is happening. I can feel it. I'm jealous and frightened at the same time.

"I think Charles is coming home with . . . with us," Jennifer says.

"Oh."

The limo and the driver with the impersonal pat await.

I swallow my pride.

"Then would you . . ." I begin. I have to swallow again before I can get the question out. "Would you ride with me back to the funeral home?"

She glances at me, then toward Donner.

She's so torn it looks like some giant hand took her face and ripped it in two.

I touch her shoulder. "It's okay. I'll be fine. Maybe sometime later this week you could help me box up Eva's clothes and things for the thrift store."

I'm giving her an out. A way to maintain two loyalties. One to Donner and one to me. Nothing else would be fair.

She catches the back of my neck and kisses my forehead. "Thank you."

"You're welcome."

I climb back into the limo, studiously avoiding touching the driver as he holds the door for me. Studiously avoiding the sight of the cemetery employees laying Eva into her final resting place. The pastor is already inside. He wipes his forehead with a handkerchief when the driver shuts the door. "Isn't—?" He breaks off, confused by a poor memory.

"Charles," I say. "He's riding back with friends."

"I hope . . . I hope I didn't cause any problems?" He ends on a hopeful note.

I look at him. Wonder whether he's worried about potential problems with the collection plate. Realize what a nasty thing that is to wonder. His brown eyes are guileless.

The whole world isn't just looking out for number one, I tell myself.

"You didn't do anything," I tell him. "My great-aunt left me everything. I didn't know. And Uncle Charles didn't know either."

He shakes his head. "It's too bad that property issues have to come between family at a time like this."

"I didn't ask for it," I say, looking out the window. "For all I care, he could pile it up and set it on fire."

"I didn't mean—" the pastor stammers.

"I know," I interrupt as the last of the pines slide by the darkened window. "But it would make one hell of a bonfire."

* * *

I skip the church ladies' potluck for the bereaved family and walk back from the funeral home to Eva's house. Charles will be angry, but I know he'll be relieved, too, if the black sheep keeps her distance. It's not far to the house, but I'm glad to reach the shade of the trees and escape the sun soaking through my black dress. Midday in late summer. The air shimmers. As I pass the spirea bushes, I look up and see my child self sitting on Eva's porch, waiting for a car to pull up in front of the house. Waiting to be swung into the air.

I blink. The air shimmers. And the ghosts disappear.

The second step groans in protest as I climb the stairs. I sit down on the top step. Too worn out to face the carnage I know the interior holds. Since Eva's death, Pearl has made sure I keep up my cleaning skills. Each night, Kitty and I have come home to a disaster. Potted plants uprooted and dirt spread like mulch over the living room floor. Area rugs collected into a single pile and pooped on. Curtain edges shredded. I keep thinking it will stop. I keep trying various methods to Pearl-proof the house. But Pearl has nothing to do with her time but dream up new and ingenious methods of torturing the intruders. For the funeral, I locked Kitty in the upstairs and left the living room to Pearl, hoping Eva's scent on the yellow chair would help the poor little mutt. I know she's just scared and lonely.

But I'm tired. Too tired to clean. Wrapping my arms around my shins and curling forward into a tight ball, I lay my cheek on my knees. The porch railing closest to me has bits of peeling paint falling from it. I close my eyes to block out the image of layers of color dating back a hundred years and find myself looking across the scuffed limo floor into Charles' angry face.

What happened today? In the limo? Does Charles think I manipulated Eva into leaving me what she has? Had, I mean.

Does he think this is what I wanted?

I'm not looking for a home. This is only a resting place. For eighteen years I drifted in this town. Using it. Abusing it. Not so different from the last three years on the road, just more . . . complicated. I don't belong here. I never did. I'm just catching my breath. I'm just resting.

I don't belong here.

"Sometimes I feel like this is where I was meant to be," Stephen said to me. We were standing on the stage of one of the club bars that made West Hollywood famous, the early-afternoon silence highlighting the creak of the wood under our feet.

From the balcony area opposite the stage, Newell clicked on the spotlight. "That's because it is."

Stephen bowed in the spotlight. Standing just outside the circle of light, I watched Stephen change from blue to red to green as Newell tried various gel sheets, and I felt . . .

. . . I felt outside.

Newell hit me with the white spot. "Kat, flash some skin. I want to make sure I can see all those naked breasts after the girls get done throwing me their shirts."

I flashed Newell a middle finger as I left the stage.

I didn't belong there.

Sitting on Eva's porch, I shiver. Goose bumps form on my bare arms. A car drives slowly past, dipping and lurching over the hollows made by tree roots pushing up from under the street. Metallic crashes announce that John the Escapist is up from his nap. High overhead, cicadas hum in the heat waves. A drop of water soaks through my dress, wetting my knee.

Blinking away the wetness, I push myself to my feet and fumble with the key until the old lock gives and I can open the door. Inside, I strip off my shoes and nylons—careful to avoid the potting soil and dog shit laid fresh in the entryway—while Pearl watches me balefully from the depths of the yellow chair. We glare at each other.

Someone knocks on the front door. Someone short. Opening it, I look down on John the Escapist.

"Hide me," he says. "I'm free."

Pearl jumps down from Eva's chair. I jump to catch her before she can pull down a kill, but stop when I see she's wagging hard enough to dislocate something.

"Hi, Pearl," John says.

"Johnny!" A short, blond woman runs up the sidewalk and grabs John's shoulder. "I'm sorry," she says to me. "He's always getting out."

"It's okay," I say, still dazzled by the miracle in front of me. Pearl is baptizing John's face with her tongue.

"I'm Gwen," the blond woman says.

"Yes." Then I stumble, realizing this must be an introduction. "Kat," I say. "I'm Kat."

"Uh-huh," she murmurs in response while bending down to pet Pearl. She straightens up. "Is Eva okay? We saw the ambulance."

"She's . . ." *dead*. Too harsh for the blue, angel eyes in front of me. "She passed away. The funeral was today."

"You must miss her," Gwen says, honest sympathy in her voice. "I'm sorry." She hands me a tissue.

And I realize my cheeks are wet.

"No. I mean, thank you. Yes. I don't know." I grind to a halt. Embarrassed because the tears aren't for Great-aunt Eva. They're for the man I left standing on the stage in West Hollywood.

"I understand," she says. "Losing someone is difficult."

Pretty words that people say when they're talking about death. Only she seems to mean them. Guilt at my lack of emotion for Eva twists my stomach.

"If there's anything I can do to help . . . ?"

"Do you need a dog?" I ask, part joke, part exhaustion, part embarrassment. "Pearl doesn't think much of me."

Pearl demonstrates her feelings by peeing on my foot.

Gwen looks up from my wet foot to my face.

"You're giving us Pearl?"

I shake my head. "God, no." My laugh is more hiccup than laugh. "That would be like giving someone one of the four horsemen of the Apocalypse."

"Pearl's a dog," John says. "Not a horse."

"Right. A horse would poop less."

"Are you serious?" Gwen asks again.

"Um . . . I was just joking, but if . . ." I let the sentence trail off, wondering whether I've done something wrong. But Gwen's eyes are distant with memories.

"I haven't had a dog in years," she says. Quietly. As if she were speaking to someone in the past. Some people might not understand her distraction, but I've just been conversing with a few ghosts of my own. Under the porch, the cricket hums. Boards creak as John shifts beside Pearl.

"Pearl's not happy," I say, pulling Gwen back from wherever she's gone. "I mean, she wasn't until now. I don't think I'm any good at canine psychology." I think about showing her and John the house, then decide that might scare off the answer to my doggy difficulties.

John is looking between Gwen and me. "Is Pearl coming home with us?"

I look at Gwen. She smiles and nods.

I squat down and look John in the eye. Realize I can offer Gwen an equal exchange for taking a problem off my hands. "Pearl's suicidal," I begin.

He looks confused.

"She can't get out," I say, trying to find words he'll understand. "If she gets out, she'll throw herself under the cars and get hurt. You'll have to stay with her. Inside the fence."

He frowns, then nods. "Okay."

As Gwen and John walk away, she turns and says, "Thank you."

The words surprise me, and I don't know what to say. I don't know whether she's thanking me for getting John to stay inside the yard or for giving her a link to her past.

"Come down for some coffee tomorrow," Gwen says. "When you get up."

Before I can respond, she's walking away again. Pearl leers at me over John's shoulder. She's obviously vowing to bite me tomorrow.

I shut the door.

Great-great-grandmother Wilhelmina glares down at me.

I turn the picture so it faces the wall and go to the bathroom to wash my foot.

CHAPTER 8

"No. Absolutely not," Lil says when I tell her I want to work. "Go home. It's bad enough I've let you work at all this week."

I shuffle my feet. "I don't know what to do," I whisper. "I—"

Lil grabs my face between her hands. "You go home and be with your family."

She must see something of what I'm thinking in my eyes, because she drops her hands from my face. The air inside the bar is cool on my hot cheeks.

"Go home, take some Tylenol PM, and go to bed," she says. "Get some sleep and come in tomorrow."

I never take advice.

After parking in front of Great-aunt Eva's house, I take Kitty inside and apologize for leaving her behind.

Then I start walking.

By the time I reach the bridge, I'm running.

Three miles used to be easy. I'm gasping after one. Leaning on my knees, I look across the bridge and down the road beyond.

I could just keep going. Running down the road with my back to the town. Instead, I turn and slide down the dusty bank until I reach the thin trickle of water. Down here in the riverbed, I can hop from rock to rock until I stepping-stone my way to the rounded lump of a hill and the big cottonwood.

From the highway, this is just a grassy ripple and bump in the landscape. But if you put your back to the ribbon of asphalt, you can see into the stretch of forever. Or at least up and down Silver Creek with its winding curves and clumps of green trees hugging the bank.

Legend has it that a young married couple died on this lump of a hill. Trying to evade a flash flood that washed through about twenty years ago. I don't know whether the story is true. Whenever I asked Eva, she thinned her lips and said we wouldn't talk about the past. I never asked Charles.

I probably never will.

But if Will and Meddie weren't the kind of people who would listen to their daughter while they were alive, they've become good listeners in death.

"Eva's dead," I say to the cottonwood, leaning my cheek against the rough bark. Above me the leaves rattle a late-summer symphony. I wrap my arms around the trunk. I don't want the human touch. I want to sink into the tree and become its spirit. Daphne turned into laurel. Something solid and immovable. Something at rest and yet still alive.

The wind slips fingers into my hair and lifts the stray bits off my neck. The sweat on my face dries and begins to itch. I can almost hear the cottonwood say *"Now, there's a benefit to being human: scratching your nose."*

The bones in my legs give, and I slide down the tree until I'm sitting in the tall, yellowing grass with the trunk at my back. I scratch my nose, then tuck my knees to my chest and watch the sun dip down the sky until it plunges into the western end of the river.

Walking home, I pass John and Pearl playing fetch in the dirt yard.

"Did you escape?" he asks.

"Almost," I answer. "But my nose itched."

He nods and throws the ball for Pearl, who scampers after the rubber toy as if she were a puppy. "It happens," he says.

I don't need any help sleeping, even though one of Great-aunt Eva's kitchen cupboards is filled to the bursting with arthritis painkillers and sleeping aids. I've rigged up a bed on the couch. It's not as comfortable as the bed at the Silver Spur, but it's better than some of the beds I've slept in since leaving L.A.

Better than sleeping in the beds upstairs. Where monsters hide under the dust ruffles.

"Kat! Kat! Wake up!"

I yanked myself out of the black hole sucking me down and found Stephen's face hovering over me. The constant hum of the L.A. freeways reached me, filtered through the curtains.

"You were having a nightmare," Stephen said. "You okay?"

"Just monsters," I said.

He rolled me over and tucked an arm around me. "You're the only adult I know who has nightmares about monsters."

I didn't bother to explain that my monsters weren't green things with pointy teeth. That in my dream I was walking on a road with no beginning, no end, and nobody beside me.

"Why did you leave today?" Stephen whispered into my ear. His breath lifted the hair on my cheek.

Still trapped by the lonely restlessness of the dream, it took me a moment to understand he was asking why I had walked off the club stage.

Because you didn't need me.

I pretended to be asleep.

The Montana sunshine filters through the curtains and burns through my eyelids. I have a vague feeling the City of Angels intruded on my dreams. My mouth tastes sour. Pulling myself into a sitting position, I see Miss Kitty watching the birds splashing in the birdbath just beyond the kitchen window. She makes a longing chatter noise at the thought of raw meat for breakfast. I ignore her pleading meow for me to open the door, and let the birds splash in peace. I don't think I could handle more death before breakfast.

I'm making coffee when I remember Gwen's invitation.

I think about pretending I misunderstood the offer of coffee. But the vision of Gwen bringing Pearl back out of spite has me pulling on jeans and a sweatshirt and stepping out into the early-morning chill blowing down from the mountain passes.

Gwen's yard has more dirt than grass. Grass would have a hard time growing inside the chain-link fence. Squirming bundles of humanity push each other around on plastic . . . *things* on wheels. Childish shrieks sink through my ears and into the headache starting behind my eyes. I don't blame John for being an escapist.

"Good morning," Gwen calls from the door.

At the sound of her voice, the squirming bundles of humanity run to hug her legs, and I realize there are only four small bodies. The noise level indicated something closer to forty.

"I run a day care," Gwen says, laughing and rumpling the hair of the nearest leg grabber. "They're not all mine."

I smile and nod around the headache. Wonder if I can get out of being caged in with the noisemakers posing as children.

"It's play time." Gwen sounds nervous. "It's a little loud."

I look up from the child beating two spoons on the side of a plastic car and catch Gwen twisting her hands together. She puts them behind her back. It reminds me . . .

"Nice dress," I said to the girl in the gym bathroom. I was leaning in to add

more mascara before returning to the dance. We were both using the mirror. The compliment was something to say. I didn't even look at her dress.

Leaning back to see longer lashes, I noticed my mirror partner was blushing and smiling and twisting her hands together in front of her. "Really? You think so?"

"Sure," I said, deciding to ignore that I'd finally noticed it was some kind of awful pink taffeta.

"Oh, *thank* you!" the girl said.

I shook my head as she tripped out of the bathroom. But deep down inside I felt . . . dark and powerful with the knowledge that even when I was lying, people cared what I thought. I stretched one hand to the mirror and touched my reflected face. And smiled.

Gwen twists her hands behind her back.

I cringe at the memory of that reflected smile.

And then I lie to make Gwen feel better.

"I knew they weren't all yours," I say. "Unless you're very fertile and have a shorter gestation period than most humans."

She laughs. "Come in." Before she follows me she sets a timer up on the window ledge. "Fifteen minutes," she says to the kids. "Then come inside for a snack."

Inside, she shoos me toward the kitchen table. As we cross the living room, Pearl darts out from under a blanket tent. I tense, but she just sniffs me politely before returning to the tent where John is poking his head through the opening.

"Hi," he says to me.

"Hi."

Pearl's head reappears under John's chin. She gives me a self-satisfied look.

I shrug and follow Gwen into the kitchen.

"The kids can be overwhelming," she says.

"No—" I begin, but she interrupts me.

"*I'm* a little overwhelmed this morning," she says, her hands shaking a bit as she pours us coffee, "so you don't have to lie to me. But Mayla is sick."

"Mayla?" I ask, trying not to notice that she caught me in a gym bathroom lie.

"Oh, sorry. Mahala. I'm so used to calling her Mayla . . ."

I smile and nod. A polite stranger in the mirror.

Her eyebrows pull together. "Don't you remember?"

My smile freezes helplessly.

Gwen's face droops a little. "Mahala and Gwen Carlyle? I thought you would remember—" She breaks off and shakes her head. "It's no big deal."

But it is. And I understand why seeing Gwen has me caught in memories I would rather forget.

"*Hi, Katherine,*" said the girls walking toward me down the hall lined with orange lockers. I smiled and said hello. Walked past them congratulating myself on what a gracious big fish I was being, acknowledging the existence of the two skinny girls who had to wear outdated dresses, black shoes, and white caps.

I don't remember one of the girls having angel eyes, but who could tell behind the thick glasses?

"You were a couple of years behind me, right?" I ask.

She smiles and it lights up her eyes with puppylike joy. The joy reminds me how it feels to be the person on top of the world. When the world looks up at you in adoration and you pretend you don't even notice.

I shiver and gulp some coffee.

I don't want to be Katherine Earle anymore. I don't want the dark, rich taste of pleasure that comes with the power of popularity and self-satisfaction. I wouldn't like me if I ran into myself in the hall.

"I hated those dresses," Gwen says, adding cream and sugar to her coffee. "My mother was German Baptist."

I shake out of the dark place her worship has put me, and she misinterprets the movement as confusion.

"Everyone calls them Dunkards," she says.

I nod.

"She ran away with my dad, but she never did change how she dressed. Or how we were dressed." She laughs, but it doesn't touch her blue eyes. "She folded all those dresses away the day I told her I was pregnant with John."

Everything sounds so final.

"You mean she kicked you out?" I ask.

Gwen smiles. "No. Nothing that drastic. Sometimes I wish she had." She sips her coffee.

I stir my spoon around in the black coffee. Around and around. Looking for the right words.

"You have the look," she says amid the sounds of stainless steel on ceramic.

I glance up.

"I heard about you leaving with Stephen McKittrick," she says. "When he came back with Newell for the wedding." Then she smiles. "The whole town heard about it, actually."

Clink. Swish. I keep stirring. Wondering—

"You have the look," she says again. "Of someone who's loved the wrong man. Like me—"

"He wasn't the wrong man," I say.

Reflexively. A foot kicking up when the doctor taps your knee with the cold hammer.

She stops in mid sentence. Blushes. "I didn't mean—"

"No. It's okay," I say. "I . . ." I what?

"You're just . . . My mother always said there was . . . something in a woman's eyes that came from loving the wrong man. She said I have it."

"You have angel eyes," I tell her, taking the spoon out of my coffee. "So whatever you felt for him must have been wonderful."

I gulp a scalding mouthful of coffee.

The timer on the windowsill goes off before she can answer. The door bangs open. Snack hunters fill the kitchen. Under cover of the distraction, I call a polite thanks for the coffee and . . . escape.

Outside, the air smells of dried leaves and pine smoke.

CHAPTER 9

Death is complicated. The spiritual and metaphysical complications should be enough. What happens? How does it feel? Is there really a hell with devils sticking pitchforks into your melting flesh? Will Virgil explain everything? Or will you simply cease to exist with that last breath?

As I said, complicated enough already.

Uncle Charles adds a few more complications.

Just for fun.

It was a bad first night back at work after the funeral. Somehow, everyone managed to get their Kat linked up with Evalene Earle, town matriarch. Maybe it was the obit that Lil showed me. There I was. Plain as day. Listed as one of the survivors. Whoever wrote the glowing pack of lies even managed to mention my place of employment.

I thought that was illegal.

It should be.

So it was a bad first night back at work. Lots of offers of sympathy. Everyone meant well. I'm just out of practice when it comes to having people know more about me than my face and my name.

Lil picked up on how I felt. She had me deal with the supplier and clean the storeroom. She meant well, too. But it probably would have been better to put me behind the bar where I could get it all over with and stop playing the dramatically grieving heroine.

And the house has started whispering—

More on that later.

I fell onto the couch around four in the morning. There's nothing magical about four in the morning. It's just dark, cold, and scary. The time when you wake up (or can't go to sleep) and your stomach has that nameless, gnawing fear that used to be about monsters under the bed, but has somehow transformed into the monsters in your head.

Four hours later, Uncle Charles adds a few more complications.

Just for fun.

Via the phone.

"Nine-fifteen," he says. "At the lawyer's office."

"What?" I ask, bewildered by the dim sky and the cotton clogging my synapses.

"For the details of the will," he says. "You should be able to clean up and be presentable in an hour."

"It depends on whether or not I can dress myself," I say, the cotton burning away in the anger at being treated like a recalcitrant child when I haven't done a damn thing to deserve it.

Recently.

"The office building on Main and Third," he says. "Second floor. Suite at the end of the hall. It looks over the street."

He hangs up.

Miss Kitty sits on the sink and listens to me moan and growl while I take a shower and use up the entire forty-gallon capacity of hot water.

All I have to wear is jeans. I can't show up in the dress from the funeral. Well, I could, but I'm not up to getting another of Charles' slow, sarcastic looks.

I tiptoe into Great-aunt Eva's bedroom. We were about the same size. On top, anyway. A nondescript silk blouse and a cream sweater from her closet make the jeans passable.

I braid my hair as I walk to Third and Main. It's only a few blocks. And I need the air.

A flock of little brown birds are fighting and singing in the tree the city planted on the corner during the attempt to beautify Main ten or fifteen years ago. It's hard to beautify a row of false fronts mixed with bad fifties industrial architecture. The office building on Third and Main is brick and square, with glass and aluminum doors and windows. The windows don't open anymore. If they ever did. The marvel of controlled interior weather made opening windows a shocking and evil thing to do during the energy crisis of the seventies. And these days, no one wants to mix fresh air with the refrigeration.

I climb the carpet-covered stairs. The window on the landing halfway between floors has a view of the town and beyond. I stop to dream about driving away into the rolling hills.

I can see the waves in the grass as the wind runs its fingers through the ripening seed heads.

Driving away.

Surfers talk about the thrill of catching the best curl. But surfing is just returning to the beach you paddled out from. Imagine the thrill of catching a wave going to somewhere new. *Out* to sea, for a change, rather than just back to the sand. Not knowing where you'll end up, what it will look like, whether you'll even get there or whether you'll get sucked down into the depths of the ocean. Down so deep the sun can't reach you.

Driving away can feel like that.

Leaving can feel like that.

But I came back to the beach of Silver Creek.

Uncle Charles would say it's just a case of the bad penny turning up again.

I lean on the wide wooden sill of the window and look at the wind ripples in the grass. After that coffee with Gwen . . . I feel even more like a stranger on a foreign shore. A stranger who has a familiar face.

And maybe that's why I'm still here. Because I don't know if I'm a stranger or a friend.

Or maybe I'm just that bad penny.

I turn my back on the waves, climb the second set of stairs, and walk down the hall to the suite where Great-aunt Eva's lawyer hides out.

"You'd be Katherine Earle," the receptionist says as I try to unobtrusively shut the main door behind me. "They're waiting for you."

I glance up at the clock. Nine-ten.

She ignores my glance. Points to a frosted-glass door.

I pause, my cold fingers wrapped around the door handle. .

"What time is the meeting?" I ask her.

"Nine," she says. "He has another appointment, so the sooner you go in . . ." She makes a shooing motion with her fingers.

I open the door. Charles is sitting in a leather chair in front of an impressive black walnut desk. Behind the desk is one of those hearty men with booming voices.

"Usually the family's on time for the handout," he booms at me. Then he laughs.

I already don't trust him.

"Just a misunderstanding," I tell him.

Charles can't meet my eye. He's looking at the blouse and sweater.

"Did you 'borrow' those?" he asks.

But his sarcasm is weak. He's already ashamed of the childish stunt with the meeting time. The shame is there in the red tint on his cheekbones. I remember how I felt outside the bank. When I called him "Chaz." We're going around and around. Bringing out the worst in each other. The child in each other.

I sit down, but I don't bother to answer his question. He knows the clothes are Eva's.

The lawyer looks at me, then at Charles. He shrugs and shuffles the papers on the desk in front of him. "Let's get started," he says.

There's a window behind him. And some pigeons perched on a long swoop of electrical wire. They're fluffing their feathers in the sunshine. The first one in the row puffs his feathers up until he's a big blue-purple ball. He shakes. A little like Miss K. when something tickles her ear. The feathers flatten. The spotted pigeon next to him scratches and preens. Every once in a while, the big blue-purple one leans over and rubs his cheek against the cheek of the spotted pigeon.

"Do you understand?" the lawyer asks me.

I focus on his beef-fed face.

"About?"

He looks over at Charles.

"The four months," he says, giving Charles a "they're pretty, but isn't it good we have the brains?" look. "We have to give any possible creditors the chance to step forward and collect from the estate."

Great-aunt Eva isn't going to have any creditors. But I nod.

"If you need help disposing of or dealing with any portion of the TOD funds," the lawyer says to me, "we can discuss that."

I wish I could ask why Aunt Eva left me everything. But I don't think Mr. Boom-voice will know.

"Is it possible . . ." I stop. Swallow. "Possible to transfer to . . . other family members?"

Because I'm not sure I want . . . this.

This beach, this connection, this responsibility.

The lawyer looks between Charles and me again. "It would be a gift," he says, "and with the limitations or taxes that would involve."

"Oh," I say. Not grasping the concept.

"I don't want your . . . *gift*," Uncle Charles says from beside me. So soft the lawyer might not even hear it.

Outside the window, the pigeons have finished their morning ablutions and are dozing in the sunshine.

"If there are no further questions?" Mr. Boom-voice taps the papers together into a neat pile and stands up.

The pigeons fly away.

Death is complicated. Maybe not so much for the people who die as for the people who are left behind.

Given my latest trend toward morbidity, it's probably a good thing there's a person standing on the front porch of Eva's house and peering in the front window. But it's a blessing wearing good camouflage.

"Well, *there* you are," she says when I stop at the bottom of the steps. As if peering in someone's window was precisely the action to expect should the someone not be at home. "I knocked, but nobody answered. And no wonder! Here you are!"

I smile. It isn't terribly genuine.

"I heard about Eva," the woman continues. She wags her head from side to side, and the wattles under her chin wag in opposite time. "I'm so sorry. You must be devastated. Nathaniel told me you were working at the Watering Hole. Are you holding up all right?"

She's put on weight. Not a little. A lot. But this is Nate's mother. From down the street. Until she wagged, I didn't recognize her.

"It's a good job," I say, deliberately taking her question the way I want to take it.

She wags her head again. "Evalene was a good neighbor and friend."

Which isn't strictly true, because Evalene Earle used to pretend no one was home when Rosemary Litwin came knocking. *"Old-fashioned, blathering, idiot busybody,"* was Aunt Eva's summation of Rosemary Litwin's *better* side, muttered one afternoon when we hid in the kitchen to avoid Rosemary's peeping eyes at the front window. *"If I have to hear about that boy's ear infections one more time,"* Eva grumbled, *"I swear . . ."*

I nod. "How's Nate doing?" I ask, choosing to not respond to Rosemary's memories of Eva.

"Didn't you see him the other night?" Rosemary asks, changing subjects without a hitch.

"For a moment."

"I wish he'd date a nice girl." She wags, the chins quivering in consternation. "You were always a nice girl."

I shiver. As if the ghost of my former self just walked by and smiled that perfect smile at me.

"People have varying opinions on that," I say out loud.

She laughs. "And a good sense of humor, too."

I smile again. It still isn't terribly genuine. And anything I say here will be repeated ad nauseam via the local grapevine. Rosemary is one of the hopeful members of the Society for the Concern of Morals (Other than Gossip) in Our Community. The Society has branches in every city in the world. Branches that collect those few small minds whose lives never get any bigger than the city limits. They probably have secret signals and decoder rings so they can recognize one another when they go on vacation to Palm Springs. I say Rosemary is a hopeful member because she has never been allowed into the inner circle. People like Rosemary aren't part of anyone's inner circle.

"Well," she says, "I just wanted to drop by and let you know how sorry I am. About Evalene, I mean. Why don't you come over for dinner tomorrow? Or tonight?"

I lift my shoulders in false apology. "I'm sorry. I work nights."

"Sunday noon, then?"

My mouth opens, but no excuse presents itself.

She comes down the steps to stand beside me. She's shorter than I remember.

"I'm being pushy, aren't I?" she says.

My mouth closes.

"Nathaniel says I've been pushing him all his life." She sighs. "I wouldn't, if he would just show a bit more . . . *oomph*. You know what I mean?"

No.

I smile.

She pats my cheek.

I almost jerk away.

Almost.

"You just drop in for any old meal you want," she says. "We keep regular hours."

"Okay," I manage.

"I'm sure you're not up for company just yet," she says, in direct contradiction to her presence on Eva's porch, "so I'll head back home. Call if you need anything. I can send Nate up if you want some furniture moved. Or anything else."

She says it in a hopeful kind of way. Like I might want Nate to move my world or something.

"Thanks," I say. "I will."

She starts to pat my cheek again, but I manage to step around it and climb the porch steps to safety.

CHAPTER 10

I would be lying if I pulled out the usual cliché and said the rest of the week passed in a haze or a daze or some such rot.

The rest of the week is crystal clear.

The nip of approaching autumn in the air—all wood smoke and drying leaves—when I step outside Great-aunt Eva's back door to carry water to the birdbath is crystal clear. The golden glow of the light as the sun slips a little farther to the south . . . crystal clear. The feel of the ground under my feet as I walk. The yeast and hops smell of beer at the Watering Hole. All of these impressions are anything but hazy.

They're sharp.

Solid.

Real as real can be.

The haze and daze happen when people talk to me. Or look at me. Or talk *about* me when they think I'm not listening.

I didn't expect this.

This lingering feeling of guilt and shame.

I find every family photo in Great-aunt Eva's house and turn the faces to the wall. When that doesn't work, I take them down and store them in a dresser drawer that used to be filled with various ancient feminine things like industrial-strength garter belts, girdles, and nylon stockings thick enough to tow a car with. I put the feminine undergarments into a paper sack and set them next to the dresser.

But sometimes, around five a.m., when the gray edge of dawn is just starting to touch the eastern sky and I'm lying downstairs on the couch, I can hear Great-aunt Eva's relatives—my relatives—whispering about the failure in the other room.

"*—Left in the middle of the night.*"

"*Couldn't even be bothered to say goodbye.*"

"*What a disgrace.*"

"*Useless.*"

"*Disgrace.*"

"*Disgrace.*"

And I roll over and pull the floppy feather pillow over my head and try to ignore the voices and the pricks from the quills some ancestor missed.

Disgrace.

I think I'm going through postmortem depression. I'm unloved and unlovable. I can't stand who I used to be and I don't know who I am.

Sunday morning comes and the sunshine finds me sitting in the yellow velvet TV chair after another sleepless night spent listening to the voices of guilt. Miss Kitty is chirping to herself as she watches a squirrel who's braved the porch railing. The squirrel digs down into the dirt in one of the railing flower boxes and buries some treasure he's found. He practically does a little soft-shoe for Kitty's benefit before leaping onto a low-hanging limb.

For three years I was like that squirrel. "Home" was nothing more than a clump of leaves and branches high up in the trees. Or a cozy nook in a pile of old masonry. My primary purpose of existence was survival.

Three years.

No.

I've been living like a squirrel my whole life.

I look around the living room and realize that I don't exist in this house. I came into it, lived in it, left it, and was neatly maneuvered back into it. But there are no school pictures of me on the wall, no bookshelves with my books mixed in, no child's plate or cup in the cupboard, no furniture I called mine . . . nothing.

Swinging up out of the chair, I startle Miss Kitty, who's still staring longingly after the squirrel. She drops down from the windowsill and follows me.

I climb the stairs.

Walk down the hall.

And open a door that I haven't opened since I came back to Silver Creek.

I'd be surprised if it's been opened since I snuck out of the house four years ago.

But it has, because the mattress is bare and the comforter has been bagged in plastic and put at the foot of the bed.

My old bedroom is a small affair. The ceiling slopes to a dormer window that lets in a dimly concentrated light. The bed is on one side of the room. The dresser with the cracked mirror I refused to let Eva replace is on the other. Under the window, the seat lifts to reveal a place for buried treasure. Not that I had pirate gold or secrets to bury. Great-aunt Eva told me it was where I should keep my toys, so they wouldn't "mess up" the room.

The bedding has been bagged up, but the walls are the same. Posters of cats hanging from tree branches, magazine pictures of popular bands that have long since faded from the scene, an old Rudolph Valentino movie poster I picked up at a garage sale.

On the hanging shelves I installed amid loud protests from Eva about flaking plaster are my books. Poetry collections, horse stories, dog stories, cat stories, children's books, and turn-of-the-last-century melodramas by authors no one remembers.

Here and there on the shelves are little toy cars and wind-up waddling geese and a backflipping kangaroo. A stuffed owl Uncle Charles gave me for graduation. A month after the ceremony. Two days before I stuffed some clothes in a backpack and unlatched the front door in the middle of the night.

I pick up the backflipping kangaroo. His tin sides are scratched and the windup mechanism is rusty. The paint is almost gone from his face. I twist the key a few turns and the spring inside grates a bit before rebelling and grinding to a halt.

Christmas. Before the baby fat burned off my arms.

The kangaroo was in my stocking.

"You knew she would leave someday, Charles," Great-aunt Eva said across the table.

I wound up the little kangaroo and watched it do backflips beside my plate. The kangaroo was more interesting than the ham and brandied cherries.

Buzz. Flip. Click. Buzz. Flip. Click.

"Why would you say that?" Uncle Charles asked Eva.

Buzz. Flip. Click.

"You're angry," Aunt Eva said. "I'm sorry. I shouldn't have brought it up."

"No, Eva. I want to hear this. What made you think Cynthia would leave me?"

Eva looked in my direction. I grabbed the kangaroo off the table, but she looked away without saying anything.

"She loved me," Charles said.

"If you say so," Eva said. "But she never wanted the best for you."

Later, I found Uncle Charles sitting at the table and playing with the kangaroo. I climbed up into an opposite chair and wound the toy up again and again.

Standing in my old bedroom, I rub the kangaroo's face.

Childhood toys always look more rusty, torn up, broken, and shabby than they do in your memories.

I look up at the shelves and the spiderwebs draped with dust that connect the books to the toys.

The adult life is too cluttered for childhood toys. If the toys are connected to good memories, you want them out where you can see them. But only if they're out of the way when you wipe down the shelves with a dust rag. Only if they're out of the way when you want to get books down from the shelf.

The adult life is too cluttered for memories. You want them out where you can see them, but seeing them reminds you how rusty, torn up, broken, and shabby they are.

Kitty rubs her chin on my leg, and I set the kangaroo back on the clean spot it's made through the years of settling dust.

It isn't until I step out into the hallway that I realize what I want to do. How I can end this manipulation and feel solid again.

"What are you doing?" a voice asks from the doorway of Great-aunt Eva's bedroom.

I scream and throw a handful of support hose into the air.

Jennifer screams, too.

Miss Kitty howls.

"Jeez," I say, pulling a flesh-tone knee-high off my head. "Where did you come from?"

"I knocked," Jen says, "but you didn't answer, so I came on in." She digs her hands into her coat pockets. "I brought some boxes from the thrift store."

"Good."

I'm nodding, but her hands are wadded *deep* into the pockets of her coat. And I'm nodding, but I'm really waiting for her to let fly with whatever it is she wants to say. She's always done that—twisted her fingers into a knot when she's upset or nervous or pissed off.

I called her after coming downstairs from the exploration of my childhood and asked if she wanted to help me box up Great-aunt Eva's clothes for the thrift store. She agreed in the enthusiastic tones of a child who's agreeing to do the dishes for a week if only she can get out of a spanking.

"At the funeral . . . the other day," Jen begins. Then she stops.

Golden autumn sunlight pokes past the clouds and through the window. The warm rectangle lands on the hardwood. Separates us.

She looks up from the floor to my face.

I almost let her off the hook by telling her to forget it. Only that's what I've been doing all my life. Telling everyone that it's okay. Letting other people tell me that *my* hurtful, hateful behaviors were okay.

"It's all right. Don't worry about it."

Two of the most dishonest sentences in the English language.

"I didn't know what to do," she says when she figures out that I'm not going to interrupt. "Charles is Donner's best friend . . ." She trails off, because we both know that she was—is—*my* best friend.

"But you've been gone," she says in a rush. "Gone."

I drop the support hose I've been holding into the garbage bag at my feet.

"I'm your friend," I say. "I understand about being pulled in two directions. I was . . ." Honesty is so *hard*. I fumble for the right word. "Hurt, I guess."

"You *left*," Jen says, her fingers working themselves into tighter knots. "You just *left* me. You ran off and left me *behind*."

I sit down on the edge of Great-aunt Eva's bed.

The tables of hurt and blame are turned so easily.

All the blood has left Jen's face. She's looking at me, and I'm looking inside of myself and wishing that I could apologize. But just like the other day at the thrift store, I know I'm not sorry for leaving and that faced with the same situation, I would repeat the past.

But that doesn't mean I ever wanted—want—to hurt Jennifer. Just that I would make the same mistake again.

No.

Not a mistake.

Just a decision.

"I'm getting rid of everything," I say into the void.

Jen bites her lower lip. She's embarrassed by her emotions.

Two friends can be honest with each other without letting their emotions get the better of them. It's like there's one place in a friendship where both parties accept dishonesty. A place where you know the other person doesn't agree and never will, so you both make a silent pact to never mention it. Where "sorry" is a word neither of you will ever say. It may not be psychologically healthy, but it's something we all do.

"What do you mean?" Jen asks.

"All of Eva's things," I say. "I'm getting rid of them."

"Charles isn't going—" She breaks off, censoring herself.

"I know. I'll call him. He can come over and take everything. If he wants it."

"I don't think that's the point," she says.

I remember Charles' face across the dining room table and the back-flipping kangaroo. I wish I knew what the point was for Charles, but I've got enough problems understanding myself.

"How?" Jen asks, bringing me back to Eva's bedroom. "How are you going to get rid of everything?"

"I think I'll just put up a sign. 'Free Stuff. All You Can Carry.'"

"You wouldn't?"

Well, I hadn't actually *thought* I would. I was just joking. But Jen's shock makes the idea seem a lot better.

"Why not?" I ask.

"Because it's valuable. You could sell it. Use the money. *Donate* the money. Give the things to the thrift store. I don't know. But just *give* it all away? That's crazy."

That's crazy.

Suddenly, the idea is the only idea I'm going to entertain. I'm going to invite it in for dinner and dancing. It's a marvelous idea.

"Help me clean out the closets, will you?" I ask.

Jen's forehead wrinkles into a frown. "You're going to do it anyway, aren't you?"

"Clean out the closets? Yes."

She sighs.

I take pity on her.

"Yes," I say. "I'll call Charles tonight."

"You shouldn't have come back," she says, shaking her head. "You shouldn't have come back."

The hurt goes deeper than I'll ever let her know.

"Too late now," I say, bright as tears. "I'm already here."

"I wonder why you bothered," she says. "You're just upsetting everything."

"Upsetting you, you mean."

She looks up from the sunlit cracks between the pieces of hardwood flooring. A hundred years ago, the flooring was practically seamless, but the cracks formed as the house rose and fell with each shift of the weather.

"Is that what you think?" she asks, looking at me. Searching my face.

I look back at her. Keep my face still. Twist a stray knee-high around and around my hand.

"I think you don't like being where you are," I say.

She opens her mouth, but I hold up a nylon-wrapped hand.

"I don't think you like being on Charles' side. You're used to being on my side. But Donner is definitely in Charles' camp. And you're on Donner's side. At least, I'm guessing—"

"You know so much about being married, huh?" she says, each word a nail.

"No," I say, not bothering to tell her about the ring next to my skin. Nine months of watching my fantasy dissolve into reality doesn't make me an expert.

"When you do, you can talk about what this feels like," she says.

I nod. "Okay. But that doesn't change anything. You don't like being the monkey in the middle."

"Fuck you," she says, which means I'm right.

"Want to help me clean out the closets first?" I ask.

She shakes her head. "You can still do it."

"What?"

"Make me hate you one minute and love you the next."

I grin and dangle the nylon for Miss Kitty to swat. "I'm just a great, big bundle of contradictions waiting to happen."

"And your ego still needs trimming."

I remember sitting across from Gwen at her kitchen table. The gym mirror and the girl in pink taffeta. I remember what a heartless little egomaniac I used to be and how being a real friend might have made all the difference to Gwen.

But if that's what I think, I'm no different now than I was then. No different now if I think one word from me would have made all the difference in Gwen's life.

"You're a little late for ego trimming," I say to Jen, pulling the nylon away from Miss K. and stuffing it into the sack with the others.

CHAPTER 11

Silence.

I stare at the fingers of my left hand and try to come up with a better way to describe what's happening on the other end of the phone.

"You want me to—"

"—come by and pick out anything you want," I finish for him.

"She left it to you," Uncle Charles says. "All of it. Do what you want."

"I am," I say, "and I want you to have any of the furniture, dishes, books . . . anything you would like to have."

Silence. Again.

Very few words in the English language rhyme with "silence" and still look good in a poem. "Obsolescence," for example. Cute word. Not good for poetry.

I start drumming my fingers on the wooden door frame.

I'm standing in the entryway to the kitchen. Across from me, my reflection is misty in the glass door of the china hutch. A ghost of the present mixed in among the solid porcelain of the past.

"Stop that noise," Charles says. "Can't you ever sit still?" He asks the question absently, since he doesn't expect an answer.

I stop drumming.

The face in the china hutch glass is pale. Dark hair mixes with the dark wood, and my white face floats alone in the glass.

"You want more money, don't you?" Charles asks after another long silence. "You want me to buy—"

"Haven't you ever just *given* anything away?" I interrupt. "Because you wanted to?"

"No one *gives* without a reason," he answers.

"You're right," I say. "I want you to take whatever you want so you won't be angry at me when I give the rest of it away."

Someone knocks on the door, keeping me from getting in trouble for drumming again, because we're back to silence and I still can't think of a word that rhymes.

"Here you go," Rosemary Litwin says as she shoves a potted plant into my free hand. "I hear you're moving things around."

"Who's that?" Charles asks. "Someone you're planning on giving the family heirlooms to?"

"If you don't get your butt over here and take what you want, I just might," I say.

Then I hang up.

"Did I interrupt something?" Rosemary asks.

"A family quarrel."

"Oh, dear." She points to the plant. "I brought this for you. And Nathaniel will be over to help you move things. He's already agreed to do it, so don't you hesitate to use those muscles of his."

I set the phone down.

Rosemary smiles. Her eyes never leave my face.

I wonder when she's planning on informing Nate of his agreement.

I look down at the potted plant. I'm guessing it's an aspidistra. Great-aunt Eva had a dozen of them until silk plants became the rage and she threw the live ones out with the garbage. The aspidistra smells like over-watering and Rosemary's cologne spray. I give the side of the pot a reassuring pat and set it in the middle of the table.

"Who said I needed help moving things?" I ask.

"Well, Irene needed some ice cream to eat with her afternoon football, so naturally she went by Donner's place. He always has a pint or two around for Sunday-afternoon regulars. And Donner *is* married to Jennifer, you know, and he happened to mention . . . At any rate, she, Irene, I mean, called Darla, who happened to be sitting in my living room. Darla just got one of those cell phone—"

"Got it," I say, not wanting to hear how easy it is for everyone to know my every move.

"Are you redecorating?" she asks.

"Sort of."

"I know how it is. When Ferrel died, I—"

"Would you like something to drink?" I ask, belatedly remembering my manners. Realizing as I say it that I've just interrupted her. A further breach. Poor Great-aunt Eva. "Tea? Coffee?"

"Oh, whatever you have on hand."

She follows me into the kitchen.

I pour water into the coffeepot. As I start to spoon coffee into the filter, Rosemary reaches out and takes the scoop from my shaking fingers.

I'm not in the mood—

"Sit down," she says. "Coffee needs a sure and accurate hand."

—for companionship. Maybe the glass reflection did it. Maybe it was Jennifer and all that hatred she wanted to hide but couldn't. Maybe . . .

I sit down at the scarred wooden table by the window. Outside, gray clouds are starting to block out the northern sky.

Rosemary finishes setting up the coffeepot, then sits down across from me. "I chatter when I'm nervous," she says.

"I never know how to say anything," I say, thinking of Jennifer and watching the fingers of storm stretching for blue sky.

She folds her hands on the table.

"I'm not a nice person," I say, not looking away from the black clouds. "Every time I talk to someone, I remember what I did. What I'm like."

"You're a nice girl," she says. "Any mother would want you for a daughter-in-law."

I smile at my reflection in the window. "Thank you," I say, realizing that this conversation isn't going to get better before it's over.

Realizing that Rosemary isn't going to be a well-hidden font of wisdom.

Realizing that I never met my mother-in-law. She took a trip to Virginia when Stephen was eight or nine. She never came back to Silver Creek. The last he heard—the last I *know* he heard, anyway—was that she had married someone in Norfolk and had two new kids to love.

The coffeepot sputters to a halt.

Rosemary hops up. "Where are the cups?"

"First cupboard on the right."

"I'm hopeless with houseplants," she says as she pours the coffee. "But Eva was always so good . . . I thought maybe the green thumb was genetic, you know."

I nod.

"Is it?"

"Is it what?"

She hands me a stoneware mug filled with coffee. "Genetic."

"I've never tried. To grow anything."

"They say plants are a lot like children," she says. And she smiles at me over the rim of her cup.

That night, lightning crackles like fireworks, and the rain fills Silver Creek to the bursting point.

Uncle Charles still has a key to the house. And he uses it to take the family silver. And the hall table. And the china hutch. And all the black walnut bedroom furniture some ancestor's bride carried from Missouri in a covered wagon.

Uncle Charles still has a key, and he uses it to spirit things away while I'm at work. So he doesn't have to face me. At three-thirty a.m., I'm too tired to notice more than the dark spots on the wall where the furniture used to be.

"We'll have to paint, I guess," I say to Kitty.

And even though I told him to come and get what he wanted, I still feel like I've been robbed. It's one thing to watch furniture leave in the hands of someone you know. Watch people sweat and strain to carry bulky items out the front door while you tell them to mind their step. There's a sense of closure.

But catching the smell of strangers in your house when you unlock your door . . . it's unnerving.

Miss Kitty's tail is fuzzy. She paces back and forth on the kitchen table, brushing her body on the leaves of the aspidistra with each pass.

Charles didn't even leave a note.

I check the dresser drawer and sigh.

At least he could have taken the pictures.

I expect the voices of guilt to wake me, but the morning alarm takes the form of knocking on the front door. I should have stayed at the motel. At least there I got five hours of sleep.

Bleary and rumpled, I open the door and practically get a fist in the face.

"Oh, I'm *sorry!*" the chubby pastor says. He tucks his hand back around the leather Bible clutched to his stomach. "Did I wake you up? I didn't mean . . . I usually make a follow-up visit to members of the family of the deceased, but if . . ."

I smile my relief that he's not Rosemary or Charles, and step back. "Come on in."

He wipes his feet on the mat. As he comes in, he looks around the entrance hall, his mouth open, then realizes what he's doing and blushes.

"I'm sorry," he says. "I used to be an architecture student. These old houses have such interesting . . . architecture."

I see it through his eyes. Look at the arched doorways on either side of the entryway, the hand-carved bannister railing gliding up the stairs, the eight-over-eight paned windows, and the half-moon of stained glass above the door. Seen for the first time, it *is* . . . interesting.

"I guess I've never noticed," I tell him. "Would you like some coffee?"

"If it isn't any trouble."

Poor Great-aunt Eva. The wishy-washy state of the universe must have insulted her idea of proper company etiquette.

"Come on into the kitchen," I say, picturing Eva's frown of disapproval at inviting guests into the seat of hospitality production. I enjoy the imagined frown. "Unless you'd like to see the rest of the house?"

"I . . . I apologize for that," he mumbles. "For being presumptuous."

I turn around and catch the edge of the arched entry into the living room in one hand.

Watch the blush of shame creep over the pastor's face.

"You've already been to see Uncle Charles, haven't you?" I ask.

"Um—"

"I wasn't asking if you'd like to look around in order to embarrass you," I say, a bit more bite in the words than I intend. But the image of Charles torturing this man is similar to the image of Charles kicking a puppy. "If you'd like to see the rest of the house, I'd be happy to show it to you."

He smiles nervously.

An evil idea takes root. A way to get revenge.

"In fact," I continue, "if you'd like some of the furniture or need something for the church, it would be my *pleasure* if you'd take it off my hands."

The blush on the round cheeks fades to white. "I . . . Well, I . . ."

I smile encouragingly.

"I'd love to," he says. And the first genuine smile I've seen pops onto his face.

"Let me start the coffee first," I say, only someone knocks on the door. I sigh and reach for the knob. "I'm popular all of a sudden."

"Maybe it's the furniture giveaway," he says. Then he blushes again. Sarcastic humor must not go over very well in his line of work, because he starts mumbling apologies, too.

I open the door before he can stammer out a "sorry," and a complete stranger hands me a casserole dish covered in aluminum foil.

"I am so sorry about Evalene," the stranger says. "I know it must be devastating for you. I'm a little late with this, but a person suffering from grief should be careful to keep up her strength." She pats my hand. "I hear you're working at the Watering Hole."

I nod, playing along until I can figure out what's going on.

"We should be careful," she says. "We wouldn't want Evalene's grand-niece hanging around with a woman—"

She looks over my shoulder and breaks off.

"Oh, hello, Pastor Bob," she continues, barely missing a beat. "It's good you can be with our Katherine in her time of suffering."

"It's Robert, actually," I hear the pastor say under his breath.

She pats my hand again. "You just give the dish back when you're finished."

Then she turns and walks away.

I shut the door. "What . . . who was *that*?"

"Darla Covington," Bob—Robert—says. And he says it with enough sorrow to make me pity him.

"Why did she bring me a casserole?"

"She heads up the Caregivers."

I stare at him.

"The Caregivers. It's a women's group at the church. My church. The Methodist one, I mean."

"Great. But what about the casserole?"

"It's a form of community outreach."

I lift up a corner of the foil. "Did she reach out to Charles with one of these?"

"One would hope so."

I look up at him, and he smiles quickly. I'm not sure whether he's joking or not. I know *I'm* hoping Charles was the recipient of Darla Covington's charity.

"They, the women, go to all the families in Silver Creek who have experienced some . . . difficulty or hardship," he adds, trying to inject a little joy into his words.

The Caregivers are starting to sound like a major branch of the Silver Creek grapevine.

"I need that coffee," I say.

I'm on my second cup, and Robert has seen the house from attic to basement. I had no idea the massive floor beams overhead could be so . . . interesting, but he spent a full ten minutes examining them before he remembered where he was and blushed again. He's looking over a cupboard that has choir-room possibilities when someone with a cheery knock raps for my attention.

Pearl waltzes into the house when I open the door.

"Hi," Gwen says. "I thought you might need a little help recovering from the community outreach. Unless you want to go back to sleep?"

I laugh and open the door all the way so she can come in.

"I saw Darla Covington's car," she says. "Did you survive?"

"She retreated after leaving a casserole."

"Don't eat it," she says. "It'll give you indigestion."

"You don't say. My, my."

"She brought one after John was born. To 'ease the workload.' Mayla threw up for a week."

"What a surprise."

We grin at each other.

It's an odd feeling.

Communion.

As if the cottonwood suddenly spoke back.

You have the look.

Last week, I ran away from her so fast, my heels were burning, but now I think . . .

"I think I understand what you meant last time," I say.

"About Darla?"

"No."

She looks at me. And something in my face must help her understand.

"It doesn't have to be a mistake," she says.

"I think that cupboard would be fantastic," Robert says from the living room arch. "If I can—"

He stops.

"This is Gwen," I say, before I notice that Gwen isn't moving.

If I ever wanted to know how Daphne looked when her soft, living flesh became the hard outer bark of the laurel . . . Now I know.

"Robert," Gwen says. Rough. Cold. Freezing. The kind of voice I always wished I could cultivate. The kind of voice that stops unwanted advances in their tracks. But somehow, even after long hours spent in front of the mirror to get the right look (and succeeding), I never managed to find the right temperature.

Eva had the tone down cold.

Robert nods. "Gwen."

He doesn't blush or stammer an apology. But he looks a little like Apollo must have looked when he reached the laurel tree a moment too late.

Pearl whines and stands up on her back legs so she can paw at Robert's knee and get his attention.

He reaches down to pet her.

"I'd better go," he says to me.

"Okay," I say.

He's gone before I can ask him if he wants the cupboard.

The rough bark of Gwen's face shimmers into flesh again.

She gives me a shaky smile. "Did I tell you not to eat Darla Covington's casserole?"

I bite the inside of my cheek.

"Yes," I say.

CHAPTER 12

Silver Creek is a small town. If you're willing to walk a few miles in any given direction, you can get around without a car. Unless you're taking a cat to work with you every day. Then you have to drive.

And buy gas.

The yellow warning light by my fuel gauge has been on for almost a week before I break down and drive out to the Silver Creek Gas and Lube. Dustin meets me with a grin.

"I figured it out," he says as I climb out of the car. "Where I've seen you before."

I raise my eyebrows.

"At school. Your picture is in the trophy case by the office."

Homecoming coming home to haunt me.

"I guess," I say out loud.

He starts the pump, then slaps some window cleaner onto the gloppy insect bodies covering my windshield.

"How—?" he begins, but I interrupt him, not feeling up to sharing stories about empty events.

"How's your mom doing?"

He switches from sponge to squeegee. "Fine. I was cleaning the rooms. I heard a lot about you while I did it." He grins at my frown, then says in a voice almost like his mother's, "'Kat dusted the bed frames.' You made my life a lot harder, you know."

I smile, but I'm still caught on the past tense. *"I was cleaning."* Still remembering Melody's swollen legs and how hard it is for her to get around.

"So you're cleaning the rooms?" I ask, after fishing around for an innocuous, unthreatening, unaccusatory way to ask if Melody is trying to do everything herself.

"Nah. She's got another renter now. Same deal as you had." He drops my wiper back down onto the windshield with a flourish.

"Tell her I'll stop by sometime."

"She knows you've been busy. What with your great-aunt dying and all." He blushes. Realizes he might have spoken out of turn.

I try to smile and hand him the money and tip. "Yeah, it's been a laugh a minute since I got back."

He folds the bills around an index finger. Oily dust has worked its way into the creases around his knuckles, competing with the nicotine stain.

"Why'd you come back?" he asks. "I mean, living in L.A. and all. Living somewhere . . . big. Seems crazy to come back, doesn't it?"

"That's the million-dollar question," I say as I open the car door.

"Which one? Why you came back or if you're crazy?"

I shrug. "Your pick."

Canada has sent a gift of cold air on the heels of Sunday's thunderstorm. The kind of cold that reminds you how the glass of your doors and windows will creak and tinkle like starlight. The kind of cold that freezes the air inside of your lungs. But when I swing back by Great-aunt Eva's house on the way to work, I have to admit that picking up my coat isn't the primary purpose.

I'm hoping to catch the Cadillac parked by the curb.

It is. I do.

I open the front door as quietly as I can and see Uncle Charles standing beside the oak dining table. He's running a finger along the surface.

"Checking for dust?" I ask.

He jumps.

Gripping one of the chairs, he turns to look at me.

"Hello, Katherine."

"You won't need that," I say, gesturing to the chair. "I won't attack."

He smiles. It's so thin, I can barely see it. "I wasn't going to fend you off."

"You don't have to wait until I'm gone," I say. "You can come over any time."

Another smile.

His fingers convulse around the wooden slat of the chair back.

"Are you implying that I'm avoiding you?" he asks.

"Aren't you?"

"I don't agree with what you're doing."

I lean my shoulder against the arched doorway between the entry hall and the living and dining rooms. "You mean giving things away?"

"I could fight you, you know," he says.

"Like with lawyers and courtrooms?"

"Something like that."

The room is chilly. Old houses let the cold seep in through their pores. I dig my hands into the pockets of my jeans.

"Why not just take everything?" I ask. "I wouldn't stop you."

"Obviously."

I'm not sure whether he means it's obvious I wouldn't—couldn't—stop him or whether it's obvious that I don't care if he takes everything because I'm about to give it all away.

He points toward the sign on the table. I found some old reflective stick-on letters in a kitchen drawer. I'm missing a few letters, so the sign says, FREE FURNIT RE: EVERYTH NG OES. I haven't decided whether I want to pay for the missing letters or just fill in the blanks with a Sharpie.

"Don't you think this is demeaning?" he asks, still pointing to the sign.

I dig my hands a little farther into my pockets. "For you or for me?"

"For Aunt Eva. This is her legacy. She wanted you to have it."

The toes of my boots are scuffed. If I don't oil the leather, they won't last through a Montana winter.

"What if I don't want her legacy?" I ask.

He's quiet.

I look up from my scuffed boots.

He's looking at me. Really looking. For the first time since that day on the bridge.

"It's not something you can decide," he says.

I think about Melody's face after Eva's phone call. The hurt she felt at being treated like so much trash. Like so little human being. Inflicting that kind of pain . . . you decide to do it. Decide to live it. Decide to hand it out to other people with a few choice insults so carefully garbed no one can actually say you intended insult instead of injury.

Or you can decide not to.

It's as simple as that.

"I think you can," I say to Charles.

"She took you in," he says. "You could have gone to a foster home, you know."

"As opposed to living with you?" I ask before I can stop myself.

He swallows.

I watch his throat work. The movement is painfully familiar. From that dark night when Charles caught me and Blaine on a gravel side road just outside of Silver Creek.

"What in God's name did you think you were doing?" Uncle Charles said through his teeth. He had shoved me into the car and was driving back

into Silver Creek. The headlights of his car flashed over the reflective tape of the guardrail. In the momentary glow, I saw his throat work up and down.

"Embarrassing you," I said, looking away from his throat and to the road beyond the windshield.

I'd been caught. Drunk, mostly undressed, and pretending to enjoy the seduction of the Golden Boy. Blaine Whatsisname. Senior, star athlete, closet alcoholic, and the fast track to high school popularity. Blaine liked alcohol about as much as he liked football, basketball, baseball, and himself. Girls barely made it into the top ten, so being female and noticed was enough to get a nobody freshman onto the fast track to being somebody. I made sure I was noticed. And found myself lying on a blanket under the stars with half a bottle of alcoholic foreplay in me. I didn't have to fuck (not much else to call it) Blaine to get noticed. I chose to go the extra step.

Because I was fifteen. I was angry. And I had just figured out that growing up was kind of like having the wind at your back. You rolled where it took you and took life as it came. Blaine had asked, *"Want to share this?"* when he'd pulled up beside me as I was walking home. He'd held up the bottle, and I'd let the wind roll me right on into his car.

Why not?

"Embarrassing you," I said again, watching my reflected lips move in the window as I said it.

"You're crazy." Uncle Charles went on talking—lecturing—as if I hadn't said anything. "Disease, pregnancy . . . Did you use . . . ?"

The sentence hung in the darkness of the car's interior. Waiting. I ignored it.

"What is Eva going to think?" Charles asked a quarter of a mile later.

I shrugged. "Who's going to tell her?"

"What will people think of you?"

Outside the car window, the autumn grass beside the road waved in the headlights as we drove past.

"Have a little respect for your family," Charles said. "Life isn't just all about you."

"I'm so sorry," I said, still looking at the grass. "I forgot that it's all about *you*. And what you need. Next time I'll try to make it to that flash flood so I won't be a problem that gets left behind."

The car nearly went off the road when Charles stepped on the brakes.

"Get out," Charles said.

I opened the door. "*Oh,*" I said before I shut it, "*if you see me by the side of the road again, don't bother to pick me up. At least that way I'll get a ride back into town.*"

I blink the memory away. Watch Charles swallow again.

"Eva took me in," I say, digging in the knife, "because no one else could be bothered."

He lets go of the chair and holds his hands out in an inclusive gesture. "Give the rest of it away if you want. I don't care."

Then he brushes past me and slams the door.

The windows rattle.

I'm still leaning against the door frame when the clock chimes a quarter to three.

I'm going to be late to work.

Families know exactly where to stick in the knife and twist it around for maximum effect. I look down on Great-aunt Eva for her cruelty to Melody, but I can use a knife with equal skill. I enjoyed hurting Charles. I enjoyed standing in Eva's living room and reliving the memory of the night when I lost my virginity to the Golden Boy and stabbed my uncle with the knife I'd been sharpening from the moment I finally understood why I was living with Great-aunt Eva. On that night, I knew just where to find the weak spot in his armor. And standing in the living room today, I found that spot again. The spot where long ago he didn't live up to a responsibility he had accepted. The spot that likes to cover responsibility with a sheen of familial affection.

I enjoyed hurting him.

I disgust myself.

Haven't I gotten beyond this bullshit?

It's not like I spent my childhood starved for love. Eva loved me in her own way. That way might have been imminently practical, but let's face it, there aren't monsters under the bed and *"the sooner you figure it out . . ."*

. . . the sooner you figure out that the monsters are inside of the people you know and talk to every day.

. . . the sooner you figure out that the monsters are inside of you.

Lovely stuff to figure out.

Lyle waves me over as I step into the bar. It's five minutes after three. Lil raises her eyebrows, but she's busy with the supplier, so I'm off the hook. The warehouse tends to mix up the Watering Hole's orders, so any anger Lil has over my guilty five will be transferred to the idiot who juggled light and dark.

"I hear you're giving away furniture," Lyle says after I've set Miss K. down on the floor behind the bar.

"If everybody knows about it," I ask, "why aren't they lined up in front of the house?"

"They're waiting for a sign," he says.

"From God?"

He smiles, then turns serious. "I'm not sure you can do it legally. Right away, that is. When my dad died . . . I mean, there's usually a period of time—"

Exhaustion swamps me and I tune him out. I've heard this from the lawyer already. Why did I think tossing the remnants from the past would be easy? Why is everyone against change?

"Can't or shouldn't?" I ask. And some of my frustration works its way into my voice. Heats it up a little hotter than I actually feel.

He holds both hands up in front of him in defense. "I didn't mean anything. I just thought since I did some work for Eva—"

"Are you beating up my accountant?" Lil asks from beside me.

"I'm thinking about it."

"Everyone wants to kill the messenger," Lyle grumbles.

Lil looks at me, and I take a deep breath and explain the whole situation.

"If you know all your aunt's records and things," she says, "I wouldn't worry about it. As long as she didn't have a secret love affair with a televangelist or make trips to Reno?"

I shake my head.

"It's just some furniture," Lil says. "I wouldn't sweat it."

Lyle leans his cheek on his fist and sighs. "I don't know why I bother."

"Because you can't help yourself," Lil says. She hands me his mug. "Fill this up, will you? It's on the house, Lyle."

"No," I say. "It's on me. Thanks, Lyle."

He smiles. "Just trying to help."

I've set the beer in front of Lyle when Lil pulls me to one side. I'm assuming she's going to give me a few lashes for being late, but she surprises me.

"Have you seen Thad?" she asks.

I shake my head. "But I don't get out his way much," I add.

Thad runs a fiber farm west of Silver Creek. That is, he raises goats and sheep for the mohair and wool. I asked him about it once and heard more than I wanted to hear about how sheep aren't nearly as dumb as the other ranchers say they are. I'll take his word for it. They don't look very bright to me. Not that the local Herefords look much brighter. They're usually leaning on the barbed-wire fence trying to reach the grass in the ditch by the highway while miles and miles of green stuff stretch out behind them.

"He hasn't been back in . . ." Lil begins. Her voice trails off.

I grin. "Miss him?"

She looks right through me.

And I realize I said the wrong thing.

Realize her skin is gray and tight.

"I'm sorry," I say, not quite sure what kind of offense I'm apologizing for.

"Never mind," she says, dismissing my ability to help and my apology. She points down the bar with her chin. "There's a guy down there trying to get your attention."

It's Nate.

"Hi," he says.

"Hey." I inject a bit more warmth into it than I might normally, trying to chastise myself for my social blunders with everyone else around me. "Corona, right?"

"No. I only drink that with Summer. It's her beer." He points to a dark beer on tap. "I'll take a glass of that."

I'm pouring when he says, "Mom told me you said something about needing some help. Moving stuff?"

I shut off the tap and look at him. "Has your mother ever considered going into politics?"

He scratches his upper lip and pays for the beer. "I don't think so."

The compressor in the refrigerator behind me clicks on. Nate blows the foam away from the edge of his glass before drinking.

"You didn't say anything to her, did you?" he asks, setting the beer down onto the bar. It's not really a question. It sounds too resigned.

"Did you tell her you'd help me move a lot of furniture around?" I ask.

He shakes his head.

"Well, I heard you did."

"I take it you're a 'nice girl,' " he says, leaning on the bar.

"So she says."

"I'm sorry about that." He sighs and swallows some more of the beer. "It's enough to drive you crazy."

I wipe a damp ring from the surface of the bar. "Don't let it bother you. She'll be happy with anyone as long as you're prepared to present her with grandchildren."

He makes a face. "You'd think that was life's crowning achievement."

I laugh.

For the first time today.

"For some people, it's their only achievement," I say.

He finishes the beer and hands me the glass to refill.

"Do you like Summer?" he asks when I set the full glass down in front of him.

I raise my eyebrows. "I thought the answer to that was obvious."

He smiles. "Right. I meant, other than that. She doesn't act like that all the time, you know. She sees you and she just . . . sees red, I guess. It's kind of fun to watch. For a bit, anyway." He rubs circles into the bar with his finger.

"I've never—" *liked her.* But I don't finish the sentence.

"She's nice," he says. "I just . . ."

I don't want to know his girl troubles. Summer managed to rub me the wrong way for all four years of high school and the two times I've seen her since. If she's a nice girl, then Nate can figure it out for himself.

Something in my face must tell him what I'm not saying.

He straightens up. "So, do you need furniture moved?"

Thinking about all that oak and walnut, I almost say yes. But the costs are too high. For me. For Rosemary. For Nate. And maybe even for Summer.

Some things should be left alone.

"I think I've got it covered," I say. "But thanks."

He nods, pays for the second beer, and leaves.

CHAPTER 13

Once I got used to the wind at my back, once I got used to rolling along like a tumbleweed, I began to like it. Life's little problems were easy when there was no responsibility. When there was no one else with needs and thoughts and emotions. When the only person I had to worry about was me.

The cold front brings a new look to the world. You hear a lot about the weather in Los Angeles. How great it is. As I slip Miss K. into the car at three in the morning, the icy Canadian breath has Silver Creek firmly in its grip. Above me, the sky is clearer, blacker, closer—dropping molten stars into my hair. My own breath puffs out of my lungs in white clouds.

My nostrils pinch together as I breathe in. And I feel alive. The cold reminds me that living is a gift. That tomorrow every leaf in town will be lined in white frost so delicate it looks like some crazed baker went around tossing confectioner's sugar into the air. It reminds me that next week every tree will pull her wild gypsy cloak of autumn reds and yellows around her shoulders and snuggle in for the winter.

I couldn't find autumn in the ozone-scented sunshine of L.A.

I didn't feel alive.

I slide in beside Kitty, who's protesting the cold vinyl seat, and wonder whether I left Stephen because of him or because of me. I wonder whether

I left because I needed to see what life before the wind could be like when there was no one to please but myself.

I'm not sure I know the answer.

I'm not sure I *want* to know the answer. The answer raises too many new questions. And I'm tired of questions.

Katherine Earle as prodigal novelty must have worn thin. Because no one wakes me up. I sleep until noon and wake up grateful for the lack of popularity. But when I hop out to the mailbox in my bare feet, toes curling in protest at contact with the icy cement, I find a note from Jennifer that she must have left yesterday or while I was sleeping.

Can we talk? Lunch? My treat.

She packed up a few boxes last Sunday. Before claiming that she had to go home. But we both knew she wanted to go home and cry on Donner's shoulder. Too bad he passed some tidbits along to Irene the ice-cream-snacking football fan, who passed it on to Darla the indigestible-casserole maker.

Yes, I'm bitter.

I'm hopping up and down on the entryway rug, trying to thaw my toes, when Jennifer's SUV pulls up in front. I consider pretending I'm not home, but the gossip isn't Jen's fault.

"I'm sorry," she says when I open the door before she can knock.

"I just got this," I say at the same time while waving the note. "Or I'd be dressed. Unless you'd like a little casserole for lunch?"

"You're pissed," she says.

"You're kidding."

She flushes. "I didn't know he'd say anything."

"You didn't, huh?"

I'm behaving badly.

I feel badly.

I want to lash out at my friend for being on the other team.

I close my eyes.

"I'm sorry," I say. "I know it's not your fault, but I'm mad at you anyway."

"That's one of the reasons I thought we should talk."

I open my eyes. "All formal and reasonable?" I say it with a smile so it doesn't come out sounding sarcastic. I have to admit that a little part of me *feels* sarcastic, but Jen is here and doing her best. It's only fair that I try, too.

"Come on in," I say. "Before I save the gas company the trouble of going bankrupt."

She comes in and stands on the rumpled entry rug.

"Want to take off your coat?" I ask, pointing toward the tree by the door.

"I missed you," she says. "When you left."

I stare at her.

Remember that one night in L.A. when I sat all night in the back-est, darkest seat I could find at a twenty-four-hour restaurant. When I sat all night with my fingers wrapped around a cold cup of coffee and wished I had the nerve, the money, to call Jen and tell her how much I needed to hear her tell me that nothing was impossible. That in every dark moment there's a candle.

I'm not sure why I didn't call. I could have scraped some change together. I paid for the coffee in cash.

"I missed you after I left," I say. "After the crazy part became sane."

"Then I got so angry," she says, as if I hadn't spoken. "I wanted you to die. After I heard that Newell died, I wanted to hear that you died with him."

"Thanks," I say, surprised by the ghosts of hate and fury in her eyes.

She rubs a hand under her nose, then looks up at the wall. "You took down the picture of your great-grandmother."

"Great-great-grandmother," I say. "And she made me nervous."

"After I got done being angry," she says, still looking at the wall, "I didn't care. Until I saw you at the thrift store."

I set the mail and her note on a little table that Charles hasn't taken.

"Did you think we could just pick up and go on from where we left off?" I ask.

She looks at me.

"Because I did," I continue. "I thought it would be easy."

"Until the funeral."

I nod.

"Maybe I should have gone with you," she says. "Maybe I should have."

And I'm not sure she means the funeral.

It's like a window just opened for me. Not a window into her soul. More like a window into her heart.

She's lonely.

She's caught.

As long as I wasn't in Silver Creek, she was happy being part of the generation that is Donner and Charles, and all their friends and mores.

Then I came back.

She's not angry because I left without a word. Oh, she used to be. But that anger has faded and would barely register past an apologetic ice cream cone in the park.

She's angry at me for upsetting the first stability she's had in her life.

She's angry at me for reminding her that she misses the time when she undermined the community pillars. For reminding her that now she supports them.

"I'm not asking you to choose between me and Donner," I say into the silence that has become uncomfortable.

But it doesn't matter if I'm asking or not. Because in her mind, it *is* a choice.

She rubs her hand under her nose again.

"Let's go get some lunch," I say, knowing that it will probably be the last real lunch I have with Jen. Unless we meet at some community function or church potluck. Unless we meet at another funeral.

And even now, this last real lunch will be a casual lunch. Between old friends who have drifted irrevocably apart.

I unbraid my sleep-shredded hair and start to rebraid it when Jen says, "Here, let me."

I turn my back to her. There was a time when I couldn't figure out how to hold three strands and twist them at the same time. Jen would always say, *"Here, let me."* And then she'd show off with some elaborate French braid. Even after I figured out how to do a simple braid, I didn't let on. Because I enjoyed the human touch, and the way Jen would hum under her breath when she did some style that was particularly difficult.

She twists a quick, tight braid and hands the end to me to tie off.

"Remember the time your aunt caught us reading that how-to sex book?"

"Remember when Miss Parsons thought you were the one who stole the master exam for the physics test?"

"Remember Summer's face when you were made homecoming queen?"

Remember the day when our friendship ended in Eva's entryway and we went out to lunch?

I'm not sure that memory will be one I laugh about over the all-you-can-eat pizza buffet.

"I'd better go," I tell Jen when it's almost time for me to be at work.

The exhausted waiter cleaning up after the lunch crowd raises a silent fist of joy. We're the last two people in the restaurant.

"I'll drive you," Jen says, even though it's only a block or two. We both know that when I step out of the SUV, it will be over. That we will have crossed the bridge that leads from our past to our future.

"I guess the mascot will have to stay home today," I say.

One of Silver Creek's two ambulances is in front of the bar. Blue and red lights twirling lazily in the wind.

"Looks like someone might have had a bit too much to drink," Jen says.

I ignore the pillar-supporting comment and thank her for lunch.

Shut the door of the SUV on my past.

I secretly thank the patron who collapsed in the bar for a distraction to ease stepping off the other side of the bridge.

Only the person strapped down by the medics is Lil. And she's yelling that she won't go until the cats get here. The medics look ready to gag her.

I grab her hand. "One cat is here," I say.

"Thank God," she says, only it's slurred a little because one side of her mouth is having trouble working. "Don't shut down the bar."

"I won't."

"The supplier—"

"I'll take care of everything," I say. "I promise." I'm surprised at how confident my words sound. I don't feel confident.

The medics wheel her out. I follow them and stand outside the door while they hoist her into the ambulance. The wind grabs my braid and pulls it apart. Strands of hair get into my eyes.

"Don't close it down!" Lil manages to yell before the doors are shut.

The ambulance drives away and I still don't know what's going on.

"She fell down," Lyle says from behind me.

I've had too many ambulances in my life.

"Do you run your business out of the bar?" I ask Lyle.

He reels back.

I reach out and grab his elbow.

"I didn't mean that," I say. "I'm sorry. I didn't mean that at all."

He catches *my* elbow.

We're both shaking.

"Come on back inside," he says. He starts to put the CLOSED sign in the window, but I stop him.

"I said I'd keep it open," I say. "And I will."

"Right."

He sits down at the bar and rubs his hands down his gray face. I pour him a dose of brandy and set it at his elbow. All I want is a glass of water.

"How did she fall?" I ask, when the brandy is gone.

"She didn't fall, exactly," he says. "I think she had one of those ministroke things. A TIA. But I don't think that's what she wants getting around."

I nod, even though I'm not sure what he means.

"Will she be okay?" I ask.

"Fine, probably. The medic said it would be fine. In a day or two."

I nod again. A bobble-head doll leaning on a bar. My water glass is empty. I fill it again. And miss—

"Where's Thad?" I ask.

Lyle buries his face in his hands and shakes his head. "He stomped out about an hour ago."

"Have you called him?"

He shakes his head again.

The door opens and one of the early-afternoon regulars shows up. "Cold today," he says, rubbing his hands together.

"Sure is," I say, injecting Lil's typical warmth into it. I lean over and tap Lyle's cell phone where it's hanging from his belt. "Call Thad," I say to him, too soft for the customer to hear.

"I don't think—" Lyle begins.

I grab his wrist. "No matter what happened between them, they're friends. He needs to know. Call him and then go down to the hospital. I have to stay here or I'd go."

The customer leans on the bar a few feet down. "Long face you got there, Lyle," he says. "Lose somebody's money?"

Lyle tries to smile.

"Call Thad," I say again. Then I walk down to the regular, who's giving Lyle a perplexed look. "Lil had a little accident," I say to him, playing down my own fears. "She'll be all right, but Lyle's kind of worried."

He looks a little ashamed. "I'm sorry," he says. "I didn't know."

"Of course not," I say, patting his arm.

More Lil behavior than mine. I tend to avoid contact whenever possible.

"So, what do you want to warm up?" I ask, moving us out of the awkward bit.

CHAPTER 14

Thad shows up during the eight p.m. rush hour. I've been working the bar and fryer alone. Sweat coats my skin and I can feel the stray hairs from my braid sticking to the back of my neck. People stepping into the bar stamp their feet and blow on their hands, but it's hard to imagine that kind of cold when you're dropping french fries into boiling oil and trying not to drip sweat in after them.

Word has spread around the bar that Lil "had a fall." Someone runs out for a piece of posterboard and some colored pens. It's enough to put a lump in my throat. Because it's not a half-drunken kind of concern, but genuine worry and affection for Lil that gets the whole roomful of people to sign the giant get-well card. Someone starts to sing "Rocky Raccoon," and soon the whole group is lifting a glass to Lil's health.

And that's about the time Thad shows up. He hangs his hat on the tap advertising a light beer and smooths his hair down over the bald spot I've never seen. The smile he gives me is pale.

"Is she okay?" I ask, pausing with three beers in my hands.

He doesn't look at me. "They're keeping her overnight for some tests. She wasn't happy until I promised to come help you out."

"I need it," I say. "Thank you."

He nods.

It's well after two in the morning—closing time—before we can draw a breath. I'm mopping the traffic-polished wooden floor, and Thad is supposed to be washing the glasses, only he's got the posterboard card in his hands and is reading the bits of bad humor some of the rowdier regulars have written. He doesn't look like he's enjoying them much.

I lean on the mop.

"Want to talk about it?" I ask.

He looks up. "Not really."

"Okay." I go back to mopping.

"I asked her to marry me," he says.

I stop mopping. "You do that a lot."

"For real this time."

He rolls up the posterboard card and secures it with a rubber band.

I swish the mop strings around a fixed table leg and wonder how many demons can wreak havoc in a town during a twenty-four-hour period. Wonder how to drive them away.

"I take it she wasn't into the idea," I say, dunking the mop in the Lysol water.

He doesn't answer. He's washing glasses. Hanging them up on the rack to drip-dry. Lil would scream about water on her bar, but I don't think Thad's in the mood for a housekeeping lecture, so I keep my mouth shut.

"No," he says.

I know when to drop a conversation. And I've had a lot of practice dropping things today. Maybe that's why I don't drop it this time.

"Want to talk about it?" I ask again.

He leans both hands on either side of the sink behind the bar. "What will it take to get you to shut *up* about it?" The words are tired and said with a small upward twist of his lips. He's not pissed. He just wants to suffer in silence.

"I appreciate the strong, silent type," I say, dunking the mop and wringing it. "But they're a pain in the ass to live with."

"Full disclosure, huh? You're as bad as—"

He breaks off.

As bad as Lil.

I slop the damp mop out onto the floor. I've said as much as I'm going to say, but he doesn't need to know that. If he wants to talk, he will. If he doesn't, he won't. I don't know why I want to hear what he has to say. Maybe because of that smile he gave me the first day I stepped into the bar.

"It's my fault she's there," he says. "In the hospital."

"She had a TIA," I say.

The only sound is the damp slap of the mop. And the water dripping from the glasses hanging over the bar. One glass is above the water-filled sink and the drips make a raindrop sound when they land.

"Lil isn't interested in men," he says. Flat. Low.

I'm done with the floor. I wheel the mop bucket back into the store-room and pretend I don't see Thad rubbing his eyes with his forearm.

"All men or just you?" I ask after I've stowed the mop.

"All men." He looks up and adds, "She's a . . . lesbian."

"Okay," I say.

He stares at me. "Okay . . . okay what?"

"It explains why you'd be depressed, but it doesn't explain why you're pissed at her."

"Because she didn't tell me!" The words come out in an explosion. "She didn't tell me. She just let me go on all this time—"

"What was she supposed to do?" I interrupt. "Advertise? Do you go around telling everyone you like girls?"

"She could have told me," he says, sinking down onto a chair behind the bar. "She could have told me."

I lift the stools down from the bar where I set them while I was mop-ping, and then sit down across from him.

"She didn't know you were serious," I say.

"About what?"

"About her."

"How could she not know? Does she think I hang around here for the beer?"

"She thinks you're her friend," I tell him. "But she thought all those things you said about getting married were just kidding around." I puff out a breath. "Or maybe she wanted to think that, because she was worried you'd act like this if you found out."

He rubs the back of his neck and says, so softly I can barely hear, "I told her to rot in hell. Before I left the bar this afternoon. Before . . ."

I stare at him.

He looks up at me. Catches the tail end of how I feel. "I was *angry*," he says. "Because she didn't tell me about . . . about being a lesbian. I was angry."

"You were embarrassed," I say, still caught in the tail end of shock and disgust.

He shakes his head. "A little. But it's not what you're thinking. I didn't mean it like that. I was angry because it wasn't *fair*. We're friends, but she didn't trust me."

I start to say *"Looks like she was right,"* but I stop myself just in time.

This is Thad. I've only been here about a month, but I've seen him six days a week. Thad may get angry, but he's not vicious or vindictive or a bigot.

"You may be right," he says, while I'm still working things out for myself. "Goddamn . . ." He says the last as he rubs the heels of his hands into his eyes. "Goddamn."

I lean my folded arms on the bar. With a fingertip, I drag a drop of water in a circular pattern until the water dries.

"I lost a friend today," I say to the dry spot where the water droplet used to be. "I always thought she would be there. It's not like I spent a lot of time thinking about her. I just thought she would be there. If I couldn't handle it anymore. If I needed her."

I glance across at Thad. He's still got his eyes buried in his hands. Looking back down at the bar's surface, I find another unsuspecting water droplet to push around.

"Now she's married to a pillar of the community," I say. "She goes to town meetings and chamber of commerce luncheons. And I don't fit in. I remind her—"

I break off because I can see Jen's face the afternoon we skipped freshman English and drank our first stolen bottle of Jack Daniels under the bridge. Before we got so drunk we were sick, she told me about the foster parent who wouldn't let her put locks on her door.

"—of who she is," I finish, swallowing the memory. "Or was."

I stop torturing the water drops and look over at Thad. His hands are in his lap and he's smiling at me.

A sad smile.

"I left Silver Creek . . ." I tell him, "a while back. With someone. I didn't tell her I was leaving. I made the decision to not tell her. Given the circumstances, I'd make the same decision again. She can forgive that. But we can't change who we've become in the meantime."

He folds his arms. "And the moral is?"

I ignore the mild sarcasm.

"For whatever reason, Lil made a decision to not tell you about one aspect of herself. That one aspect doesn't change who she is to *you*. As your *friend*. But if you don't forgive her and patch it up now, you'll both change. Then it will be too late."

"Thanks, Aesop."

I snort. "Aesop was into morality. This is a cautionary tale."

"I'm going back to the hospital," he says. "Do you want to come?"

The clock says it's three in the morning. "They won't let us in."

"My brother's the head nurse on Lil's floor tonight. He'll let us in."

He does. But only after Thad bribes him with a few skeins of wool for the wife. The bribe sounds more like a long-standing joke.

"Go on," Thad says to me. "I need to figure out what I'm going to say."

I nod.

Lil is sleeping when I step into her room, but her eyes open. She looks at me. "Who's at the bar?"

"It's after three," I say, sitting down in the chair by the bed. I twist my gloves together and wish the room wasn't so hot.

"Why aren't you in bed?" she asks.

"Because I'm here."

"Smartass."

I hand her the roll of posterboard. "The people at the bar made this."

She opens it up and looks at the drawing of her fire hosing the patrons with beer. "Idiots," she says, but she's smiling. "I'll read the dirty limericks tomorrow."

"Some of them are pretty good," I say.

I try not to look around the room or let her know that I'm nervous to see her like this. She's smaller in the hospital bed.

"Thad helped out with the rush," I say.

She doesn't answer.

I want to tell her what Thad said, but I know it's up to them to work it out.

"Did he tell you?" she asks.

"Tell me what?"

She rolls her head back and forth on the pillow. "Good political response, there. Did he tell you about my . . ." Her mouth twists into a small sneer. "My 'sexual persuasion'?"

"Yes."

"And you don't care?"

"Should I?"

She shrugs.

"Thad's here," I say.

Her body stiffens. "Tell him to go away."

But I'm halfway between the bed and the door when she says it. I pretend I didn't hear.

I pass Thad in the hall and tell him I'll see him tomorrow. I'm grateful he forgets I'm on foot. Stepping through the hospital's automatic doors, I walk between the cars in the parking lot, past the sleeping houses with their porch lights and bundles of warm humanity, past the edge of town . . . I walk until Silver Creek is a glow behind the hill. Walk to the bridge where Jen and I shared that bottle. Where Uncle Charles found me thirty-six hours after I rolled back into town. Where Stephen and I . . .

It's calm. The early-morning hours when the wind dies to a whisper. Not even enough to rustle the frostbitten prairie grass. Far-off smoke from someone's fireplace mixes with the icy scent of stars stretching from one edge of the world to the other. Under the bridge, water plays with the rocks. Every day grinding off a little more, rounding a little more, dragging bits of sand to the sea.

Maybe I should follow the bits of sand. Not to the ocean. I've already been there, and the water is cold when it rolls up onto the sand and swamps the river grains. Maybe I should just . . . leave.

Maybe it's time to go. Time to follow the southern stars. The migrating birds that have been massing in the bare fields around Silver Creek.

What's holding me down?

A promise. I told Lil I would take care of things.

But that promise isn't enough to keep me here, because Lil will be back tomorrow or the next day. Lil can find another person to mop the floor and provide a mascot.

I'm not driving away this time because I'm not sure I *want* to leave. Because I'm tired of having the wind at my back.

I sit on the guardrail and look up at the stars. Orion is here again. Announcing the coming of winter.

CHAPTER 15

Someone was banging on the door.

Beyond my bedroom windows, I could hear the L.A. evening rush hour winding down. The ozone scent of exhaust was still strong, but the sea breeze would push it on up into the mountains in a few hours.

The banging came again. Refusing to be pacified by my pretending to not be home. I had to be at work in a few hours—I had the night shift at an all-night restaurant—and would have appreciated the extra sleep. Pulling on a pair of sweats, I answered the door.

"Stephen here?"

"Hi, Newell. He's at work. You know that."

"Can I come in?"

I shrugged and opened the door. I didn't know Newell all that well. He had grown up in Silver Creek, just like Stephen and me, but he had been a high school senior when I was twelve or so.

"How much longer do you think you're going to hang around?" Newell asked.

"Until I have to go to work."

"You know what I mean."

I did know what he meant.

"Go away, Newell," I said.

"You're just in the way," he said.

I pointed to the door. "So are you."

He left. But he hadn't said anything I didn't already feel.

I wake up to the predawn gray of an autumn morning in Montana with Miss Kitty leaping from the back of the couch onto my rib cage. She likes the hurly-burly of the Watering Hole and didn't appreciate fifteen hours of being alone and bored in Eva's house. Now she's taking her pound of flesh by practicing gymnastic moves on my body. I roll over and scratch an apology between her ears. The dream—memory—of Newell sits sour in my stomach.

Outside the windows, gray shadows mix with Jack Frost's artistry. Feathery crystals outline the leaves, reflecting back the pink tinge from the east. I shuffle Miss K. into the pile of warm blankets and go to the kitchen to make coffee, even though my stomach rebels at the idea of additional acid. While it brews, I lean my hot forehead against the iced-up glass of the window.

"*Newell was here,*" I said to Stephen as I crawled into bed during the morning rush hour.

"What'd he want?" Stephen mumbled around a yawn. He worked days. And I'd just woken him up. He was three steps away from the shower but still scratching the night beard on his face and rubbing sleep from his eyes.

"You," I said. "Alone."

Stephen rolled his head on his neck. "He's worried about the recording contract. Just ignore him."

I pushed myself further into the blankets. I didn't know how to tell Stephen I was afraid and lonely. So I didn't say anything at all.

Behind me, the coffeepot splutters to a halt. My forehead still pressed against the cold glass, I take a deep breath and blow it out, fogging up the window. Fogging up the promise of dawn and a new day.

The last few years, I've seen the far side of midnight more than most people. I haven't seen a lot of sunrises. Jobs that hire on a moment's notice tend to be jobs with odd hours. So I've been either working through sunrise or sleeping through it. The pink dawn pokes through my window and invites me out into the frost-scented air.

An old coat hangs beside the kitchen door that opens onto the backyard. It is—was—Great-aunt Eva's coat for grubby work, like gardening, taking out the trash, filling bird feeders, or checking the rain gauge on a misty morning. It's an old wool dress coat that probably belonged to one of her brothers or her father. Now it's patched and a seam in the shoulder is ripped, displaying the striped-silk lining that was the pride of some Chicago clothing manufacturer. I pull the coat on, slip my stockinged feet into a pair of Eva's rubber boots, and take my full coffee cup outside as a hand warmer.

Miss Kitty joins the fun, attempting one last act of revenge by darting between my oversized boots and nearly tripping me. She stops at the edge of the back patio and washes her paw.

Outside, the gray shadows are bluer. The band of pink is brighter. I sit down on the wooden bench under the old elm tree that survived when all the other elms collapsed in the wake of the Dutch elm disease epidemic.

A sunrise is not a sunset in reverse. The colors are different. Softer, less flashy.

I wrap my fingers around my coffee mug.

Candy orange takes over from the pink. A flotilla of round, popcorn clouds passing overhead are blue above, pink on the edges, and flaming gold underneath. In the distance, I can hear the lonesome call of a crow announcing the dawn. The sunshine collides with the windows, and reflected light falls across my face and makes me blink.

I understand why I cried in the Watering Hole's storeroom after having ice cream with Jen. I cried because, no matter what Lil said, I haven't changed. I'm still a child. Frustrated, lashing out, furious at Eva's last act of manipulation, blaming fate for the course of my life. And when life goes where I'm afraid to go . . .

. . . I still throw everything away.

I break up with my past instead of confronting it.

A few inquisitive sparrows drop down to inspect the iced-over birdbath. They notice Miss Kitty and fly up into the elm branches.

If I'm going to stay in Silver Creek, in this house, even just for a while, it makes sense to gut the place and start over.

But only if it's what I really want to do.

Only if it's not just a childish tantrum. Only if it's not a childish way to get even with the family that didn't know what to do with me.

The wind comes up with the sun and slinks in through every buttonhole and rip in the brown boiled wool of the coat. I tuck my chin down into the collar and breathe coffee breath on my face to warm my nose. The coat smells like old lining and a touch of mildew from being hung up damp. Underneath is a faint hint of violets from Aunt Eva's cologne. I close my eyes.

"I'm just going out for some daffodils to brighten things up," Great-aunt Eva said as she pulled on the old coat. A misty rain was falling and soaking into the spring earth. "Get down that blue vase, won't you?"

I pulled the wooden step stool over to the shelves by the window and carefully reached for the blue vase sitting on the top shelf. Through the window, I could see Eva bending over the barely opened yellow trumpets and singing as the rain soaked into the back of the old coat.

I close my eyes and decide the coat is one thing I won't throw away.

The color show is over. The wind is cold. My coffee mug is empty. And Miss K. is waiting by the back door so she can go get warmed up in my vacated blankets.

Standing in the door between the kitchen and living room, I look around with sunrise musings in my thoughts. And understand again how little of *me* there is in this house.

But I understand something else for the first time.

There's precious little of *Evalene* Earle in this house where she spent her youth caring for her invalid mother. A special mug. A hen and rooster salt-and-pepper set I remember her carefully washing and filling each week. The TV chair.

But everything else is . . . distant. The house is a house of ancestors. *"That table belonged to my aunt,"* Eva said every Saturday as I gave the oak dining room set its weekly dusting with Pledge. *"That cupboard was your grandmother's."*

I wonder whether the pictures whispered to Eva.

I shiver in my socks and reach out for the coffeepot and a refill.

I wish . . .

But even if Eva were alive, it wouldn't make any difference. What would I ask? *Was this the life you wanted? Did you want to live like this?*

The rim of the mug is touching my lower lip, but I don't actually drink the coffee. What if Eva doesn't have to be alive to answer my questions?

I pick up the phone and punch in Uncle Charles' number. He'll be shaving about now. But he keeps his cell phone with him wherever he goes.

"Hello?" a shaving-cream-muffled voice says.

"When did Aunt Eva change her will?" I ask.

Silence.

Here we go again.

"Katherine?"

"No, it's the Cat in the Hat."

I hear him swipe the razor through the cream on his face. Water gushes as he runs the razor under the tap to clean it.

"I'm sorry," I say. "I didn't mean that to sound . . . rude."

"Well, it did."

I don't say anything.

He sighs. "I don't know." He's wiping his face with a towel and the next words come out muffled. "Before she died, the last time I saw the will was . . . before you left, I think."

"So you weren't . . ." I trail off, not knowing the right words to ask if he had any power to do anything, any knowledge.

"Her attorney usually told me . . . if she made serious changes, I mean." His voice is quiet, a little guilty.

"Isn't that illegal?" I ask. There's a thing called attorney-client privilege. I know that much.

"We take golf trips together," he says.

Meaning he and Mr. Boom-voice go on vacation together to the links nestled in the foot of the mountains. Meaning some things are said off the record over whisky and sodas at the nineteenth-tee clubhouse.

"Just not this time?" I ask.

He coughs.

Hangers rub on a bar.

"What's this about?" he asks. "I have an early meeting, so if it's not important . . . ?" He leaves the question hanging.

"Not so's you'd notice," I say. "Thank you."

He hangs up.

I wasn't being flippant. I don't think Uncle Charles *would* notice the importance of my question. Dear old "happy to be me" Charles. Furniture is a legacy. Proper etiquette involves having the car washed once a week, weather permitting. Life is a round of business meetings, town council appointments, and voting at every election. Uncle Charles takes care of all the details.

Uncle Charles would buy a new coat to hang by his back door.

I sit down at the table. I'm not trying to beatify Great-aunt Eva. She was a difficult, frustrating, strict, no-nonsense, manipulative . . . *annoying* human being. I spent the first eight years with her believing that if I made her upset, I'd be given away. Totally untrue, of course, but you wouldn't have been able to convince me otherwise. I spent the next eight years making up for lost time by trying to upset her at every turn. I hated her more times than I can count.

But I left.

And she left me everything.

I thought it was just simple manipulation.

Leaving my coffee on the table, I start emptying every impersonal drawer of every impersonal piece of furniture in the house.

Like Eva should have done.

Like Eva knew I would.

Gwen drops in as I'm dumping out the last drawer. She looks around but doesn't say anything, just hands me a hot serving dish that's emitting good smells.

"Chili," she says. "I always make too much. I thought you might like some."

"Who's holding down the fort?" I ask, sniffing the chili, wondering if it would be rude to eat it in front of her. I'm starving.

"Mahala. And you can eat it, you know. You look like you've been working on your appetite."

I lean over and see my dust-smeared face in the hall mirror. "Attractive."

"Oh, very. Go call Clinique."

We smile at each other in the mirror.

"Want to join me?" I ask, holding up the chili.

"Yes."

I find two bowls I'm keeping—some bright Fiestaware things—and hand her one.

"I heard about what happened at the Watering Hole," she says. "Is your boss hurt?"

"She had a TIA," I say. "But don't tell anyone."

"Oh."

The chili is good. Gwen is practically silent. And practically not eating. She's just pushing the beans and tomatoes and hamburger bits around with her spoon.

"I guess you're probably wondering about Robert and me," she says after a few determined pokes at a piece of celery.

I'm still trying to figure out who Robert is when she starts crying.

What am I supposed to say? *No, I haven't actually wondered about what you and the Methodist minister have been up to.* That sounds like I don't care.

Gwen has lived in Silver Creek too long. There are places in the world where no one gives a . . . no one cares who you are or what you are. As long as you don't cause any trouble or call attention to yourself. But that doesn't mean people dislike you or don't give a shit about you. I like Gwen. I give a shit. But I would never ask who John's father is or why she's crying into her chili.

Besides, I have the feeling I'm going to find out whether I ask or not.

I get up and locate one of the myriad boxes of tissues floating around the house.

"Here," I say, handing her the box.

She nods and keeps crying.

I'm still hungry, but it doesn't seem right to keep on eating while the cook is filling her bowl with salt water. I push my half-full bowl to one side and try not to give it longing looks.

"He's not John's father, if that's what you think," Gwen says from behind her hands.

"It never crossed my mind," I say.

She drops her hands and gives me a watery glare.

"Okay, maybe once or twice," I amend. "But I figured it was your business if you wanted to give him the ice-princess treatment."

Reaching out for a tissue, she begins to wad it into a little ball. "Did I do that?"

"Sort of."

"He just feels sorry for me." She blows her nose in the wadded tissue and reaches for another.

I decide we're at a point where I won't be rude if I start eating again. I missed supper last night, so I haven't eaten in . . . oh, twenty-four hours.

Lunch. Yesterday. With Jen. A lifetime ago.

"How do you figure that?" I ask.

"He just does."

"He looked more frightened than sorry."

"Is the chili any good?" she asks.

"Yes."

"I thought maybe I got too much tomato sauce this time. John doesn't like tomato sauce."

"It's perfect."

"I didn't mean the other day in your hallway," she says. "He asked me to marry him."

I chew and swallow. "Marriage is a sign of pity?"

"Sometimes."

If you think about it, she's right. Not in all cases, of course. But sometimes. I wonder if Stephen felt pity for me when we stood on the beach and the sea sucked the sand from under our bare toes.

We were both laughing.

As preteens, Jen and I spent a lot of time giggling over those guides to better marriages (especially the parts about sex). But when it came to the actual ceremony, the guides made it sound like a solemn, awesome, and joyful occasion. None of the guides mentioned laughing too hard to say the vows.

Stephen and I had sand, surf, and Drumstick the mail-order minister.

It wasn't solemn, but the sand felt good as I dug my toes down into the beach.

No pity in sight.

"Not always," I say.

"I said 'sometimes,'" Gwen says.

"Okay." I set my empty bowl aside. "What made you think Robert's asking was one of those times?"

"It was right after I told my mother about John. Well, not John. The baby. He wasn't John yet."

She blows her nose again.

I wait.

Miss Kitty jumps up and starts to lick out my empty bowl. Gwen stares, and I realize other people might not have lived with a feline family for three years. I think about setting Kitty and the bowl on the floor. But Kitty is my friend.

"She's human," I say.

"I was just thinking of what Eva would say."

I grin. "I try not to think about things like that."

Miss K. decides tomato is not her favorite food and proceeds to wash her face.

"I'm not making the connection," I say to Gwen when it's obvious she isn't going to continue. "Between Robert and pity and your mother."

"I found Mama folding my dresses away," Gwen says. "She didn't say anything when I told her about the baby, but she folded and put away my clothes." She smiles at me, but it isn't much of a smile. "It was her way of telling me that I was a disappointment."

I try to imagine how that would feel. Aunt Eva was happy to let me know when I was a disappointment. Somehow, having it said made it easier to ignore. It's the quiet things that hurt.

"Behind the Methodist church," Gwen continues, "there's a little garden.

For sitting. It's open. I sat there for a long time. And Robert came out. I didn't know him. I thought he was the janitor or the gardener." She smiles. I don't think she realizes that the smile has the soft quality of clouds in a blue sky.

"And?" I ask.

"He asked me to marry him," she says. Then the smile disappears. "He felt sorry for me."

I lean back in my chair and pick at the edge of the table, remember . . .

"Hey," the man tapping on my car window said. *"Are you okay?"*

I was fifty miles from nowhere. At a service area along the freeway. I needed two dollars to buy enough gas to get to somewhere, but I couldn't even find fifty cents. I'd just searched the entire car for the possibility of a stray quarter and come up empty.

I was fifty miles from nowhere, sitting in my car, and sobbing into my hands. Because it looked like the end of the road to me. I didn't want to call Eva or Charles or Stephen. I wasn't ready for that. I wasn't ready to be told what a bad little girl I'd been.

"Hey. Are you okay?" the man tapping on my car window asked.

I rolled down the window. "I'm out of gas," I said.

He nodded. "And out of money."

"Yes."

"I have a daughter your age," he said. "Here. It's all the cash I have. I hope it's enough." And he handed me five dollars and his cup of coffee. Then he walked to his car, got in, and drove away. Before I could stammer a thank-you for the kindness of a stranger. He didn't know it, but that five dollars kept me tumbling along for two more years. I wonder whether he would have given me that five if he knew it stood between me and a collect call of shame.

I lean back in my chair. "I've been pitied," I say aloud to Gwen. "But the guy who pitied me didn't propose."

I stop. Wait for my point to sink in.

"He didn't ask me to marry him," I say, when Gwen just frowns at me.

"Of course not."

"He felt sorry for me."

"You're making fun of me, aren't you?"

"No," I say.

At first I think she's going to get mad, but she starts laughing. I kind of had the impression that I was making a good point. Gwen's laughter ends that little fantasy.

"I can't believe," she says, still laughing, "that I cared about what you thought. In high school. I worshiped you. We all did."

I frown through the heat reddening my face. "Who's 'we'?"

"Us girls. Us outsiders. And all the guys . . ." She trails off.

I pick at a speck of wax or dirt or something that mars the perfect finish of the table. Her words call up the moment of triumph when Blaine the Golden Boy stopped me in the hall in front of a gaggle of senior girls and said, *"Hey, are you okay? You didn't get into trouble last night? Great! I'll see you round."* The moment when I brushed past the gaggle of girls as if they didn't exist. The moment when I thought that now, *now*, I controlled my life and my place in the world.

I pick at the speck of wax or dirt and try to smile at Gwen. "I worked at it. I was a bitch."

"You were."

It hurts to hear these things said. I can think them, believe them, wish they weren't true. But hearing them from someone else . . . It makes my stomach twist and turns my skin clammy. A combination of pride, anger, and the sickening knowledge that what I thought, believed, and wished *wasn't* true is very, very true. Because no matter how many times I say *"You were an awful person"* to myself, it isn't really true until someone else agrees.

"I didn't mean to hurt your feelings," Gwen says.

I pick the imperfection off the table. "I hope you're not pitying me," I say. "I don't think the state of Montana would approve of us getting married."

She shakes her head. "I can't believe you think I'm so . . . *stupid* that I would believe something dumb like that."

"That Montana wouldn't approve?" I ask. Being facetious. To cover up things like embarrassment.

She rolls her eyes.

"I meant *Robert*," she says. "Only Robert. You know him. He's kind and he's got the softest heart—" She breaks off.

"I know he likes architecture," I say. "And that he's scared of Uncle Charles. Other than that, I barely know the man."

"He likes architecture?" she asks.

"How well do *you* know him?"

"Enough to recognize pity when I see it." She smooths a fresh tissue. Folds it into a triangle. "Besides, he's in the ministry. And I don't think I want to go there."

I hug my arms around myself and wish I could feel the shifting sand between my toes. Even with the sucking waves, the sand was firmer ground than this.

CHAPTER 16

"Why is Humpty Dumpty an egg?"

I asked Great-aunt Eva that question one Sunday night when I was doing the dishes and she was cutting up the leftover pot roast for Monday-night stew.

"How can horses put something back together again?" I asked before she could answer the first question. "They don't have any hands."

I could barely reach over the sink, so Eva had bought me a little wooden step stool to stand on. *"It's never too early to learn good habits,"* she said when she showed me how to wash a plate on both sides. The stool made me taller, but the bubbles still tickled my nose.

"Can you put an egg back together?" Great-aunt Eva asked me.

"No."

"Then that's why Humpty Dumpty is an egg."

"What about the horses?"

"The king's horses just came with the king's men."

Eva and Lewis Carroll obviously thought alike, since it was *Alice in Wonderland* where poor Humpty Dumpty turned into an egg. Nobody really knows who or what he was before that. But whoever or whatever he was, the king's horses and the king's men couldn't do anything for him.

The king's horses and the king's men can't put my friendship with Jen back together again, either. We're an egg that can't be fixed. But friendship is a funny thing. It may disappear in your entryway, but before you've had a chance to turn around, it will appear again. Usually where you least expect it.

On your porch. On the heels of an escaping child.

On the wings of a glance during a wedding reception.

On an early-summer night while sitting on the guardrail of a bridge.

Gwen calls Mahala and asks for a few hours off to give me a hand. She doesn't ask me if I want a hand first. She just asks if she can use my phone.

"I can help," she says, hanging up the phone.

And that's the first I hear about my needing another pair of hands.

"You're getting rid of all this stuff?" she asks, pointing to the various piles of linens, towels, and old upholstery covers I've got scattered around the room.

"Do you want any of it?" I ask.

"No." She picks up one of the hand-embroidered flour-sack tea towels from a small pile. "Well, maybe these. Can you imagine spending all that time to do this? Make this? So you could wipe the dishes with it?"

"If I needed an excuse to sit down for a few hours. After hoeing the garden, canning the beans, and changing Timmy's diaper for the fiftieth time this morning, embroidery would probably look pretty darn fun."

Gwen laughs. "I think it's why pie was so popular. Picking berries was a good excuse to take a walk."

I remember the time I spent a whole afternoon watching a bird build a nest. It was at a rest area somewhere in eastern Washington. I'd seen nests before, of course. But I'd never taken the time to watch one being built. I'd always had a good excuse to not bother. I'd always been too busy, too full of myself and my own importance to take an afternoon off and just sit—

"Have you ever watched a bird building a nest?" I ask Gwen.

She smiles. "Of course. Every spring on my parents' farm. Did you know barn swallows build their nests out of mud and straw?"

I shake my head.

"What made you think I had the look?" I ask. "What made you think I'd loved the wrong man?" I add when Gwen looks confused.

She sets the embroidered tea towel back down onto the pile. "It's your eyes."

"You said that before. What do you mean?"

"You look into a person, but you don't let them look into you," she says.

I shake my head. "I don't do anything."

"You don't have to."

She's done talking about it. The finality is in the way she snap folds a tablecloth and sets it into a box. I have a vague image of what her mother must look like during an argument.

"I didn't mean to make you angry," I say. "I was just curious why—"

"I never told anyone about Robert," she interrupts. "Just you."

I don't know what to say. I dislodge Miss Kitty from a pile of crocheted upholstery thingamajigs—the little ovals to keep sweaty arms and greasy hair from staining the couches and chairs—and start bagging them up.

"Why?" I ask. "Why tell me about Robert?"

"I don't know."

She sits down beside the box and starts laying in cloth napkins and table runners on top of the tablecloths.

I keep stuffing thingamajigs.

"You're not what I expected," she says.

"You expected something?"

"You used to walk down the halls . . . like you knew who you were and why you were here on this planet."

I crush the crocheted yarn between my fingers. I can almost hear the cicada song from a long-lost summer.

What do you think? I asked Jen. It was hot in my bedroom. Outside the window, cicadas trilled in the elm tree. In one month, Jen and I would be freshmen.

"Push your boobs out a little more," Jen said. She was lying on my bed and eating a carrot—we'd both vowed to lose ten pounds—while I practiced my "walk."

I flipped my hair back. "God," Jen said, "don't do that. You'll look like Summer."

Reaching up, I slid a hand through my hair and pushed it back, then walked across the room again.

"*Perfect*," Jen said. "*You look like you know where you're going.*"

Gwen smiles up at me. "You looked like you belonged. Like you knew where you were going."

"I didn't know shit," I say, hot and a little frightened. I can still hear the cicada song outside my bedroom window. "I didn't know shit then, and I don't know shit now."

My sunrise confidence is disappearing fast. How did I ever think I could start over by tossing some ancestral belongings? I don't want to go where Gwen is trying to take me. High school isn't a pleasant thing to reminisce about. I worked too hard to be somebody everyone else wanted to be.

I close my eyes.

"I don't want to talk about this," I say, the words falling quiet among the crocheted doilies and embroidered bits of linen.

"I'm sorry," she says.

I open my eyes and find her watching me. "I wanted something I couldn't have," I say.

She smiles. "Did you know I wouldn't have come over to see you if John hadn't run up to your door?"

My eyes are stinging, but I shake my head from side to side and go with the change of topic.

Gwen tilts her head to one side. She purses her lips, pretending to be lost in thought. "I figured you were as snot-nosed as you used to be."

"Snot-nosed?" I ask as the wetness behind my eyes stops stinging.

"Definitely. Your nose was so high all a person had to do was look—"

"Okay, okay." I stick out my tongue in mock disgust. "You've been hanging around with little kids too much."

We snicker.

And a little part of what I used to be cracks off and floats away down the river.

Never to return.

It's the first time I've opened the bar alone. Usually, Lil is there and we have a cup of coffee before customers start trickling in. I stop inside the door to set Miss Kitty down so she can begin her usual routine of inspecting the place for nonexistent mice. Reaching for the switch beside the door, I turn on the red-shaded lamps.

It's quiet. The thick, obvious kind of quiet that a public place has when the public isn't present.

In an hour or two, the pool balls will be clacking together, someone will start up the old jukebox in the corner, and the laughter will grow along with the body heat and flushed faces. Every once in a while, a grizzled Beatles wannabe brings his acoustic guitar and sets up shop in a well-lit corner. If that happens tonight, rude people will add money to the jukebox in a futile effort to drown him out, while his fans will join in the singing whenever they can figure out which song he's muttering.

But for now, it's quiet.

The air smells of yeast and wood. A faint hint of grease from the fryer where we make the fries and chicken tenders. If I breathe deep, I can even smell the Lysol from last night's mopping. Scents that come together and create an atmosphere I'm beginning to love.

It's not a pretty room. Dark, grooved paneling supports a few framed photos of Silver Creek in its rough-and-tumble days and a tin sign of a red-winged Mobil horse from the station that used to be where the Gas and Lube is now. The furniture is mismatched. A collection of garage sale items.

And staring at a chair missing one of its spindles, I find myself wondering how my unnamed great-great-aunt's table would look—I squint—over there. And maybe the chairs. Maybe even the old pie safe in the kitchen—

The door opens and Lil walks in.

"Why aren't you in bed?" I ask without turning around.

"Why are you just standing there?" she asks.

"I'm rearranging the furniture."

"Over my dead body."

"Almost."

We grin at each other.

"How are you feeling?" I ask.

"Lousy."

"But you didn't trust me to handle it for another night?"

"Looks like I was right. You're messing with my furniture."

"Actually, I'm thinking of adding some."

She sits down in the nearest chair. "The great Earle furniture giveaway?"

"Yes."

"What's the catch?"

I frown. "Catch?"

"What do you want?"

And I remember that I'm just an employee.

I smile one of my cover-up kind of smiles. "I'm giving the stuff away, remember?"

"It's still my bar," she says, proving that I was right to think I'd over-stepped my station in life.

"I know," I say. I start to turn away, start to go behind the bar, start to switch my mind to "opening the bar" thoughts—

But I stop.

Turn around.

And lean back against the bar.

Because last night I made a decision to not leave. And this morning I made a decision to not act like an angry child. I decided to not act like a child who didn't speak until spoken to, but kept all the insults deep in her heart until she could exact revenge when revenge no longer mattered. I decided to not wait for all the king's horses or all the king's men or any other put-me-back-together sorts to do the job.

"Look," I say, "I have this furniture." I stop and give myself a moment to think before I speak words that can't be recalled.

Lil opens her mouth, but I beat her to it.

"You're the boss," I say. "I'm not arguing with that. But I'd like to tell you my ideas. Once you've heard them, you can tell me this is still your bar. But I just want someone . . . *you* to listen to the ideas." I let my too-tight chest relax on a breath.

Lil leans back in the chair.

Rests her elbow on the table.

Looks at me.

I can feel my face begin to heat.

"I like it here," she says. "But there's not much point in changing a place. Something always comes along to make you enjoy leaving more than you enjoy staying."

Miss Kitty jumps up onto the table and rubs her head against Lil's hand. Even ten feet away I can hear the purr.

"The last town I lived in," Lil continues, "I had a partner." She looks up. "Not a business partner."

"Right," I say.

"I owned a bar there, too, and got up to my ears in debt turning the place around. I thought I'd live, love, die, and be buried there. But something happened and Julia . . . wanted out." She scratches Miss K. on the head. "I went by her place one night, thinking we could patch things up, but—"

Her mouth twists into silence. I can feel sweat collect in the hollow of my back.

"Julia belonged in the town," Lil says after a few silent moments. "I didn't. And some of her mother's friends made it unpleasant to stay. So I don't see much point in fixing up the Watering Hole."

I think of Darla Covington and her casseroles. People like Darla Covington always win. You can *say* that you "aren't going to let them win," and pretend that you will live your life as though they don't exist and can't hurt you.

But they exist.

And they can hurt you.

"I've always run away," I say out loud. "It's easier than trying to fix things."

Lil glares at me.

"I'm not being sarcastic," I say. "Running away isn't a bad thing. Sometimes."

"It's only a matter of time," she says.

"I'm not asking you to do anything," I say. "I just want you to hear my idea."

She stops scratching Miss Kitty's head. "Fine. Let's hear the idea."

I take a deep breath and point to the dark corner of the bar. It's an open area with nothing but benches lining the wall. Relics of the day when the Watering Hole had two pool tables and enough people waiting to use them to warrant giving them a place to sit while they waited. The only decoration on the wall is the rack of pool cues. One of them is broken. Blue chalk dust has drifted down into the cracks of the paneling and stained the wood.

"That's wasted space," I say.

"We don't get enough people in here to use it," she says, shrugging my idea away before she's heard it.

"You said you'd listen."

"I said I'd 'hear.'"

She's trying to make me angry. Great-aunt Eva always used that bait and switch technique.

"Clean out the benches," I say, ignoring her tactic. "Move the cue rack. Bring in the squishy chairs my aunt Eva never used that are cluttering up the living room. Lay down one of the rugs. Some of the side tables. A few lamps. It's like . . ." I struggle for a description. "A British club or something."

I've been looking at the corner, trying to picture it as I saw it just before Lil came into the bar. When I turn to look at her, she's looking at the corner, too.

For one moment I think she's—

Then she shakes her head.

"It won't work. They'll just fuck up the furniture. Spill stuff."

"I have a thousand-years supply of those little covers," I say. "The ones that go over the arms and back."

"Do I look like the thrift shop?" Lil asks.

Afternoon sunshine reaches the front windows and highlights the fingerprint smears on the glass in the door.

Lil stands up. "How badly did the supplier mess up yesterday?"

I pull my aching body away from the bar and step back into the role of employee. "He didn't," I say, walking around behind the bar.

"Impossible."

"He started to, but I made him a plate of fries and chicken and the dark beer mysteriously disappeared."

"I suppose you wiggled your ass a bit, too," she says. "Lucky you."

I recognize bait and switch.

That doesn't mean I don't fall for it.

"How wonderful it must be," I say, "to have the sexual persuasion that allows you to be a sexist pig despite your sex."

Lil stays next to the table.

Standing straight.

Still.

I'm shaking all over.

My face is hot, my brain is fused, and my fingers tremble so much all I can do is grab a rag and push it meaninglessly over the polished surface of the bar.

All I did was make a suggestion about bringing in some furniture.

Wipe, wipe.

Lil sits back down.

Her chair creaks.

Wipe, wipe.

I think about how it looked. To her. Coming in, seeing me thinking about moving things around, changing things, doing things to something that doesn't belong to me.

A gust of wind rattles the loose pane of glass in the storeroom window.

I think about how she must feel. After Thad. After last night. Why she told me about what happened in the last town. How I didn't understand the significance of what she was saying.

The compressor clicks on and the bottles inside the fridge make glassy noises as they rub together in the vibration.

She doesn't put down roots.

Wipe, wipe.

I asked her to put down roots.

It isn't something I have the right to ask.

"I'm sorry," I say.

"I'm sorry," Lil says at the same moment.

We look at each other. Across ten feet of worn hardwood floor. Across golden sunlight squares.

It's disconcerting. I'm not sure I've understood a person this well since Stephen and I spent the hours after the wedding reception sitting on the bridge and talking about dreams. All kinds of dreams. Simple ones and big ones and crazy ones and pie-in-the-sky-never-gonna-happen dreams.

"I like your idea about the furniture," Lil says. "I'm not so sure about bribing the supplier—"

"Just the driver," I say. "And I'm not sure it was a bribe."

"It was a bribe."

"It was a bribe," I agree. "But he was hungry."

She shakes her head. "Next thing you know, you'll be giving free food to the whole state."

I push the rag aimlessly, deep in another idea—

"Free food," I say. "It has possibilities."

"No," Lil says, holding up a finger. "We're not going there."

"We bring in the furniture," I say. "Do a little remodeling. Then we offer free tenders and fries between five and seven. One week only."

"You're nuts," she says.

But she likes the idea.

CHAPTER 17

The bar shrinks and Aunt Eva's house expands as the furniture changes locations. I keep the yellow TV chair, the cupboard Robert might want for the choir room, the desk, bed, and dresser in my bedroom, and the scarred wooden kitchen table that doubled as a work island all my life. Eva's bed sits lonely and abandoned in her empty room. I guess Uncle Charles didn't want the bed, even though he took the rest of the suite. Some of the customers might like the idea of a bed in the bar, but the bed stays put. Everything else Thad and Lyle load into Thad's pickup and transport to a new life.

"It looks like a set for *All in the Family*," Lil says, shaking her head and looking around the bar.

"Whatever we don't want we can . . . raffle off," I say.

Lil gives me a sideways look.

"Or not," I add.

The ideas are pouring out of my head faster than I know what to do with them. So fast I don't have time to think them through. Lil thinks them through for me and does the discarding. But ideas are infectious. Like a disease.

Pretty soon Lil is shutting the bar down FOR REMODELING (at least that's what the sign says) and buying cans of paint to "brighten things up." Thad almost pleads farm work to get out of painting. He and Lil are tender around each other. Like fresh, pink scar tissue rubbing together. A little stiff. A little sore. Feeling their way.

It's painful to watch.

Lyle and I find ourselves on the opposite side of the room if they're together.

"Do you think it will ever stop?" Lyle asks me as we scrub the blue chalk stain off the wall. I was getting along okay on my own—the stain isn't really wide enough for two scrubbers—but when Lil handed him the paint can, Thad started grumbling about needing to get back to his sheep in a mock-frustrated kind of way. Lil muttered something about sheep being too stupid to live on their own. Somehow it ended painfully, and Lyle scooted over to my side of the bar to help scrub.

"You mean, will they kill each other?" We look over our shoulders at Lil and Thad. Lil swipes paint onto Thad's nose with a finger.

Lyle and I let out a shared breath.

"Do you think they'll be all right?" he asks.

"Looks like it."

"No," he says. "I meant, do you think it will ever get back to normal?"

I scrape blue chalk from one of the grooves. "Not like it was. Thad's still in love with her."

"He always will be."

"How do you know?"

"I've known him since he was a kid. He's never been in love before. Well, he's in love with that fiber farm of his, but that's not the same."

I sit back on my haunches and look at the wall. Think about all the boys I imagined I was in love with from about sixth grade on.

"Is that even possible?" I ask, before the memory hits.

"*I have to ask,*" Stephen said. We were lying on the beach, looking up at the sky and the few stars that shone through the orange glow of the city.

We'd been married for five hours and twenty-seven minutes. "I have to ask; did you come with me because of me or because of the van?"

I scrunched my back into the warm sand and hoped any stray crabs would take the hint and move along to find supper somewhere else. "The van, of course. It's such a prize," I said, picturing the rusty, shag-carpeted Econoline van in my head. Then I laughed.

He rolled over onto his side to look at me. "Did you just want to get out of Silver Creek? Is that why you came with me?"

"I was going to college in August," I said.

"Sometimes I think I'll wake up one morning and you'll be gone."

An airplane growled by overhead. I pointed to it. "Look, a shooting star."

He shook his head and rolled onto his back again. Reaching down, I caught his hand and brought it to my stomach. "You're here," I said. Then I laid it just over my breastbone. "And here. That's all I know."

We stayed on the beach until dawn.

Lyle is saying something about Thad and Lil, but I'm not listening.

Blue chalk dust dribbles out from under the screwdriver I'm using to clean the grooves in the wall. The dust sifts down onto the floor.

"It's too bad Thad met her," I say. "He would have been better off loving the ranch."

"You think?" Lyle asks. "You didn't know him then."

Lil is on the phone, torturing some poor employee at the hardware store, so Lyle risks going back to the other side of the bar and the rotting window frame he was fixing before the argument sent him scurrying over to scrub blue chalk.

I poke at the groove. Jab it with the screwdriver.

"Do you have any pictures?" Lil asks from behind me, making me jump.

I imagine Great-great-grandmother Wilhelmina's outrage at finding herself hanging on the wall of a bar. "Only ones that would scare away the customers."

Lil pulls up a chair and sits down beside me, straddling the seat and resting her elbows on the back.

"That groove's clean," she says after a minute or two.

"Could be," I say, but I stop poking at it.

"What's up?"

"Nothing."

"Okay."

"I don't have any pictures," I say, hoping she'll take the hint and leave me alone with my thoughts. Not that I'm sure what the thoughts are about. The vague impressions seem less clear and colorful the longer she sits beside me. Fading away like old photographs.

"Billboards? Watercolors? Movie posters?" Lil asks.

"None I want to part with." I give up trying to recapture the vague impressions and let them drift away. "I take it you want something new on the wall?"

"Just thinking about it." She shifts in her chair.

I look up at the wall. "I found an old Polaroid camera," I say. "In one of the closets. Why don't you just put up a big bulletin board, then let everyone take pictures of each other on opening night."

"That idea is going to get me locked up for posting obscenities in a public place," she says.

I think about the mentality of a few of our customers. Try to imagine looking at Polaroid shots of Buddy Swinson's crack for the next few months.

"You're right," I say. "And it might make us sick."

We stare at the wall.

"Postcards," I say, remembering Melody's glass counter. "From Montana to Maine."

"That leaves out the whole West Coast," Lil says.

"I was trying to be alliterative," I say.

"Uh-*huh*."

"Let's make it the whole world."

"From Montana to Mozambique?" she asks.

Miss Kitty walks in front of me. I reach out to scratch her head and she ducks away. Yowls. I ignore her.

"What's up with Kitty?" Lil asks.

I shrug. "She's been nervous lately. I don't think she likes all the changes."

Lil sighs. "Before we're done, I may agree with her."

A few days ago, I would have used Lil's sighed comment to flagellate myself in the wee hours of the morning. I swallow hard and ask, "Do you think it was a bad idea? Doing all this to the bar? Are you going to blame me if you end up not liking it?"

She leans her chin onto her arms.

I stare at the chalk-free wall.

"Having regrets?" she asks.

"About?"

"About speaking up?"

I scoot around and lean my shoulders against the wall. "I'm just not used to being the one with the ideas."

"Meaning?"

"Meaning I'm used to making decisions for myself. Me. No one else. But lately, it seems like I'm getting caught up in everyone else's life. It makes me nervous. What if what I say to them is all wrong? Then I've screwed up their lives as well as mine."

I'm not sure I'm talking about the remodeling project anymore.

Lil's forehead wrinkles. "Remodeling the bar isn't going to make me commit suicide or anything. Even if it *is* a mistake. And I don't think it is. If I'd known you were going to be so sensitive about it, I wouldn't have said anything."

"Don't do that," I say.

"What?"

"Don't watch what you say."

"Okay."

She scratches her chin.

From the other side of the room, Thad mutters curses as he tries to pry the lid off one of the paint cans.

"Want to talk about it?" she asks after a moment or two, unconsciously echoing my conversation with Thad the night she was in the hospital.

I push myself to my feet. "No. Thanks, though."

She nods.

I'm exhausted.

When Robert knocks at eleven, I almost roll over and ignore him. But . . .

"Did I wake you up?" he asks. All nerves and hands twisting. "I'm sorry—"

"It's okay," I say. "You're here for the cupboard?"

"Sort of."

I let him in. "Sort of?"

"About the other day . . ." He trails off.

I wait.

"Do you know Gwen well?" he asks, surprising me. Or not, actually. I think I was expecting him to ask.

"Not well. I like her. I think she likes me."

He seems confused. I don't want to explain that some friendships grow more slowly than others. That sometimes people are cautious. Afraid of getting hurt.

"I love her," he says.

I turn around and walk back into the living room. Collapse onto the couch that Lil didn't want. The couch I'm still sleeping on because even boxed and stuffed into the attic, the pictures still whisper.

"Sit down," I tell Robert.

He perches on the edge of the yellow TV chair. Just "the yellow chair," now. It can't really be a TV chair with no TV. I left the TV in the alley behind a repair shop. If the guys in the shop want it, it's theirs. If they don't want it, they can throw it away. I don't want to end up with a couple of copies of *TV Guide* by the lamp and knitting at my feet.

"How do you know?" I ask Robert. "That you love her?"

"I just do."

"Love at first sight?"

"Yes."

"That kind of thing makes people uncomfortable," I say.

"But not you."

It's not a question. I can feel my face begin to harden. Freeze. Fear.

"What do you mean?" I ask. All casual and clean.

Miss Kitty yowls. She jumps up onto the couch back and begins rubbing against my head. She hates fear. It's upsetting. It smells funny. It might attract predators.

Robert moves forward, perching even more precariously on the seat's edge.

"Charles . . ." he begins, looking at the floor. He coughs.

"You don't need to say anything more," I say. It doesn't take a lot of imagination to imagine what Charles has to say about me and my—how did Eva put it?—"carryings on."

"He just said you ran off with someone. In the night."

Miss K. tries to bite my ear. I pull her down and settle her into my lap. Robert looks up from the floor.

"I'd give up everything for Gwen," he says. "I knew it the minute I saw her. I'd go anywhere. Do anything. But living this half life . . ." He shakes his head. "Charles said you were crazy to leave like that, but I knew—"

"I thought pastors were supposed to feel called by God," I say, interrupting him. Throwing up a roadblock.

It's a cruel roadblock. But I meant what I said to Lil in the bar. I'm frightened by what I'm becoming. All the crap I've been saying that people might take seriously. I want to be the master of my fate, but I don't want to mess with anyone else's decisions. Anyone else's fate.

I've already done that.

And God knows, I wouldn't wish love at first sight on anyone. Even Charles.

I stand up. "Let's get that cupboard," I say.

For one long moment, I expect him to protest. Then he nods. "All right."

I've been working more than I've been sleeping. And Kitty doesn't want to sleep at all. She paces all night. Nervous pacing. I'm nervous, too. I think it's because tonight there's a possibility for rejection. Rejection of the bar's new look. Rejection by Lil and Lyle and Thad. Because no matter what they say, if the idea flops, I know they're going to be angry. And the idea is my fault.

And I can feel something strange down deep in my stomach. It was there before this morning's conversation with Robert.

Now it's worse.

Something is different.

It's in the smell of the wind.

Maybe Great-aunt Eva is haunting the place.

I shrug away the chill.

When Miss K. and I get to the bar, Lil is almost as nervous as we are. She keeps tapping the OPEN AGAIN sign and pacing the floor.

Summer Jones slaps down a *World's Largest Ball of Twine* postcard onto the bar. Everyone has to bring a postcard. A postcard is their ticket to free fries. "I can't believe you bothered to fix up this dump," she says.

I hand her a paper holder filled with steak fries.

I think about all the things I could say.

But I don't say them.

Because I'm picturing Summer's future Sundays eating dinner with Rosemary Litwin and having several Nathaniel Juniors running over her toes after long days working the floor of the thrift store.

"What do you think?" I ask. "Of the fix up?"

She sniffs her fries. "These are underdone."

"Want me to drop them back in the fryer for a minute?"

"So you can burn them? No."

Behind the bar, I wring a rag between my hands. "Would you like the usual Corona?"

"Is it free?"

"Just the fries."

"Cheap." She looks at the taps. "I'll have a Bud Light."

I pour half a mug.

"Sorry," she says. "I changed my mind."

I dump the beer into the sink. "Don't change, Summer," I say.

"What?"

"You're a nice girl," I say. "Perfect for Nate. Don't change. His mom is going to love you."

"Just give me a Corona," Summer says, but the words sound more confused than belligerent. She takes the fries and Corona over to the plush chairs.

"If everyone likes the free fries that much," Lil says, leaning in so she can be heard over the noise of the latest customers to walk in the door, "it will save me a lot of trouble."

"And fries."

"Hey, Lil," says one of the new arrivals as he pushes an old Stetson back on his head, "did you see God when you had that fall?"

"No," she says, leaving him to his impression that her TIA was only a trip over the rug. "I just had a chat with one of my former lives."

He looks around. "It's nice. The place needed a change." He hands me a postcard of Glacier National Park.

By happy hour I'm back in the storeroom praying we stocked enough fries to make it through the night. I'm digging in the freezer for a new box when Lil taps me on the shoulder.

"There's a guy here looking for you."

I heft the box of frozen fries onto my hip and shut the freezer door. Holding onto the door's handle, I start sifting through the possibilities and come up with nothing.

Nothing I want to contemplate, anyway.

"Is he still here?"

She nods. "He's at the bar." She must see something she doesn't like on my face, because she adds, "You can see him from the door. If you open it a crack."

She does.

The light is behind him.

"Do you know him?" Lil asks.

I'd know him anywhere.

"He's my husband."

CHAPTER 18

The world is a frightening place. Because no matter how many times you dream a scenario, imagine a scenario, walk through it in your head and heart and soul . . . when the time comes, you won't be prepared. The world is a frightening place. Because the world can't possibly care about one fragile human being out of six billion.

I can feel the numbness where the box of frozen fries sits on my hip bone. I can feel the sweat on my palms. The sweat is colder than the box. I can feel the sandwich I had for lunch begin a slow revolution of my stomach. I can feel the trembling in my knees and ankles and back and hands.

Dear God—

"Kat? If you don't—" Lil begins.

But I can't hear her through the rush of blood inside my skull.

I push the stockroom door open and set the box of fries on the counter beside the fryer.

Stephen is sitting a few stools away from Lyle. He keeps his hands below the bar and twists back and forth on the seat. Absently. His cheekbones are sharper than they used to be. Older. His eyes are tired. His hair is a little longer, a little rougher.

Over by the pool table, someone cheers as they sink a hard shot.

I pour Stephen a mug of coffee and set it down in front of him.

"How did you find me?" I ask.

He wraps one hand around the heavy porcelain. His fingers are shaking. "I just kept going."

I nod, even though I'm not sure I understand. "It's not like I went in a straight line," I say.

"I know."

"I took the scenic route. To get here."

He nods, but I don't think he understands.

"I have to get back to work," I say, gesturing toward the customers sitting around the bar, toward the storeroom, toward Lil.

"Okay."

Miss Kitty saunters down the length of the bar and sits down.

"Hi, Kitty," Stephen says.

She blinks at him. A long, slow blink.

He'll be here when I'm done mopping and throwing away the last crumpled french fry holder that missed the trash can basketball hoop.

"You don't have to wait," I say. "I can catch up with you wherever you're staying."

He blows the steam away from the surface of the coffee. "Would you leave?"

I deserve that.

"No," I say.

He nods. But he doesn't tell me where he's staying.

I turn my back on him and Kitty.

But I can't stay out . . . here . . . right . . . now.

In the storeroom, Lil catches me before I can topple into the new boxes and kegs the supplier dropped off this morning.

"Kat?"

"Someone needs to watch the bar," I mumble as I sit down on the nearest keg and put my head between my knees. Just like the picture in Great-aunt Eva's Red Cross handbook of emergency medical procedures.

Lil steps out, and I bless the darkness as the storeroom door closes behind her.

The darkness doesn't last. She comes back, turns on the light, and sits down on a nearby keg. "Lyle and Kitty have it," she says. "Now what's going on?"

"I ran away," I say.

She digests the words.

"You mean he's abusive?" she asks, getting up. Her fists ball up and she's ready to go out and take Stephen on.

I catch her hand. "No. I was young."

"And you're ancient now," she says, a gentle smile in her voice. She sits back down, warms my limp, damp hand between hers.

"Is he the reason you left Silver Creek . . . before?"

"I left *with* him," I say, resting my cheek on my knee. "He wasn't the reason." I sigh on a defeated laugh. "In a way . . . maybe part of it. He was my courage. To go. I didn't leave *because* of him."

She nods and keeps rubbing my hand. It hurts a little when her rough fingertips scrape the scars Pearl gave me the day Great-aunt Eva died.

"The past has teeth," she says. "But it's a lot like monsters under the bed. More painful if you have to face them alone."

My stomach is clenched around a hollow spot. I try to smile for Lil's sake. "Aunt Eva told me that the monsters under my bed were nothing but my imagination and the sooner I . . . 'realized the monsters were in my head, the sooner I could go to sleep.'"

"Your Aunt Eva was an idiot," Lil says. "The monsters under the bed shrivel in daylight. They're child's play compared to the ones in your head."

I squeeze her hand. "Thank you."

"Do you want me to run him off?" she asks. "Or would you rather have some time to talk to him? Here. With Lyle, Thad, and me for backup?"

I shake my head and sit up. "He doesn't bite."

We look at each other in the dim glow of the overhead bulb.

"I'll be okay," I say.

She catches my face in her hands. "You're important to us," she says. "To me. I've gotten used to having you and Miss Kitty around. If I had a daughter—"

She drops her hands from my face.

"Thank you," I say. Because I don't know how to tell her what I feel.

I feel like the cottonwood on the hill by the river just opened its branches and wrapped me up in safety and love.

I said something about scenarios. About coming up with them and rolling them around in my mind.

It wasn't true.

Odd as it sounds, I haven't rolled any scenarios about Stephen around in my head. I've rolled plenty of scenarios about what might happen if the car ever quit on a back road a hundred miles from the nearest gas station. Or if some stranger with strange notions figured out I was alone, and strange to the neighborhood and not likely to be missed. Or if a meteor fell from the sky and landed on me.

But not about Stephen.

My brain rolled away from that kind of scenario.

Until it bumped into reality.

Tonight.

And came to rest.

I force myself to leave the storeroom. I force myself to pour Stephen another cup of coffee and pretend that he's a regular customer.

"Thank you," he says. In that quiet voice. The same one he used at Newell's funeral. The same one he used when he talked to Miss Kitty.

Miss K. jumps onto Stephen's shoulder. He nods to me, and they retreat to a corner of the room, where he sits down in one of Great-aunt Eva's comfy chairs.

I can't feel jealous. Miss K. owes Stephen. He found her under a car in the apartment parking lot. She was thin, oily, and wretched. Stephen coaxed her out. One inch at a time. When I came home from work that night, I found them both asleep on the kitchen floor where he'd been feeding her our last can of tuna.

I can't feel jealous.

Or sad.

Thad meanders over to Stephen after a short conversation with Lil. I know they're trying to help. I wish they wouldn't. But I don't know how to tell them to stop helping.

So I finish the night.

Mop.

Search the corners for wrappers. Search again.

Think about crawling through the window in the storeroom.

Lil watches me. "You'll be okay?" she asks.

I nod.

"If you need to talk . . . after . . ." she adds, leaving the offer hanging.

"Thanks."

Miss Kitty winds herself between my ankles.

"What about Kitty?" Lil asks.

"Can she stay here? For now?"

"Of course. You have a key?"

I nod.

I look up from Miss K. and across the room to the corner.

Stephen stands up even though I didn't say a word.

Outside, the stars flirt with the moonlight and the drifting scraps of cloud. The wind is sharp, but it doesn't cut. I wrap my scarf more tightly around my face and look up at the waning crescent moon.

"I keep expecting the clouds to catch on the moon," I say. "They look so close. So close together."

"I've missed the sky," he says.

I turn and walk down the street. Away from the blue neon light of the beer sign in the Watering Hole's window. He falls in beside me. We're walking toward the bridge as if we had discussed where we wanted to go and made a decision. It rained in the mountains the other day—all black clouds and lightning—and Silver Creek is washing sand and rock and mud between its fingers.

I swing a leg over the cement guardrail and let my feet dangle above the moon-washed rocks and dark water.

Stephen's feet dangle beside mine. Black against the gray-white of the bridge.

Cold from the cement seeps through my jeans. I can feel the warmth from his shoulder. Or maybe the warmth is just an illusion. A memory.

"Why didn't you file for divorce?" I ask.

Cottonwood leaves swirl over us, and I have to close my eyes against the dust.

"Why didn't you?" he asks after the wind dies down.

I look at the riverbed under my swinging feet. Look at one rock. It's out of place. Gleaming black and oily among so much sparkly, glacier-rolled granite.

"I don't know," I say, after the silence has stretched too long.

He shrugs. I catch the movement in my peripheral vision. I used to hate that shrug. I thought he used it to brush me off. But it's only a form of communication. No more and no less than *I don't know*.

"Has there been anyone else?" I ask. I'm not sure why I'm asking. I'm not sure I care. Three years is a long time.

"Maybe." He says it without any defensiveness. Like a person might say *"Let me think about it."* As if he weren't sure.

"Maybe, but you've forgotten? Or maybe, but you don't want to tell me?"

Beneath our feet, the water churns to foamy butter as it splashes against the rocks. A lingering and chilly cricket burrowed into the warm dust under the bridge rubs a rough bow over his violin.

"No one," he says. "There's been no one."

This doesn't make me feel good. It makes me feel worse. I wish I hadn't asked. "I'm sorry," I say.

"Sorry because there's been no one? Or sorry you asked?" he mimics, a smile working its way through his words.

"Sorry I asked."

"Then I won't," he says.

"Won't what?"

"Won't ask."

"I almost wish you would," I say. "Just so the guilt will be even."

"Guilt is never even. Has there been anyone else?"

"Once. Because he wasn't you." It feels good to say it. As if I've just cleansed myself of sin. I didn't even know I was carrying that . . . cross around with me.

"I was a bastard," he says.

I automatically open my mouth to say he wasn't, then I remember the way his lips would twitch when I said something he thought was stupid. Remember the casual acceptance that he was a god to be worshiped. Remember how I was so ready to worship.

"You were," I say. "But I was weak."

A owl chuckles a hoarse call in the distance. His mate answers.

"And you aren't anymore?"

"No, I'm still weak. But I'm trying to recognize it. In myself, I mean."

He laughs. Not a happy laugh. "I wish I could," he says.

"Why?" I ask, frowning.

"I thought I was done with you."

I struggle for the right words to say. Something is slipping away from me. I don't know how to catch it.

"Would you do it again?" I ask.

"Do what?"

"Take me with you?"

He looks up, and the moon catches her fingers on the bones of his face and the dark hollows of his eyes.

"Yes," he says. "Would you do it again?"

He doesn't mean leaving with him. He means leaving him behind.

"Yes," I whisper. And it nearly chokes me.

His footsteps are soft as he leaves me sitting on the bridge.

I'm still sitting on the guardrail when the waves of grass swallow the moon.

CHAPTER 19

Leaving in the midst of a microburst of anger . . . that's easy. All you need is fifteen minutes of white heat and raging storms boiling up inside of you. Just enough time to get far enough away that going back is harder than going on. If you can pass that point, get that far, it's over. The deed is done.

But there's only one catch. You can't let what you left behind catch up to you.

You can't let the guilt and regret catch up to you. So you keep the wind at your back and you keep rolling, staying as rootless as a tumbleweed.

I pick up Miss Kitty from the bar and drop her off at Great-aunt Eva's. She scowls at me as I shut the door. Her dignity is ruffled by all the recent changes. I ignore the scowl and walk to the house bordered by chain link and knock on Gwen's door. It's six in the morning, but I know one of her day care kids is dropped off at five-thirty.

Even if she weren't awake, I'd be here, knocking on the door and hoping for some reassurance.

"Kat?" she asks when she opens the door.

"What if John's father came back?" I ask.

She opens the door a little wider, and I step into the heat of the morning kitchen. Oatmeal and coffee and fruit. The five-thirty kid is sacked out in a playpen. John and Pearl are nowhere to be seen.

"Do you sleep anymore?" she asks me.

"No."

"I wondered."

She stirs the oatmeal. Little glassy bubbles form on the surface. Thick and shiny, then bulging thinner until they pop oozily and sink.

"Want some breakfast?" she asks. "Coffee?"

My stomach growls. "Both? Please?"

"Sit." She points to a chair.

Pearl yawns and stretches in the kitchen doorway before sauntering—wagging, of all miracles—over to me. I scratch her ears. I can see the healing scars on my wrist from her teeth.

"Why doesn't she bite me anymore?" I ask.

Gwen sets a cup of coffee in front of me. "Wouldn't you be cranky after living with an old lady who banged her cane at you all the time?"

"I *was* cranky."

"Point made." She goes back to stirring the oatmeal. I feel a small stirring of guilt. Because Eva didn't bang her cane at me.

"You were nervous," I say, changing the subject. "The first time I came over. Now you're not."

"I don't care what you think of me anymore," she says. She looks up from the oatmeal and grins at me. "I'm surprised I ever did."

"Thanks." I say it wryly, but I *am* thankful.

She fills two bowls with the cooked cereal. "The nuts and raisins are in front of you," she says when she sits down.

The oatmeal is good. Scottish, I think. The kind that takes twenty minutes and doesn't turn into a gooey paste. And Gwen uses half-and-half in place of milk. I raise my eyebrows.

"We had a milk cow when I was a kid," she says, pink in her cheeks. "And more cream than we knew what to do with. It's my only animal-fat vice."

"The rest of the time it's broccoli, right?"

"Of course. With a little cheese."

We grin at each other.

I'm starting to thaw out. Warm up. Feel normal. As normal as I can, I guess.

Gwen breaks the warm spell.

"He wouldn't come back," she says. "John's father. He has other kids."

"Before or after John?"

"After."

"Does he know? About John?"

"Yes. And no."

I finish the last of my oatmeal and wait for her to continue. To explain.

"I told him. That I was pregnant. He wasn't sure what to do. I think *that* said more than anything he actually *said*."

I nod. "And 'no'?" I ask, when she doesn't continue.

"I broke it off. And I haven't tried to contact him since. Not that he's tried to contact me. He doesn't know anything. About John. Not even that he's a boy."

I knock a handful of raisins and nuts out of the box. Gwen refills our coffee mugs.

"Was it a mistake?" I ask.

"Loving him or leaving him?" she asks.

"Either. Both."

"I loved him," she says. "I left him. As to whether or not it was wrong, I don't know."

"Not 'wrong,'" I say. "I didn't mean it like it was a sin or evil or something. Was it a mistake?"

"Why do you ask?"

"Stephen is back."

She frowns. "When?"

"Last night."

"Was it a mistake to leave him?" she asks.

"It was a choice," I say. "It felt—still feels—like the only choice I had."

Gwen nods.

And I realize I've answered my own question.

"Robert dropped by this morning," I say. "Yesterday morning, I mean." I pick a walnut out of the raisin and nut mix. Walnuts are my favorite. Oily enough to coat your tongue with flavor, but without any sweetness.

Gwen grips her mug. "Oh?" she asks, trying to freeze the conversation in place.

"Yes. He wanted to talk about you."

Her eyes narrow. "How nice."

"I didn't," I say. "But I think *you* should talk to him."

"Are you on his side?"

"We're supposed to choose sides?" I ask, opening my eyes wide in mock astonishment. "Nobody told me."

She throws a peanut at my head. I duck, and it lands on the floor. Pearl dives on it and chews it slowly and luxuriously.

"You don't know what you're talking about," Gwen says.

"That's true."

"You don't know anything about him."

"That's true, too."

"Or me."

"True again."

"Shut up with that 'true' stuff," she says. "It's annoying."

"True."

I deserve the raisin in the eye.

"You need more sleep," she says. "You're annoying like this."

"Talk to him," I say. "Or let him talk and you just listen. Really listen."

"You're not exactly an expert in this area," she says. Eerily echoing Jen.

"You're right," I say. And I realize I could sleep for a long, long time. I need a castle surrounded by thorns so no one can slink in and wake me up.

Stephen is sitting on Great-aunt Eva's front porch. He hasn't slept either. Three years and I can still see the lines around his eyes and recognize them as exhaustion. It's a strange recognition.

"Hi," he says.

"Hi."

"Melody told me you were living here."

"Are you cleaning rooms?"

He smiles. "Yes, but I'm told I don't dust the window ledges. Like you did."

I smile. "I should have stayed there."

"Why, when you can stay here for free? Assuming it's free."

"The whispers," I say.

I don't bother to explain, just climb the steps and open the door. Miss Kitty raises her head when we walk in, but she stays snuggled down in the blankets on the couch. Maybe it's the echoing bareness of the floor and walls, but I can hear her begin to purr. Sort of like those underground caverns where a whisper can be heard twenty yards away.

"I thought you'd be staying with your dad," I say, leaning back against the closed door.

"He got married again. They live in Missoula."

"Oh."

Stephen looks around. I see the bare house from his perspective. Dark patches on the walls. Light patches on the floor boards. A lonely couch and chair. Nothing but sunlight in the old dining room where the unnamed aunt's table used to sit.

"It's all at the bar," I say. "The furniture. I couldn't live with it anymore."

"It wasn't you, huh?"

"No. Nothing like me."

"And the whispers?"

"Disapproving relatives. They're in a box upstairs."

He reaches out a hand toward my face . . .

Bones, tendons, long fingers, guitar-string calluses.

Recognition.

I freeze.

. . . and pulls a leaf out of my hair. One of the last crumpled-yellow leaves from a cottonwood. A leaf that floated on the moon's wind and landed.

He hands it to me.

Someone knocks on the door.

Loudly.

I blink.

"This," I say, then swallow. "This is the other reason I should have stayed at the Silver Spur. At least I got to sleep in until nine."

"Hello, hello," Darla Covington says when I open the door. "I came by to see if you have that casserole dish. There's a potluck at the church this Sunday . . ." She leaves the sentence dangling, hanging, waiting for someone to rescue it with conversation.

I think about shutting the door, but she's already got her head inside.

"Well, who do we have *here?*" she asks, seeing Stephen.

"I'll get that dish," I say.

She's giving Stephen the once-over. When I get back with the oblong slab of Pyrex, she's giving him the twice-over.

"Dish?" I say, pushing it into her arms. Then I go to the door and open it. "Thanks for coming by."

"My *pleasure*," she says, touching Stephen's shoulder.

I shut the door behind her.

"You have twelve hours," I say.

"You underestimate her," he says. "I'd say four at the most."

"Do you want some coffee? Food?" I ask, not wanting to think about the grapevine having a field day with this latest tidbit of gossip. Gossip with ties to the past is so much juicier than gossip that stands all by itself.

"I'm sorry," he says. "That I left this morning. On the bridge."

Given the circumstances, given the past, the apology borders on the absurd.

"Are you trying to make me feel guilty?" I ask, only half teasing.

He smiles. "I hadn't thought of it that way. Is it working?"

"Some."

"Coffee sounds great."

He follows me into the kitchen. I'm surprised when my fingers don't shake as I spoon out the coffee. Surprised to realize that beyond an acceptable level of discomfort and embarrassment, I feel . . .

. . . happy.

"You kept this table," he says.

"I like that table. It had something other than ancestry to offer."

Miss Kitty jumps up onto said table and drags her tail across Stephen's nose. Three years disappear in a wink. As if they never happened.

It was a hot morning in L.A. Like so many of the mornings in L.A. I could hear the music from the neighbor's radio coming through the open window. And Miss Kitty was rubbing her tail under Stephen's nose, walking across the newspaper while he tried to read the employment ads. I poured a cup of coffee, then kissed the top of his head before sitting down.

Just for a second, as Kitty's tail rubs across Stephen's face, it's like time hasn't happened. Then the years separating us are back again. Like a barbed wire fence between us.

"Ancestry?" Stephen asks.

I sit down across from him. Scratch Miss K.'s head. "Some things don't have much to offer. They don't make life . . . better. They're just clutter."

"So you got rid of the unnecessary stuff."

It takes me a few seconds.

"Is that what you think I did?" I ask. "You think I thought you were unnecessary?"

He shrugs. "I wondered. After all the wondering, it was as good an explanation as any. Don't you think?"

"No." The whirlwind of heat and rage. It had nothing to do with necessity. Or the lack of necessity.

He leans back in his chair. He's waiting for something more. I don't have anything more to offer.

"If I thought you were unnecessary," I say at last, "I would have filed the appropriate paperwork."

"I feel so much more important now," he says.

He's angry. Every emotion during the last three years is swarming together and getting ready to take flight in a firestorm. But he's controlling it to the point where it will break him.

And I don't have any defense.

I don't mean a board or a rock or a baseball bat. I would never need that kind of defense from Stephen. I mean, I don't have any defensive ground to stand on. It's slipping out from under my toes like the sand being sucked away by the ocean.

"Uncle Charles says you're living in Seattle," I say.

"You can't see the sky in L.A.," he says.

"And you can in Seattle?"

"Sometimes. Enough."

"I thought it might be for the music."

He shrugs. "I do a lot of session work," he says, almost reluctantly.

"You make it sound like a crime."

"Did I?"

I nod. When he doesn't say anything more, I get up and pour coffee for us. Maybe I'll start using half-and-half. I don't like cheese on my broccoli, and with the healthy hearts in my family line I can afford the extra animal fat. In front of the back door, Miss Kitty stands on her hind legs and paws at the doorknob, wanting to be let out so she can chase the squirrels on the patio. I almost miss Stephen's next words in the sound of the squeaking hinges.

"I play other people's music," he says.

"And that makes it a crime?"

"It makes me . . . It's like living someone else's success. You can't enjoy it."

I sit down and wrap my cold fingers around the stoneware mug. Let the heat sink into my bones and knuckles.

"If you play the best you can," I say, "it's a success. If you feel—"

"Do you still copy down poetry?" he interrupts.

I look up from the mug and into his face.

"Yes," I say.

"But you never write your own?"

"No."

"Don't give me advice."

My fingers are tight around the cup. Too tight.

"Point taken," I say.

"I'm sorry," he says.

"No," I tell him. "You aren't. And you shouldn't be."

He sips his coffee, watching me through the steam. "Is this like 'it's all right, don't worry about it'?" he asks. "Because we both know 'it's all right, don't worry about it' doesn't mean shit."

I can't stop the smile. "No, this is more like 'it's all right, I was making an ass of myself.'"

"As long as you say it and not me."

This is comfortable. Easy. Simple. Nothing harsh. Even though the anger is bubbling down there like the glassy bubbles on Gwen's oatmeal, the pot hasn't come to a full boil.

It's a little like sitting in a vat of oil and knowing that someone is going to turn up the heat to deep-fat-fry in the future, but right now you're comfortable.

This is denial at its best. Gotta love it.

Miss K. yowls to be let back in. I start to get up, but Stephen beats me to it. She rewards him by allowing him to demonstrate his affection through petting. "I missed you, Kitty," he says. She buzzes.

I swallow some jealousy with my coffee. Kitty is *my* friend.

Someone knocks.

"You're popular," he says.

"It's a real thrill."

I'm hoping for Gwen. I get Rosemary Litwin.

"Is it true?" she asks.

Darla must be on speed. "Yes," I say.

"I can't believe it."

"Come in and see for yourself."

"They're here?"

"Who?"

"Them!"

I stand in the cold draft flowing over my feet.

"Why don't you come in and have some coffee," I say.

"I can't believe you didn't tell me," she says as we walk to the kitchen. "It's just—" She sees Stephen and stops. "Oh. You're . . . entertaining."

"Yes," I say. "It supplements the income."

The poor woman looks confused. She starts crying.

Miss Kitty jumps down from Stephen's lap and seeks refuge in the living room.

Stephen stares.

I grab Rosemary's shoulders and push her into one of the kitchen chairs. Then I pour her a cup of coffee and hand her a box of tissues.

"Done this before?" Stephen whispers.

I haven't, but Great-aunt Eva has. Had. One night—I don't know how old I was, but I was wearing one-piece jammies with footsies still—one cold night I sat on the steps going up to my room and listened to Great-aunt Eva console Rosemary. *"You wouldn't want him back, if that's the way he treats you,"* she said. *"Your life isn't over. It's just beginning."* Rosemary's wails drowned out the rest.

I ignore Stephen's question and chew my lip. Why does it feel like Eva is in the room with me? Clumsily, I sit down and put my arm around Rosemary's shoulders.

"I'm sorry," she says, wiping her eyes. "It wasn't what you said, it's just that . . . She's *not* a nice girl."

Things begin to click.

"I take it Nate and Summer are—"

"Not waiting to get married before they . . ." She trails off and hiccups. "Where did I go wrong?"

Stephen clears his throat.

I look over at him.

"No, you can't leave," I say.

"I was going to ask if she means Summer Jones," he says. "If you don't mind."

"Yes," I say.

"Yes," Rosemary says, hiccuping again. "Summer Jones."

"Oh."

"She's a nice girl," I say to Rosemary. "Wait and see."

I'm not sure I believe this lie. But it sounds good.

"Darla Covington is going to love this," Rosemary says, her face drooping.

"I think Darla's busy right now," Stephen says.

Rosemary gives him a sad smile. "Darla never sleeps."

"Neither does anyone else around here," I say.

It's not true.

That no one sleeps around here.

I finally get Rosemary calmed down enough so she can go find Nate and Summer. And have a talk about locks on doors and walking in on your grown son and his "lady friend," as Rosemary puts it.

"Do you think Nate did it on purpose?" I ask Stephen after Rosemary leaves and I've shut the door. "Because he can't stand up to his mother?"

He settles down on the couch beside Miss K. The couch sags softly, warmly, drowsily.

"Is that what you think?" he asks.

"I think it would take a visitation from a choir of angels to get Rosemary's attention."

"They're hard to find these days."

The couch's pull is too strong. I sit down.

"Do you have to work tonight?" he asks.

"Every night. Except Sunday."

"Try and sleep."

"I've tried."

"Try again."

I snuggle down into my corner of the couch.

"Keep the whispers away," I say, already halfway into dreamland.

As I fall asleep, his fingers touch mine.

The dragons stay in the attic.

CHAPTER 20

I expect Stephen to be gone when I wake up.

But he isn't.

I'm cramped from sleeping in an upright ball on the couch. When I open my eyes, I see Stephen's sleeping face. I don't think I've ever woken up this way. The trip to L.A. was a whirlwind of driving and emotion. The motel stops were few, and Newell and the others were draped over the furniture and floor. In our own apartment, our schedules were crazed. One of us working days, the other working nights.

It's a strange sensation to wake up to someone who is still asleep and at their most vulnerable. A strange sensation of embarrassment and fear and protection all mixed up and all at once.

I pull my fingers from underneath his.

He shifts and rolls a bit, but doesn't wake up. I ease up from the couch, trying not to disturb him. The exhaustion lines are still sharp around his eyes and mouth.

The clock says two p.m. My hair is heavy and tangled. After starting a new pot of coffee, I braid it as best I can, dislodging another cottonwood leaf and a small stick while I'm at it.

Outside, the sky is heavy and tangled. A homogenous thickness of gray on top with fast-moving blacker puffs floating along underneath. A flock of brown birds sweeps away from the elm tree, their wings whispering to the wind and anyone willing to listen. *"Get ready!"* the wings whisper. *"The cold is coming."*

I sit down at the table and rest my head in my hands.

I can hear the bubbling oatmeal pot of anger. I just don't know what to do about it. I could turn the heat up and force a confrontation, but the idea frightens me.

Because I know I'm guilty.

Because I can't admit that I was wrong.

Leave.

I swear someone said it.

Just leave. He won't try to find you.

But I didn't leave Stephen because I wanted to get him out of my life.

I left because . . .

. . . I don't know.

It's all tangled up like the leaf and twig in my hair. All tangled up like the clouds and the sky. Lost in the little details of a sarcastic smile, rolling eyes, hero worship, and harsh reality. Lost in the subtle way I felt excluded by Newell and the others. Lost in the jealous ache in my chest when Stephen would leave me behind to go with them. Lost in the realization that I was as much use to him as the fancy hood ornament Newell bought for the band's van. Especially lost in the huge rush of a city populated by concrete and asphalt and metal and so many lights its glow drowned out the moon.

I wasn't a little fish in a big pond.

I was a mouse running on a wheel.

Just like all the other little mice.

I left because . . .

. . . I didn't like going nowhere. Going nowhere while trying to go somewhere. I left because I didn't belong.

The coffeepot gurgles.

I pour two cups and carry them in to the couch.

"Hey," I say when I see that his eyes are open. He's been staring at the ceiling. For a while.

"Thanks," he says when I hand him one of the cups.

I sit down beside him.

"Did you really come here to find me?" I ask.

"Yes."

"Why?"

"Your uncle."

"Charles?"

He shrugs. "Not really Charles. He called. Looking for you."

"And?"

"I was doing fine," he says, anger pushing up into his voice. Just a thread of anger. "Fine. Things were aimless for a bit."

I nod.

"I threw all the stuff from the U-Haul away." He says it defensively.

"I didn't expect you to set up a museum in my honor," I say. "I just thought you should know where it was."

"When I threw away your books," he says, "I knew you weren't coming back."

He's looking at the yellow chair sitting all alone in the middle of the living room. Not at me. In another person, I might think he threw my books away to hurt me. With Stephen, I'm not sure.

I try to remember what the books were. Most are dim shadows. But I can see the spine of a Robert Frost collection in my mind. A used bookstore find. Classic cloth binding. Yellowed pages. Smudged from love and use. I mind losing it. But I abandoned it. You can't protect something you discard.

"Things are still aimless," Stephen says.

"There isn't always a point," I say. "Sometimes, I went to a town because there was a sign on the highway. Or because the name sounded like pine trees and smoke. One time, I wandered into a town by accident and ended up staying for a month. Because I liked the way the bricks and stones fit together on the false fronts."

"One time, I drove off the Coast Highway," he says. "A year or so ago. Just a gravel road. But I found a clearing. With sun rays coming down through the needles. The wind made the needles sing."

He smiles at the chair, seeing the sunlight on the grass instead of worn fake velvet.

"Exactly," I whisper. "Sometimes there isn't a point and you're still happy."

The clock on one of the downtown churches chimes the half hour. Usually, I can't hear the clock from here. Today, the wind is just right to carry the unfinished sound.

"Stay here," I say, soft and quiet.

His face tenses.

"In the house," I add. "Rather than the motel." I don't want him to think I meant he should move to Silver Creek and put down roots.

"Why?"

"Because we've both wandered aimlessly back to where we started."

He nods. Once.

Existential bullshit, of course. I feel stupid. Walking down the sidewalk to the bar, I can hear my syrupy conscious prattle on and on. "*Oh, please stay, Stephen. Perhaps the universe is showing us the way.*" What was I thinking? I was spouting drivel. Syrupy drivel.

I kick a rock in my path and the wind buoys it up in the hands of angels. The cold the birds' wings told me about this morning is almost here. It will arrive on the back of the wind twisting my hair around my face.

I jog the last hundred feet or so to the Watering Hole. To warm up. To escape my thoughts.

The bar is a scene from hell. Flames leaping from the fryer and demons stoking the fire. I blink my wind-wet eyes. Not demons. Lil is beating ineffectually at the flames with the remains of a damp towel. Thad is trying to put the fryer covers down and he's getting the full benefit of the towel's efforts on his arms and shoulders.

I grab the towel away from Lil and pull her back.

Thad gets the covers on.

The smoke alarm screeches. Now. After the fire is out.

"If you're cold," I say to Lil, "there's a heater."

"Just shut that damn alarm off," she says. "Then you can make whatever smartass remarks you like."

I shut the alarm off. But I'm smart enough to keep the smartass remarks to myself.

"Wouldn't that have been ironic," Lil says, collapsing into a chair. "I remodel and the damn thing burns down."

"Nothing burned down," Thad says. "The wall isn't even scorched. Well," he tests the soot on the galvanized tin behind the fryer, "maybe a little."

Lil ignores him. "I forgot I turned it up. Just like my mother used to do with the teakettle. She was senile. She had an excuse."

"I've let the teakettle go dry," I say before I figure out how condescending it sounds. "We'll have to get a timer or something," I add.

"I'm old," Lil says.

"One foot in the grave," Thad agrees. "Tottering about." He clutches his back and taps an imaginary cane.

Lil grabs the greasy, scorched towel from me and throws it at him. "Sheep lover."

Thad laughs the first truly happy laugh I've heard in weeks.

"Why are you standing there?" Lil asks me.

"I'm thinking existential thoughts," I tell her.

"You'll be *nonessential* if you don't get going."

"Ooo." I pretend to quiver in fright.

"Where's the respect?" Lil asks Thad. "No one respects age anymore."

He grins. "I guess you're not old yet, Grandma."

"I'm going to go scrub soot," I say to anyone who cares to listen. No one does.

The Watering Hole is back to normal.

"I hear you're in the market for a pool table."

I know that voice.

It's the dinner slump. The time when we catch our second wind and get ready for the night crowd that trickles in after the sitcoms are over. I'm washing glasses.

I know that voice.

I paste a smile onto my face.

"One doesn't seem to be enough anymore," I say to Mr. Boom-voice the lawyer. "What would you like?"

"Light beer for me." He pats his belly. "Have to watch my figure or the girls won't like me." He winks.

I ignore the wink.

"I have one down in my basement," he says. "A pool table. Bought it for the kids, but it never really caught on." He picks up the beer and takes a swallow or two.

I wait. Wonder what it is he wants. Because he wants something.

"I'd let Lil have it for a song," he says, leaning in close, "if you'd do me a favor."

I've done a lot of service jobs. Waitress. Maid. Cook. Busboy. Even valet parking. I've also had my share of indiscreet pickups, discreet pinches, and a full-service line of innuendos.

This isn't any of those things. Boom-voice has his sexist quirks, but after hearing the real thing enough times, I can tell the difference.

"What's that?" I ask.

"Charles. His golf game is off. Terrible. It isn't even fun to be on the course with him. He threw a club the other day and practically totaled the cart." B-v's laugh echoes off the walls and the fresh-scrubbed tin behind the fryer.

"I don't play golf," I say. "I'm not sure how I can help you."

"I think it has to do with the family," he says.

"I *am* the family."

"Exactly."

"What's your point?"

He scratches his upper lip. "Kiss and make up?"

I pick up his empty glass and refill it. "What makes you think I'm the one who needs to do the making up?"

B-v cocks his finger at me as if it were a gun. "You're a firecracker," he says. "Sometimes a girl should swallow her pride." He reaches for the glass.

I pull it away.

"What is he saying?" I ask.

"Now, now. No tales out of school."

I let go of the glass. He downs the beer in a few swallows.

"Drop by the office," he says. "I have some papers you need to sign."

"For what?"

"Routine. Nothing to worry about. Remember that pool table," he says before he leaves.

I walk over to where Lil and Thad are tacking up postcards. "I need an hour," I say to Lil. "Can you spare me?"

"No." She looks up into my face and her teasing smile dies. "But I'll do it anyway."

"Thanks."

The fire inside of me keeps me warm on the long walk to Uncle Charles' house. It's on the prissy side of town. The side of town where houses are built to look like something out of a Zane Grey novel, only with more glass and a hot tub.

There's a familiar SUV in Charles' driveway.

I ignore it.

I disdain the doorbell for a few solid thumps with the brass knocker cutely crafted to look like a horse's head.

"Hi," I say to Charles when he opens the door.

He steps out onto the porch and shuts the door behind him. "I have guests," he says.

"Donner and Jennifer. Yes, I noticed that."

He folds his arms across his chest.

"I had a visit from the family lawyer this evening," I say. "He says your golf game is off."

"It's a slump."

"He says it's because I'm behaving badly. I had no idea."

Charles shifts from foot to foot. I'm not sure whether he's cold or nervous.

"Why do you hate me?" I ask, surprising myself with the question. "I didn't ask for Aunt Eva's things, you know."

"I don't hate you," he says.

I fold my arms across my chest. We stand across the little cement entryway from each other. Two garden gnomes with folded arms.

"Okay," I amend. "You don't hate me. But it's a reasonable facsimile."

"You figure it out, if you're so smart."

I look at him. Try to construct a bridge over the past and the anger, and try to look at him as if he were a customer at the bar. Or even a customer at some other long-ago service job where I wouldn't even share the same geographical knowledge I share with a stranger at the Watering Hole.

A wind-tossed candy wrapper flops up onto the porch and scrapes across the cement. Charles glares at it. He doesn't want me here, but he doesn't know how to stop me from saying what I have to say without physically removing me from his manicured property.

"You're angry because I remind you of your own failure," I say. "Because you didn't do what you were supposed to do."

Charles goes white. Then red. Then white again.

"And you always do what everyone expects you to do," I finish. "You always keep your promises. It's your image of yourself. Except one time you were selfish. You let Aunt Eva pick up the slack. But Cynthia left anyway. And Aunt Eva didn't even respect you enough to leave you in charge of her things."

He grabs my arm. Hard. Until it hurts and my fingers tingle.

A bit of fear works through. Instinctive fear. Not fear born of logic or reason.

I stare him down.

"Go on," I say. "Do it."

His hands are trembling and he wants to haul off and hit me. His fist balls.

The door opens.

Donner grabs Charles' arm. I guess Donner has less faith in Charles' self-control than I do.

"Kat?" Jen asks from behind Donner.

Charles shakes off Donner's hand. "It's all right," he says.

"What's going on?" Jen asks.

Donner puts his hand on Charles' shoulder. "Maybe you two should come inside."

"No," I say.

"Katherine was just leaving," Charles says at the same time.

"No, I wasn't."

"Yes, you are."

I look at Jen.

Silent appeal.

Being friends for ten formative years has its advantages. Jen shakes her head in a confused, unhappy way, but she touches Donner's arm and says, "They need to work this out. Alone."

Donner's eyebrows pull together. But he lets Jen lead him back inside.

"You have influence everywhere," Uncle Charles says, bitterness in his voice.

"Maybe I'll open a credit union of my own."

He frowns. Then—when he realizes I'm shifting us to neutral—the frown breaks down into a hint of a smile. "My bank would pound your bank like a leftover steak."

"Not a pretty thought."

Our smiles are brief.

I pull the edges of my scarf up a bit against a gust of early winter.

"You're wrong," he says. "You're completely wrong."

I nod, even though I don't agree.

His lips tighten. He knows I'm playing along.

"I don't need any of Eva's money," he says. He looks at my worn coat. "You certainly do."

"I'd be fine without it," I say. Stung. Wondering if he thinks I've been living off of friends the last three years. Or stealing.

"Oh, I'm sure," he says. Only a hint of sarcasm.

"And I know you don't *need* her money," I say, deciding to ignore the sarcasm. "It's a matter of pride. You're the good sheep. I'm the black sheep. Eva left the black sheep everything. It stings your pride."

"I didn't want her money or her things," he says, pulling back from me. "It's hardly enough to bother with."

"If that's the case, why do you care what I do with it? Why do you care at all?"

"It's the principle of the thing."

"We're going around in circles," I tell him. "You don't want it, it's not enough to bother with, but you want to interpret Aunt Eva's 'legacy' and tell me what she wanted and how to take care of things—"

"No, I don't."

"Fine. Stop telling all your friends I'm behaving badly."

"Stop behaving that way, then."

I close my eyes and let out an audible huff of frustration. This whole situation is *tired*. Old aggression. Worn out. Reheated. Who's naughty, who's nice.

Who gives a shit.

I step forward.

He steps back.

"You're my family," I tell him. "I love you. For all the Sunday noons you picked me up and swung me into the air. But I'm not going to have you over for Sunday dinner. And I'm not going to invite myself here for Sunday dinner. You don't have to protect yourself from me or what I remind you of. I'm not going to come around and embarrass you in front of your friends." I try to smile. "Unless I want a checking account."

He laughs. "I'm not embarrassed."

I shrug.

"Good night, Uncle Charles. I'm sorry I interrupted your evening."

He opens his mouth. Closes it.

I'm partway down the sidewalk when he says, "Good night, Katherine."

CHAPTER 21

I walk back toward the center of Silver Creek. Walk on straight-edged, broad sidewalks that give way to tree-root-broken cement sidewalks that give in to narrow, lumpy brick sidewalks laid down before brick became fashionable and historic. The horn honks twice before I notice the truck. And notice how cold I am. The wind has picked my scarf apart and reached my neck.

The truck is a broken-down pickup outfitted with an old-fashioned crane and winch for towing, and a bright modern logo advertising the Gas and Lube.

"Do you need a ride?" Dustin asks after he rolls down the window.

"It's close," I say. "I'll be fine."

"I have a heater."

"In that case . . ."

I climb in and turn the two passenger vents my way.

"It's cold out there," he says, pulling the truck back out into the street.

"Yeah."

"You going to the Watering Hole?"

"Yes." My mouth feels funny after walking into the wind for a mile. I can't seem to get more than a few syllables out at a time.

"Mom says to tell you hello," he says. "And to stop stealing her maids."

I'd forgotten what taking Stephen away from the Silver Spur would mean to Melody.

"I'm sorry," I say. "I didn't—"

Dustin shakes his head. "Don't worry about it," he says. "She was just kidding."

"What about you?"

"You mean, what about me having to do the cleaning?"

"Yes."

"I'll leave vacuuming under the beds for the next person."

I've warmed up enough to laugh.

"Did your car break down?" he asks.

"No," I say. "I had an emergency visit to my uncle."

He shakes his head.

"What?" I ask.

"He has a fit if I leave the tiniest smudge on that Caddy of his."

I lean back into the seat. "Uncle Charles is like that."

"I'm surprised he lets those new colored bills out of the vault," Dustin says. "Someone might get them dirty. Then they'd be dirty money." He starts to laugh.

I would laugh, but I'm thinking about the bathroom just off of Charles' master bedroom. The shaving implements carefully lined up like the leaden soldiers on Robert Louis Stevenson's counterpane. The toothbrush—faithfully changed every six weeks—in the spotless glass. Soap dispenser. Paper towels for wiping recalcitrant drops of water from the edge of the sink.

A flash flood and the responsibility for a toddler might have been enough to break any up-and-coming young loan officer, much less one facing the loss of what he thought was the love of his life. You can't control floods and children no matter how hard you try. Neither one pays the slightest attention to your need to control your life. You can't control love or fate either.

And maybe it's seeing Dustin again. Because seeing him makes me remember that day I bought gas and then went back to Great-aunt Eva's and caught Charles looking over the furniture. How he swallowed a thick, unhappy lump of guilt when I reminded him that Eva took me in because he chose Cynthia over his promise to his brother. And Cynthia left him with nothing but guilt and a desperate need to control his reputation.

What looks like relief when you're twenty-five can turn sour by the time you're forty-five.

Because you can't control guilt.

All you can do is get angry. And bitter.

"Are you okay?" Dustin asks.

"Yes," I say. "Could you drop me off here?"

"It's a whole block yet."

"I know."

I stand on the sidewalk and watch the taillights of Dustin's truck disappear on down the street. A giant upside-down bowl of night sky painted with stars presses down on Silver Creek. The universe presses down on Silver Creek. Compresses the town and the rolling grassland until they blend into one dark mass.

And I'm in the middle.

Turning into the wind, I walk the block to the Watering Hole. Through the front windows, I can see the usual post-sitcom crowd. Warm and cozy on Great-aunt Eva's furniture that Charles is punishing me for because he can't control his own guilty conscience.

My hand is on the door and ready to push it open. But for the first time since I started working here, I don't want to go inside. I can hear Lil's laughter through the door. She laughs just as the Beatles wannabe strums the strings of his acoustic guitar and strikes up a tune that might be

"Daytripper" or "Drive My Car." It's impossible to tell which through the door. A howl or two from a heckler until he's shushed by Wannabe's friends. A crash of pool balls as someone makes a break.

I take my hand away from the door and lean back against the wall. Tuck my arms around myself and give in to the misery of the universal compression.

The door squeaks.

I wipe a hand over my cheek, but my face is so cold, I can't tell whether I'm crying or not.

"Hi," Summer Jones says.

I nod. And wait for the attack.

"I thought I'd come out here for a smoke," she says. "It's hot in there."

"Hot isn't a problem out here," I say.

She smiles.

It looks painful.

We stand together in the doorway, the blue neon light from the beer sign illuminating our feet. I can see her shift from foot to foot.

She holds out a pack of cigarettes, waving them in my general direction. It's a peace offering. Summer Jones has never offered me anything in her life.

"Thanks," I say, taking one even though I don't smoke. The wind drags the flame away from her lighter, and we have to shelter it with our bodies before it will stay lit.

"The stars are pretty tonight," she says around a mouthful of smoke.

I never thought of Summer as someone who would look at the stars.

"Yeah," I say out loud. "The sky feels heavy."

"Heavy?"

I shrug.

"How come you aren't working tonight?" she asks.

"I am. I just went out for a bit."

"Stephen's in town."

"I know."

She cups her elbow in one hand. Her cigarette flares as she inhales. Mine still dangles from my fingers. I pull a little smoke into my mouth. If I inhale too deeply, I'll start coughing.

"Nate asked me to marry him," she says.

"Congratulations."

"Because Rosemary caught me . . ." She trails off, but I can figure it out.

"I heard about that," I say.

"Everyone did." She blows out a long plume of smoke and vapor from warm lungs. "I don't think I want to."

I take a deeper breath of cigarette smoke. It goes well with the faint scent of burning pine logs that has colored the air.

"Why not?" I ask after it's obvious Summer isn't going to keep talking on her own. I'm not sure I really care why a former adversary doesn't want to marry a former friend. But it seems impolite to not ask.

"He doesn't fight back," she says. "He just pretends he does."

She drops the butt of her cigarette onto the sidewalk and crushes it into the blue neon glow. "I'm cold. Guess I'll go in."

I nod. "Thanks for the cigarette."

She disappears back into the heat and noise and yeast of the bar. Warm air curls around my toes before it's swallowed by the hungry wind.

He doesn't fight back.

It's a tired, cliché kind of thing to say. Not that it isn't true, just that it's a tired, cliché thing to say. I pull cigarette smoke into my lungs and indulge in a coughing fit. Summer's peace offering is hard on my system. I wonder if her answer will break Nate's heart. Somehow, I don't think it will. He's still too interested in what Rosemary wants for his life to figure out what he wants for himself.

But I may be wrong.

I drop the cold, dead butt of the cigarette into the trash can. Cringing a little, I pull off my thick glove and pick up Summer's butt and throw it away.

What do *I* want?

The trash can is a skinny cylinder with a swinging lid. Lil puts it out so people like Summer—people who want to smoke outside in the fresh air—will have something to drop their butts into. The bottom is filled with clay kitty litter. The swinging lid rocks back and forth over Summer's trash. My face is a pale oval in the shiny lid. Rocking back and forth.

I close my eyes.

When I open them, the lid is still.

I dust my fingers, put my glove back on, and reach out for the handle of the door. Almost automatically, I look up at the sign. Just like I did that first afternoon. The afternoon I came back to Silver Creek.

I smile. And enter into the heat and noise.

"That was more than an hour," Lil says when I walk around behind the bar.

"It got complicated."

She raises an eyebrow.

"Uncle Charles thinks I'm behaving badly. We . . . had a fight."

"Charles Earle indulged in a fight?"

"A polite fight," I add. "He feels guilty."

"Why?"

"Because he was supposed to be my guardian, but he was in love, so he gave me to Aunt Eva."

"Write the script of your life," Lil says. "It would make a good soap opera."

"Thanks."

She grins and pours a beer for a warrior brandishing a pool cue.

If I wanted to take the credit, I'd say that the Earle family heirlooms have managed to make the bar even more popular than before. I'm not sure I deserve the credit. Cold weather turns a good bar into a cheerful, welcoming kind of place. The lamplit walls combine with cold beer and warm whisky shots to form a cozy nest. Add a few comfy chairs, Hank Williams on the ancient jukebox, the Beatles in the corner, and the nest becomes a second home. So the Earle heirlooms can't take all the credit.

But they help.

"It's late," Lil says as I wheel the mop into the storeroom after closing.

"No later than usual."

"I want to talk to you," she says. She yawns.

"Ooo, I'm in trouble."

"Could be."

"Now or later?"

"Later. I couldn't whip a flea right now, much less you."

I lean against the frame of the storeroom door. "Are you sleeping all right? Is the doctor—"

She waves her hand at me to make me shut up. "Don't hover. Thad does enough of that. Lyle encourages it."

"They care about you."

"That's a nice way to say they think I can't take care of myself."

I laugh.

"Does Stephen hover?"

"No."

"Hang on to him, then." She looks at me sideways. Like Kitty looks at the feather on a string when she doesn't want me to know she's interested.

"If that's what you want to talk about," I say, "I think it's past my bedtime."

CHAPTER 22

"*I don't want to play the piano,*" I said to Great-aunt Eva. I was sitting on the slippery piano bench and my feet swung free a few inches above the hardwood floor.

"Everything is difficult until you know how to do it," Eva said. She was sitting in her chair and trying to read over the sound of ten clumsy little-girl fingers picking out the dulcet tones of "Here We Go to Musicland."

"But I don't *want* to know how to do the piano!"

Great-aunt Eva laid her book in her lap.

"Life is full of things you want and don't want. Someday you may want to know how to play the piano."

"I won't."

"The sooner you start practicing, the sooner it will be over."

"I don't *want* to!"

"Well, you don't always get what you want." She picked up her book.

I don't think Great-aunt Eva wanted me to practice the piano any more than I wanted to practice. It's possible both Eva and I *wanted* me to fail at piano and succeed at saving us both pain. But music was a skill she firmly believed a little girl should attempt. Even if the little girl never managed to sound better than a cat walking on the keyboard.

Being a child . . . it was simple. I wanted an ice cream cone. I didn't want to practice the piano. I wanted to dig a hole to the center of the earth. I didn't want to wear the frilly dress with the lace collar. Being a child meant that someone with more power held the keys that would open all the doors and give me what I wanted.

Being an adult . . . Being an adult means I finally realize that the only one between me and what I want . . .

. . . is me.

Being an adult means I no longer know what I want. Because every fulfilled desire contains so many frightening possibilities that desire itself becomes frightening.

I'm standing on the sidewalk in front of Great-aunt Eva's house. Which I didn't want. Didn't ask for. But got anyway.

Inside the house, there's a dim light. I can see Stephen's shadow on the curtain.

The first time I truly rejected this home was when I left it for the man behind the curtain.

Now I don't know what I want. I've been twisted and manipulated so many ways I'm not sure where rebellion ends and desire begins.

Eva's door opens and the rectangle of light blinds me.

"Are you going to stand out there all night?" Stephen asks.

"I was looking at the stars," I say.

He comes to the edge of the porch and looks up at the heavy clouds that have rolled in since this evening and are blotting out the sky. "Is that Taurus?" he asks. "The stars are so bright I can't tell."

I take a deep breath. Of the pine-smoke-scented night.

What would happen if I climbed the steps and touched his cheek? I know what his skin feels like after a long day and night. His beard grows faster now than it did when he was twenty-two, but I know how his skin feels under stubble.

How would I feel about this house if Stephen standing on the porch . . . was every night instead of just tonight?

"Can we go in now?" he asks.

I climb the steps.

But I keep my hands in the pockets of my coat.

Inside, I bend down to scratch Miss Kitty's head. She purrs forgiveness for my thoughtless behavior in leaving her behind this afternoon.

Stephen is watching me. His hand is tight on the wooden frame of the arched doorway Robert admires so much. Knuckles white against the oak.

"I have to go back to Seattle," Stephen says.

The words fall quietly into my infant dream. Rippling. Lapping. Tugging. Ripping.

"When?" I ask, my lips numb and clumsy as ten chubby little-girl fingers.

"Tomorrow. Early Sunday morning at the latest."

I reach for the ripped possibilities and try to pull them into a dignified cloak.

"Come with me," he says.

And it throws me back to the Silver Creek bridge. After the wedding reception. The long night on the bridge looking at the stars and talking about dreams and the possibility of power and glory and greener grass somewhere out there where people talked fast, drove fast, and lived fast. Not like Silver Creek with its cows and gossip and flat grassy hills and flat people. And that crazy moment when Stephen caught his hand in my hair and said into my ear, *"Come with me."* When I knew he meant *"Come with me forever,"* even though that isn't what he said.

The night when "want" was so clear and defined and hadn't been . . .

. . . twisted into reality by clumsy attempts to make everything perfect when we were anything but.

Twisted by children who hadn't reached adulthood and didn't understand the paralyzing fear of actually getting what we wanted.

"Come with me," Stephen says again.

I swallow.

"We're not children anymore," I say.

"We weren't then."

"Yes, we were."

"Do you think it was a mistake?"

Echoes. Everywhere I go, I hear echoes. Inside of me. Outside of me.

"I missed you," Stephen says. The words are harsh. And I realize why he threw away my books. He threw them away because I wasn't there.

And I realize . . .

"I missed you, too."

It's not an answer. He knows it. I know it. But I don't have an answer. On the bridge, it was easy. The future was nothing more than possibilities. Now I know too much. I know how it feels to be neglected or pulled into a conversation like a token voice rather than an equal. I know how it feels to not have a dream of my own because I'm living someone else's dream. I know how it feels to not belong.

I left once.

I don't know if I could leave again.

I want to rest.

I want a resting place.

"I missed you, too," I say again. Softer. Because I don't have an answer.

He leans the side of his head against his hand, which is still white-knuckled on the entryway frame. "Do you think it was a mistake?" he asks again.

"Getting married?"

"That's a formality. Paper and metal. Do you think leaving Silver Creek with me was a mistake?"

I can feel the moonlight and warm air. Hear the spring-filled water rushing under my swinging toes. Remember the absolute certainty—

"No," I say out loud. "It wasn't a mistake. It never will be."

"But now . . ."

"I don't know. I'm not sure what I want anymore."

He nods, his temple rubbing against his hand.

"Do you write?" I ask. "Songs. Music."

"You said I had no sense of rhythm."

He smiles.

I smile.

Because I'm remembering one hot L.A. afternoon. I was sitting on the bed, the sounds of cars and trucks on the street just beyond the window, while he played a song and I said—

"I said you needed something other than a straight four-four beat," I say. "Nothing about your rhythm."

He shrugs.

I scrunch my hands down into my coat pockets. "Do you write?" I ask again.

He picks at an imaginary speck on the trim. "Sometimes."

"Why not?"

"I said, 'sometimes.' "

"Never."

"Okay, seldom."

"Never."

"Okay. Never." He keeps picking.

"Don't pick the trim clean off the wall," I say.

"The poetry is gone."

He says it softly. I almost don't hear the words.

"You were always lousy with the words," I say.

"I didn't mean words. The poetry is gone in the music. Nothing fits together. It's . . ." He smiles a twisty little smile. "It's aimless."

I unzip my coat and take it off. "Play me something," I say, tossing the coat onto the back of the couch.

I look up as I'm unlacing my boots. He's white and still.

"Go on," I say.

"No."

"Yes."

"I'll play one of the things I recorded recently."

As a session player. The unspoken words hang.

"Fine," I say, toeing off my boots. I flop down onto the couch, bouncing Miss Kitty from her comfortable position. She yowls grumpily, then jumps down for the peace of Stephen's empty guitar case. Even Kitty slips back into the old habits. I'm not sure whether that is a happy observation for me.

Stephen sits down on the floor and fusses with the strings. Tightening, adjusting, tuning. Just like he did on those lazy Sunday mornings. I curl up and rest my cheek on the arm of the couch. Just like I did on those lazy Sunday mornings when I would pretend to read while I listened to him play everything from Vivaldi to Elvis Costello. Just like I did before things got twisted up and tightened like a steel string over a bridge.

This time, I don't pretend to read. And he starts out nervous. I've never known Stephen to be nervous. You can't be a session player if you get butterflies from playing in front of strangers. Maybe playing in front of strangers is easier.

The melody is catching, but nothing spectacular. Something dreamed up by a band that usually goes for power chords rather than skill, so they hired Stephen's skill. A tiny forgotten part of me flares to life. It's the part that . . . believed.

Believed in Stephen.

Believed in me.

Believed in something out of the ordinary.

I almost miss the change. Stephen's touch on the strings changes. It starts out dreaming, then flares into firelight and the passion of a wild dance around a bonfire. Above the dancers the sky stretches forever between the grass and hills. And under it all, I can hear Silver Creek rushing past until the music dies. . . .

"That was yours," I say as the last shivery note fades away.

He pulls back from that place where music is born. In anyone else, I'd be scrambling for something they could write on. But once Stephen finds the song, he doesn't need to find paper and pen. Not like me. I've had poetry flow into one side of my snooze-button dreams and right on out the other side. No amount of wishing can bring back the perfect word combination once it's gone. I've tried writing them down, but while I'm concentrating on remembering the first line, the others disappear.

"That was Silver Creek," I say. "And the sky."

"Moonlight," he says. "You can't see the moonlight in the city."

I reach out and lay my fingers over his, which are still curled around the neck of the guitar.

"Sometimes," I say, "sometimes wandering isn't aimless. Being rootless . . . sometimes you need—"

He cups my jaw in his hand. "I need you," he whispers. "You're my poetry."

And I believe in me.

I believe in him.

I'm just not sure I believe in us.

CHAPTER 23

I wake up frightened.

I blame the fear on sleeping in my old room.

"Why aren't you sleeping in one of the beds?"

That's what Stephen asked last night—this morning—as I sat with my hand over his on the neck of the guitar. It was his attack. To cover up the whispered words of need. Need we both felt but couldn't talk about. I think he knows why I don't sleep upstairs, but I wasn't ready to explain.

"It's cold up there," I said, taking my hand away from his and tucking it into my armpit.

"Heat rises," he said.

"It's more convenient down here," I said.

"You'll sleep better in a bed," he said. "That couch has more lumps than oatmeal."

"Oatmeal doesn't have to have lumps."

"Fine. But the couch is lumpy."

"I can't hear people knocking up there," I said. And even I admit that was a lousy excuse, since avoiding Darla Covington would be a pleasure.

"Wouldn't that be a good thing?" he asked.

"Fine. I'll sleep upstairs. In my room. I don't want to sleep in Eva's bed."

And so I ended up here. In this room. Where the monsters still whisper from behind the dust ruffle.

I slept better on the lumpy couch.

I left the light on all night.

Stephen didn't ask why.

He spent the night in Eva's room. Where monsters fear to tread, but Eva didn't . . . so it doesn't make that much difference when it comes to whispers.

I wake up with my back to the room and my face to the wall. I wake up looking at a little, discreet, pen-drawn heart. Stephen's name is inside the heart in spirally, loopy, love-potion writing. I'd just met him. At Summer's sister's wedding.

"Just met," isn't really true. He was a senior when I was a pimple-faced freshman. But he was just a pimple-faced senior who didn't play any sports so he wasn't terribly noticeable. Until he ran off to L.A. with some other guys. L.A., where everyone recognizes your true greatness and appreciates it. Not like the small-town hicks of Silver Creek, who wouldn't know true greatness if it came up and bought drinks all around.

Or so says every small-town hick kid who dreams of something bigger and brighter than the moon in the night sky.

And in Stephen's case, it was sort of true. Four years of hard work and they had a recording contract. Until Newell went and slid off the road doing ninety-five.

But before that, Summer's sister got married and Stephen came back to Silver Creek. Only he was worth noticing now. And I noticed.

I rub my thumb over the heart and wish I could erase the shallow gully that used to be me. The shallow person who couldn't tell a real human being from a stereotype. Who wouldn't notice the difference.

"Hey," Stephen says from the door. He taps it a couple of times in a pretense of knocking.

I roll over and look at him. Realize I'd notice him now if he were a bald monk with leprosy.

Not that a bald monk with leprosy wouldn't stick out in Silver Creek.

But it isn't all about noticing. I still want to make plans and talk about dreams and know who he is behind the shutters he shows everyone else.

"It's after two," he says. "In case you want a shower or want to eat or anything. Before work."

I sit up. Keeping the blankets over my bare legs. Sweeping the hair back out of my face. "Thanks."

Silence laps between us like high water in spring.

"I haven't done anything original in three years," he says. Meaning original music. "Anything worth much, that is."

I pull my knees to my chest.

I never was any good at writing poetry. During sophomore English, one of the class assignments was poetry. Writing it, not reading it. I spent the whole night in my room scratching out lines. I took an F on the assignment because the poem never matched my expectations. For it. For myself.

Which means I can't really say that I've been in a creative wash for the last three years. I can't match his statement. Can't match the guilt with an accusation to even out the scales.

If guilt has scales.

It has claws. And teeth.

Sharp ones.

"Are you blaming me for that?" I ask, feeling defensive.

"I'm not sure. Sometimes. Sometimes I blame myself. Or the crap I play to make a living."

His life is unbearable. I can see it. In his eyes. In his shoulders. In the way he's standing in the door with his hands in his pockets. He may have stayed on the West Coast for three years, but he's been rolling and tumbling. Just like me.

"Sometimes you have to stop," I say. "Aimless is good. For a while. But at some point you have to stop. Even if it's just for—"

"A week? A year?" The anger is there. The implication is there. I stopped with him for a year. In L.A.

"Sometimes a week. Sometimes a year."

"And then you move on?"

I hug my knees tighter. "I don't know," I say. "Maybe."

I hug my knees tighter and wish that possibilities could be more possible. More certain.

"And it's all your decision?" he asks.

"Isn't it?" I ask back, defensive again.

His shoulders tighten up. "You'd better get going," he says, "or you'll be late for work."

I throw the blankets back and put my bare feet onto the icy boards of the floor.

"Fine," I say. "Then I guess you'd better get out of my way."

"I don't think that matters."

I open my mouth, but he's gone.

I don't bother with a shower, just splash water onto my face, braid my hair, and call it done. Stephen is sitting at the kitchen table when I tiptoe through the living room. His back is to me and he's got his head in his hands. The last time I saw his shoulders slumped over a table was after Newell's funeral. Memorial, rather. Same thing.

I touch his shoulder.

I want to ask if he'll be here when I get home. But I'm afraid of the answer.

It's easy to scuffle and fight and act like you don't care.

It's easy to scuffle and fight and act like you don't care when you care more than words can express.

"Stephen . . ."

He leans his head on one hand and smiles at me. The kind of smile that you see behind shutters. "Hey."

"I have to go to work," I say.

He nods.

I swallow. Force out the words that admit too much.

"Can you . . . will you . . . wait? Until I get . . . back?"

The words admit that I need him to do something I couldn't do. Admit that I need him to open up and give me the chance I didn't give him. Admit that I need him to be a bigger person, a better person, than I was.

If he thinks it's worth his time to care about what I need, anyway.

He catches my hand and touches it with his lips.

"You'll be late for work," he says.

Then he drops my hand.

I leave Miss Kitty behind again.

I need to walk.

I need the air.

Even if the air is frigid and smells damp with incoming snow.

I don't know whether Stephen will be at Eva's when I get done tonight. He has every right to roll on through and keep going. I put my head down and walk into the wind.

"It's cold out there," Lil says when I walk into the bar.

I stare at her.

"You didn't notice, did you?" she says.

"It's going to snow," I say.

"It happens this time of year."

I take my coat off and hang it in the storeroom.

"How are you doing?" she asks as I shut the storeroom door.

"Fine."

"You don't act fine."

"I'm fine."

"Bullshit."

I turn around. "Is this what you wanted to talk about? Whether or not I'm fine?"

She puts her hands on her hips. "Is that lip?" she asks under raised eyebrows. "I do believe you're giving me lip."

"At least it's not a fat lip," I grumble.

She cups a hand around her ear. "Did I hear a threat?"

I lean against the bar and look at her. Think about the man sitting in my kitchen.

"I don't know what to do, Lil," I say.

"Nothing involving people is simple," she says. She fiddles with the knobs on the fryer.

"I'm old," she says.

"Forgetting the fryer once does not make a person old."

"I'll be sixty in five years," she says. "That makes me old."

"As old as you want to be."

She smiles. "Says the twenty-two-year-old who doesn't know shit about living."

I swallow a retort. It's true, after all. Lil was breathing air and sorrow and joy and trouble for thirty-three years before I was born.

"I like you," Lil says. "I liked you the moment I saw you."

"Me, too," I say. "I liked you, I mean."

"I had a horse once," Lil says. "I liked him on sight, too."

"Thanks," I say.

"Shut up and listen. I've always liked horses better than people, so it's a compliment."

"Okay."

"This horse . . . he was all gangly and lost. Stumbled over his own feet. People laughed at me when I bought him." She taps her belt buckle. "Two years later we were state barrel racing champions."

She's looking over my shoulder and smiling a little. I know she's seeing that horse, savoring that moment when everyone had to swallow their words.

Her face tightens as she shifts from the past to the present. Her eyes narrow.

"You've spent some time tripping over your own feet," she says.

"And now you're going to fix me up right and tight?"

I'm not angry. Yet. But there's a bit of a flare starting at the back of my skull.

Everyone wants to fix Katherine Earle. Their way.

"Do you need fixing?" Lil asks.

"No. If I need fixing, I can fix myself."

"Good. I don't want a fix-it project."

I shove my hand into my hair and rip the braid out. Start braiding again.

"So what the fuck was the story for?" I ask as I tie off the braid.

"Tango and I were partners," she says.

"And?"

"And I'd like to be partners with you, too."

I bite my lip.

"In the bar, you idiot," she says. "I'm offering a business partnership. Fifty-fifty."

I stare at her. The bar's heater clicks on and a rush of cold air pushes past me, warm air following in its wake. The glasses gleam. Sunlight drinks deep in the caramel and opalescent swirls inside the bottles behind the bar.

Fear and joy do a little dance in my chest.

Fear and joy die a quick death.

"I can't afford a fifty-fifty partnership," I say. "Reports of Aunt Eva's fortune must have been exaggerated on the gossip circuit."

"I didn't think you had two dimes to rub together," Lil says. "Other than the house and furniture."

I frown. "So why—?"

"I like you," she says, shrugging. "And I need to cut back."

"You've been to the doctor, haven't you," I say, worry closing in on my jugular. "Are you—?"

She waves a hand and cuts me off. "I've been to the doctor. I'm fine. Unless being decrepit will get you to accept . . . ?" She bends over and grabs her back. "Oh, the pain."

I don't laugh.

She straightens up.

"This is the first place I've felt at home," she says. "I have friends here. But it's not exactly a booming economy where you can just switch jobs and still stick around. I hired you because I liked you, but I put the 'help wanted' sign up because I can't do it alone."

I look at her. And I realize that this isn't about Lil needing help. This is just another manipulation game.

"And you're worried I'll leave," I say.

She's watching the dust motes swirl in the last rays of afternoon sun sliding through the front windows. "I've gotten used to having you around."

"You're worried I'll leave."

"You need choices," she says. Quietly. Softly. Gently.

You need choices.

I rip my braid out again. Feel like sobbing into the crook of my arm. I thought Lil was different. I thought Lil wouldn't be like Great-aunt Eva— giving something in order to manipulate me into doing what she wants. I thought Lil was my friend. I braid my hair tightly, tie it off, drink a glass of water.

Lil is still watching the dust motes. They're fading as the sun sinks lower. The light is changing from gold to orange. Her face is bathed in the orange glow.

"This is about pity, isn't it?" I ask.

She turns to me and smiles. "No. I just want you to make the right choice for you."

"And you don't think I can do that without some kind of incentive to even the scale?"

"I didn't say that."

Liar.

"Fuck you!" I scream at her.

She smiles again. "I imagine that's what Tango thought the first time I showed him the barrels."

I rub the heels of my hands into my eyes. "Goddamn you, Lil."

"Probably. If Darla Covington has any pull in high places."

I laugh through my tears and wipe my eyes on my sleeve.

"Don't manipulate me, Lil," I say, when I trust my voice. "And don't pity me."

"I'll manipulate you as much as I want," she says, "because I love you and don't want to see you screw up your life. But if this is pity, then you haven't had enough pity in your life."

"You don't know anything about my life."

She shakes her head, and now there's genuine pity in her eyes. "Someday, maybe before you're fifty-five, you'll realize how much a person can tell you without saying a word."

Through the sunlight, we look at each other. Lil's chin has that stubborn tilt to it. And I realize I love this woman like I would have loved my mother if she were still alive. Maybe I love Lil more. Because even if she *is* manipulating me, at least she's honest about it.

And it's done out of love.

And maybe Great-aunt Eva's manipulation was done out of love, too.

But the wounds haven't scarred over enough for me to look at my memories of Eva without all the pain and fury getting in the way.

The door opens and frostbitten leaves swirl in ahead of the evening's first customer.

"Do I have to give you an answer right now?" I ask.

"Will you say yes if you answer right now?"

I didn't look into my rearview mirror as I drove away from the gas station, but in my mind, I can see Stephen fading into the distance. I made the decision to drive away alone.

I made the decision to change my life—his life—alone.

Not again.

"I have to talk to someone first," I say.

CHAPTER 24

The bar is crammed with bodies. Live ones. Laughing, singing, drinking, playing pool, draping themselves over the furniture. . . .

Only one incident mars the joy of being a human pack animal in a warm spot on a too-cold night. It happens during the late-night lag. Well, usually it's a lag. Tonight, the whole town is here—minus those members of the local Society for the Concern of Morals (Other than Gossip) in Our Community.

I'm pouring one of the infinite number of beers the town of Silver Creek is sucking down when Nate taps his knuckles on the bar to get my attention.

"Have you seen Summer?" he asks.

Summer is cavorting like the last leaves of the cottonwood in the first breezes of fall. She's snuggled down by the pool table. Holding court.

I point my chin in her direction. And hope I won't be sorry.

When the first glass explodes against the wall, I am. Very sorry.

"We'll never get the shards out of the felt," Lil will say when the night is over. *"But we'll have a riot if we get rid of that pool table."*

"What do you mean no?" Nate screams at Summer. Her eyes are huge, but it might just be the dim light and all that mascara.

"I meant no," Summer says, her chin out. "N-O, no."

Nate grabs her arms. Thad, Lil, and I step forward, but he's just hauling her up out of her courtier's lap. After she's standing, he smooths the sleeves of her shirt down.

She slaps his hands away. "Leave me alone," she says.

"You're just embarrassed," Nate says.

"Because you're touching me? You bet."

"Because my mother has a big mouth."

Someone giggles.

It's an unfortunate choice of words, since that's exactly what Nate's mother has been saying about Summer.

Summer goes white.

Nate goes red.

"Go away," Summer says.

"No," Nate says.

"Run home to mommy," Summer says.

She drops back down into her courtier's lap. He's looking worried, but the code of macho ethics won't let him show it.

Nate picks up a second glass. It follows its sibling with near-perfect precision and smashes into the wall over the pool table.

"Maybe you should talk to him, Summer," the courtier says.

"There's no point talking to a man who has to get caught by his mommy before he'll move out of the house." Summer says. "Just ignore him." She grabs the courtier's hand and puts it between her thighs before giving him an open-mouthed kiss.

Nate picks up a third glass.

I put my hand on his arm. "Nate."

He almost tugs free before realizing who's talking to him.

"You're breaking all the glasses, Nate," I say. "And I'll have to sweep that mess up."

He sets the glass down on the table. "I'm sorry, Kat."

"No problem." I take his arm and pull him toward the door. The faces of the people standing around the room are still. Watching. Waiting. I get Nate out the door and away from all the questioning eyes.

The ice in the wind tears through my shirt. I might as well be naked. I wrap my arms around myself.

Nate slumps against the wall. "I just made a fool of myself," he says. "What a loser."

I automatically start to agree, then catch myself.

"You're a nice guy, Nate," I say. "But you used Summer to get at your mom. People don't like being used."

He turns on me. "Yeah, you're just Captain Courage, aren't you? Couldn't leave town until someone asked you to go."

We stare at each other.

He drops back. "I'm sorry, Kat. I just . . ."

"You're right," I say.

The church clock chimes the half hour.

"I'm freezing," I say as the wind snatches the last of the tones away. "Talk to Rosemary, Nate. It won't kill you."

He nods. "Go inside," he says. Then he turns and walks away.

"We'll never get the shards out of the felt," Lil says.

"Strapping tape," I say. "But it might take off some of the fuzzy, too."

"Go home," Lil says.

I don't want to go home. I'm not sure which is more frightening. Finding Stephen. Or finding him gone.

"I want an answer tomorrow," she says. "About the bar."

At the front door of the bar, I turn around and look at the room. The scuffed wooden floors and red-shaded hanging lamps. The warm, yeasty breath smelling of night after night of draws. Thad steps out of the storeroom and smiles at me.

"Take it easy, Kit-Kat," he says.

I lift a hand and wave.

I can't talk around the lump in my throat.

Outside, the clouds are low and reflect the glow from the streetlights along Main. I hunch my shoulders against the frosty dawn's breath and walk toward home.

Home.

Not Great-aunt Eva's.

Not just a place to lay my head.

Home.

I feel the first splinters of snow falling on my face like shards of glass as I stop on the sidewalk in front of the stripped house. No curlicues of gingerbread. Plain. Solid. Just a building, but one that I'm starting to appreciate for the first time in my life, because for the first time in my life, it feels like I might belong.

The house is dark, but Stephen's car is still parked behind mine.

"You need choices," Lil said.

Gwen's light is on, so I risk knocking.

It might be avoidance. It might be fear. I'm not up to deciding which pop psychology reason has me knocking on Gwen's door rather than walking through my own.

"Hi," Gwen says. She's bundled up in thick socks and sweats. I always imagined her in one of those flannel granny robes.

"Did I wake you up?" I ask, even though I know I didn't.

"No. Come in."

"Why are you awake?" I ask, shutting the door behind me.

"Robert was here."

"You talked?"

She shrugs and sits down on the couch. I sit down on the edge of the matching chair.

"When I was little," she says, "I always stayed awake to watch for the first snowflakes."

"What if the first snow came during the day?"

She looks down at her toes, then up at me. "I don't remember. I only remember it coming late at night."

"It's snowing now," I say.

"I know. I saw it in the window. I was waiting for it to come."

"Lil offered me a partnership tonight," I say.

"That's great!"

"I'm not sure."

"Why?"

"Stephen is going back to Seattle. Today."

"Oh."

I lean my shoulders into the chair. Rest my head on the stuffed back.

"What did you and Robert talk about?" I ask, staring at the ceiling.

She's quiet.

I roll my head until I can see her.

"I'm comfortable," she says. "Here. Now. John and I are happy."

"I know."

"I'm not ready to change that."

I nod.

"I like Robert," she says. "I'm just . . . not ready to upset the balance of where I am right now."

"But you're up all night," I say, because deep down I don't believe she's waiting for the snow. Not when she's expecting her first toddler in two hours.

"I don't like hurting people."

"And you hurt him?"

"Anything other than a straight yes would hurt him, wouldn't it?"

"Can you be friends?" I ask.

Her smile twists.

"Never mind," I say. "I get it."

But even though I understand, I still feel the chubby pastor's pain. Rolling in on top of Nate's pain. The unfairness of it all.

Love does not necessarily beget love.

I wonder whether Robert will leave Silver Creek. If he'll continue to listen to God or if he'll give in to the demons that drive him.

I let the air out of my lungs in a long shuddering sigh.

"You have to do what's best for you," Gwen says. More to herself than to me.

"You think?"

"How else can you be happy? Make anyone else happy?"

"How do you know what's best for you?"

She frowns.

"What if you're just scared?" I ask. "What if fear is making the decision about what's best?" I'm asking myself as much as I'm asking her.

"I'm not scared," she says. "I don't know about you."

I'm too tired to argue.

"I'm sorry," I say. "I didn't mean to be insulting."

"I'm not insulted," she says.

I force my lips into an exhausted smile. "You're fibbing."

"Okay, I'm insulted."

The snow falls past the living room window. I can see the light gleam white against the flakes.

"I'm scared," I whisper. "There's so much to lose."

"Just don't lose yourself," Gwen says.

The lock clicks loud in my wake. I stand in the entryway and wait for my eyes to adjust from the snow-bright street to the interior dimness. Soft music flows toward me from the living room. Music that's unbearably sad and unbearably beautiful. Bits of it I recognize from the wild wash of water, waving grass, and sky that was the music last night. But now it's softer. Walking instead of running. Sitting instead of dancing.

"I saw you on the sidewalk," Stephen says over the sound of the guitar strings quivering across the bridge.

I step into the living room. Find him sitting on the yellow velvet chair. In front of the window.

"Just now?"

"Before."

"I stopped to see Gwen. She was awake."

I sit down on the window seat. My back is to the frosty window, and the yellow-white glow from the sky turns his face into a network of highlights and shadows. The music slides into my chest and wraps my lungs up in its fingers.

"I thought you might be gone when I got home," I say.

"I left once," he says. "I came back."

"Why?"

He smiles and bends a string into a parody of its proper note.

"Leaving seemed a lot like something somebody did to me once."

He pops the string in a snapping pull-off. So hard the string thwacks back on the fret board and cries.

Miss Kitty jumps up onto the window seat and bumps my elbow. We're having unpleasant feelings. Unpleasant feelings bring predators. We should stop having unpleasant feelings. I scratch her head to reassure her and myself.

Stephen lifts his guitar off his lap and sets it gently into its case.

"Lil offered me a partnership tonight," I say.

Snow plops against the cold-crackling window at my back.

"In the bar?"

"Yes."

"Fifty-fifty?"

"Yes."

"It's a good deal. Take it."

"That's all you have to say?"

"I should say something else?"

"Don't you have anything else to say?"

He stands up. "Not really."

"Hey!" I say, but he's gone, leaving the door wide open and the snowy wind dusting the floor.

I slip on the porch steps and stumble into the layer of wet, white snow on the sidewalk. Stephen's footprints stretch down the street. He's past Gwen's yard.

"Hey!"

When he doesn't turn around, I scoop up snow and throw a snowball at his back.

He stops.

I catch up, practically falling as the snow slides under my boots.

"I need to know—" I begin.

"Did you give a rat's ass what I thought when you left me at that gas station?"

"No," I say. "I just wanted to be gone."

"Then fuck you," he says.

"That was three years ago."

"Well, excuse me. I didn't know I was breaking the statute of limitations. How long do I get before I have to shut up? Five minutes? Ten?"

"I'm sor—" I start to say.

"You left me," he says. "You just drove away and left me standing there with no chance to argue and no explanations. You just left."

"I'm sor—"

"And now you want to talk about what I think?"

"I want—"

"Why the fuck should I care what you want?"

"I'm *sorry*," I cry out into the snow-damp darkness. "I didn't think about leaving you at the gas station. I just wanted away from . . . I was just a shadow. There wasn't a place for me with you. I was just hanging on, hanging around. I had to go. I had to find *me*. I had to find my place. But I couldn't find *anything* in L.A., and—"

"I loved you," Stephen says. "You were worth everything to me."

"—all I wanted was you, but I didn't think it could possibly go both ways."

"It went both ways," he says.

"I was too scared to ask," I say, closing my eyes for a moment to drown the resurrected memories. "Too scared of what you'd say."

Snowflakes hiss as they land on the fences, trees, and roofs around us. The wind swirls glitter up into the rectangle of light falling through the open door of Eva's house.

Stephen reaches out a hand and wipes the melting snow from my cheek. "I love you," he says.

His voice shakes. And the answer is so clear I don't even have time to be scared.

Because Gwen is wrong. Sometimes you have to lose yourself. Sometimes you have to step off the comfortable road. Sometimes you have to be brave enough to find a new path.

"I love you, too."

We wrap our arms around each other and hold on tight.

Snow falls around us and covers our tracks, smoothing over the past until it disappears.

CHAPTER 25

Miss Kitty rubs my shin and twirls her tail around my knee.

"We're heating the state of Montana," Stephen says into my hair. "Why didn't you shut the door?"

"You're the one who left it open."

"I thought you would shut it."

"You thought I would follow you?"

I feel his sad smile on my temple. "No. I wanted to leave before you could tell me to go."

"Maybe I should have just shut the door," I whisper into his shoulder. "It would have been easier."

Kitty yowls and stands up on her hind legs to paw at Stephen's thigh.

"California sissy," I say to her as Stephen reaches down and picks her up out of the snow. She shakes a damp foot at me in disgust. Shakes her foot in disgust with the wet, cold stuff on the ground.

"It's cold out here," Stephen says.

"Even though we're heating the state."

Snow has blown into the entryway and piled up in the creases of the rug in front of the door. I shake the rug over the bushes by the porch while Stephen sweeps the snow out of the house. The floor is streaked with water, but I can't find the energy to care about water spots.

He shuts the door. The heater is roaring, working to blast the first taste of winter out of its mouth.

I sit down on the arm of the couch and look at Stephen. At the damp-dark hair falling into his eyes. My chest squeezes in the grip of the haunting music he was playing when I first walked into the house.

"What are we going to do?" I whisper.

Because I don't want to give up this newfound, newly rediscovered home. I don't want to give up Lil or Gwen or the bar. I don't want to give up my resting place. And because I don't want Stephen to give up . . . to *give up*. And for him, moving back here would be giving up.

He leans a shoulder against the door frame. "I don't know."

"Why does this have to be either/or?" I ask, angry at the universe and fate. "Why does it have to be either I give up my life or you give up your life?"

"Maybe it just looks that way."

I scrunch under the thought. Try to understand.

"You mean, you live in Seattle while I live here?" I ask. "The bar is a six-day, sometimes a seven-day, job. It's not like I have weekends off."

"You have a partner. There are slow days."

"You can't record if you're living in Silver Creek."

"I wasn't exactly writing music living in Seattle."

"This is *crazy*," I say. "Back and forth. Seeing each other a little at a time. What kind of life is that?"

"What kind of life do we have right now?" he asks. "Living with the ghosts of each other? I'd rather have you one day a week than the ghost of you twenty-four hours a day."

I stare at him. Fear has my chest in its claws. If I love him, shouldn't I be willing to leave and go with him? But I tried to live his life before. And it didn't work. And God knows, I don't want *him* to be the one driving away. Leaving me at a gas station because he's lost himself giving up his life for me.

"Will this work?" I ask, grasping for reassurance.

"I have no idea," he says, giving me none. He doesn't have any to give.

The windows creak in the wind. Crackle in the cold.

"Do you want to try?" I ask. "Try to make it work?"

"Yes."

"Me, too."

He steps forward and squats down in front of me, rests his hands on my knees. "Can I have your ring?" he asks.

"How did you know—?"

"It was outside your shirt this morning. This afternoon. When I woke you up."

I slip the hemp thong over my head. Hold it out in front of us. The ring spirals on the end of the braided thong. Catches the lamplight and tosses light shadows into the corners of the room.

Stephen takes the string from me. Standing up, he unties it and slips the ring off. I'm not sure what he's planning. He reaches down and pulls me to my feet.

"Come on," he says. "Put on your coat."

Shutting the door this time, we walk along the street toward the bridge. The snow is falling thick and fast. Snowflakes stick to my eyelashes and melt, running down my face and into my scarf where they freeze again. I'm glad when we reach the bridge and I can turn my back on the wind.

Stephen takes my ring out of his coat pocket. He pulls his arm back and I realize what he's planning.

"Wait!" I say, catching his arm.

"You want to do it?" he asks.

"I throw like a girl."

"Actually, so do I."

I laugh.

Standing on a snow-covered bridge and laughing, I feel the guilt, the fear, the loneliness, the sadness . . . *everything*, just slide away with the dark water gurgling between its banks of snow and overhanging ice.

And I understand what Stephen is doing.

"Where's *your* ring?" I ask.

He hands it to me. I don't know where he kept it. Why he kept it. It doesn't matter.

"Ready?" he asks.

I nod.

And we wind up, lean back, and throw the rings as far as we can up the river and toward the black silhouette of the lone cottonwood. Two splashes, so close together they almost sound like a single snowflake falling into the water.

Stephen drapes his arm over my shoulders.

"Let's go home," he says.

Everything is going to be fine.

THE GIRL
SHE LEFT
BEHIND KAREN
BRICHOUX

A CONVERSATION WITH
KAREN BRICHOUX

✤

Q. *What inspired you to write* The Girl She Left Behind?

A. A gas station. I was filling up the gas tank of my car and thinking about how all towns look alike near the freeways. And since the tank was nearly empty to start with, and the pump was slow, I had time to wonder if anyone had ever just filled up, paid, and driven away. This happened a while back, but it worked its way into Katherine Earle's story. I asked myself what, exactly, would cause someone to drive away? And would it be the current situation or something deeper? Something more long-term.

Q. *"More long-term." What do you mean by that?*

A. Let me answer this in a roundabout way. I think every author has a theme that continually works its way into his or her writing. In my writing, that theme is the discovery of self; discovery of identity, purpose, and meaning. Who are we? What makes each one of us different from the people around us? What makes us the same? Why are we here and what do we want from our lives? I think the search for meaning and a meaningful existence is something every human experiences. Katherine is unable to find that more meaningful existence as long as she is living by other people's rules. She drove away from Stephen, but she was really driving away from everyone's expectations of her. I pick up the story three years later, after she has learned to be self-reliant and after she has had a chance to discover who she is. Now she is, essentially, finding out who she has become by interacting with her past.

Q. So she is testing herself by going back to Silver Creek? Back to her past?

A. In a way, yes. She claims to not know why she is going back to Silver Creek, but I think all of us have, at some point, a desire to see who we have become in relation to the past. But there's an added element to Kat's story, and that is her rootlessness. Being rootless was a perfect contrast to her very rooted life in Silver Creek and in Los Angeles. She needed that contrast. But nothing stays rootless forever without dying or, like a tumbleweed, running into a fence. So Kat returns to Silver Creek—to find out if she's any different and also because, underneath it all, she is searching for a place where she belongs.

Q. Bridges and nature both seem to play an important part in The Girl She Left Behind. *Was that intentional?*

A. Bridges, the ocean, tumbleweeds, fences, the river, and the high plains all play an important part in creating the atmosphere of the novel. I was intentionally trying to create a feeling of motion in order to contrast that with solid objects. The river is constantly moving toward the ocean, but the bridge is a solid object between two banks. The waves created by the wind in the tall grass of the prairie mimic the waves of the ocean, only the ocean sucks the sand away while the grass helps create the solid earth that nourishes it. Tumbleweeds roll until they hit a fence. That motion/solidity aspect was intentional. The concept of bridges—spanning the gap between the past and the present—was also intentional. There are probably a lot of unintentional things in the book that are only happy accidents. If everything in a book were intentional, I wouldn't find it much fun to write. It would be like a paint-by-numbers kit.

Q. All of your books are in first person present. Is there a reason for that?

A. Definitely. For two reasons. The first is immediacy. For me, third person past (she said, he walked) removes the reader entirely from the action. It's not that different from watching a movie. You can feel the tension and the emotions, but you are still outside looking in. First person past (I said, I walked) has a similar problem, because the past tense conveys the feeling of the story having already been told and the outcome having already been reached. First person present (I say, I walk) has a quality of immediacy. The person telling the story is experiencing the story at the same time as the reader.

The second reason has more to do with first person vs. third person. First person is unreliable, because the reader is seeing the world through the eyes of the narrator. It requires the reader to receive input from the narrator—her impressions, emotions, decisions, and rationalizations—while at the same time being actively engaged in deciding whether or not those impressions, emotions, decisions, and rationalizations are true. For example, Katherine has a lot of "emotional baggage"—I dislike that term—with Great-aunt Eva. Because of that "baggage," Kat's impressions could lead the reader to see Eva as a horrible person. But the details of Eva's life—providing live-in care for her mother, taking Kat in—should alert the reader to the fact that there is more to this story than what Kat is describing. Eva is human. Kat is human. Humans are rarely all good or all evil. They would be pretty darn dull if they were.

Q. So you are using first person present in order to engage the readers?

A. Yes. And myself, as the author. When I start working on a novel, I generally have only the barest idea of a beginning and an end. Nothing else is clear. Writing in the first person present allows me to become the main character. It's a little like improvisational theater. Only with a delete key if something too off-the-wall happens.

QUESTIONS FOR DISCUSSION

�֍

1. Have you ever just wanted to drive away from your life? Have the time to focus on finding out what is important to you? Do you think Katherine is selfish for what she did? Could she have handled the situation differently?

2. A number of objects are meaningful for Katherine. The bridge over Silver Creek, the river, the cottonwood, even Great-aunt Eva's coat. Why do you think Katherine clings to these objects?

3. Uncle Charles' feelings of guilt have destroyed his relationship with Katherine. And Katherine hides the pictures of her relatives in the attic to stop the accusatory "whispers" that remind her how guilty she feels about running away. Do you find it realistic that a guilty conscience could dissolve a family relationship or keep a person awake at night? Would Charles have felt guilty about letting Great-aunt Eva take charge of Katherine if Cynthia had never left him?

4. Katherine is unable to apologize for the choices she made to leave Stephen and Jennifer because she realizes that given the same circumstances, she would make those same choices again. Does this knowledge alleviate her feelings of guilt or merely increase them? Did she make the right choices?

5. In Chapter 24, Katherine makes the argument that sometimes what seems the best choice is merely the choice with the least personal risk, that fear of the unknown can keep a person from making what is really the best choice. Do you agree? Have you ever taken the risky, unclear path and been rewarded?

The daughter of American missionaries, Karen Brichoux was born and raised in the Philippines. While taking the exams for a PhD in European history, she started writing a novel to stay sane. Discovering that sanity was a great deal more fun than taking exams, she dropped out of the PhD program to pursue writing full-time. She currently lives in the Midwestern United States with her spouse, three cats, and a large dog who suffers from debilitating separation anxiety. Her Web site is www. karenbrichoux.com.